THE PERFECT DOUBLE

Suddenly, the other cab screeched up. A woman in her early fifties bolted out.

"Kitty!" she shouted. "My Kitty!" She slammed against Carly, embracing her while breaking down in tears. "Kitty, baby, why did you leave us?"

Carly was dumbfounded. "Ma'am," she said quietly, "I think there's a mistake."

The mother began to look frightened, as if Carly were speaking a quiet truth. Carly placed her arm around the crushed woman. "Now, please tell me what this is all about."

The mother took a deep breath. "Laval," she said. "He was Kathleen's plastic surgeon."

The name hit Carly like a thunderbolt. In a fraction of a second, she knew that something had exploded, that her world had been invaded, that everything would change. . . .

FACEMAKER

WILLIAM KATZ

AVON BOOKS ◆ NEW YORK

AVON BOOKS
A division of
The Hearst Corporation
105 Madison Avenue
New York, New York 10016

Copyright © 1988 by William Katz
Published by arrangement with McGraw-Hill Book Company
Library of Congress Catalog Card Number: 87-26288
ISBN: 0-380-70685-7

First Avon Books Printing: March 1989

AVON TRADEMARK REG. U.S. PAT. OFF. AND IN OTHER COUNTRIES, MARCA
REGISTRADA, HECHO EN U.S.A.

Printed in the U.S.A.

K-R   10   9   8   7   6   5   4   3   2   1

Prologue

He stopped the car on a desolate road high in the hills. It was one A.M.

"Why did you stop?" she asked.

"I just wanted to look at you again," he replied. "It's one of life's great pleasures."

She laughed, delighted by the compliment, especially coming from *him*.

He snapped on the interior light, then surveyed the heavy bush on the side of the road. The area was perfect. In daylight, no one would be able to see into that bush more than a few feet.

He gazed into her eyes, then took in her entire face. To her, he seemed mesmerized. The look on his face was the look of a man obsessed, a man who was giving this one face his total concentration.

"I hope you're as happy as I am," he said.

"Of course," she replied. "And it's all because of you."

Nothing he saw in her face changed his mind, which had been made up long before. Casually, he reached into his jacket pocket. She didn't bother to look down to see what he was doing. A few moments later he leaned toward her in a gesture that she mistook for affection. Suddenly, she felt something sharp in her side. She lurched back. "What did you do?" she asked.

He looked baffled and hurt. "Nothing," he replied.

"I felt something."

"Are you all right?" he asked.

She barely answered as her head began to wobble. Her eyes started to close. "Something's happening to me," she whispered, as if appealing to him.

Now he smiled. "This is best," he said to her. "This is necessary."

He buried her deep in the bush. He left her—but not before doing the one thing that would allow her to serve him in death, although she had failed him in life. He knew she would have been proud.

And his thoughts turned to another woman.

1

"I want to be just another pretty face," Carly said.

"You'll be much more," André Laval replied. And Carly knew, as she listened to his cultured, reassuring voice, that he was right. Why had she been lucky enough to find this man, she asked herself. Why had Providence been so generous?

She had gone through three operations in the year since her accident, and Dr. Laval had in fact become her salvation, gradually giving her a new face, using the plastic surgeon's art to turn a nightmare into the beginnings of a dream. She had barely gone outside during the ordeal, remaining a recluse in her small Manhattan apartment. *Allure,* the glitzy women's magazine for which she worked as a reporter, had sent her editing to do at home, sparing her the stares of the curious.

Her mind raced back to the day the accident happened. *Allure* had sent her to Kennedy Airport to cover the introduction of a new jetliner as part of a travel feature. Funny, she recalled, she hadn't even wanted the assignment. It had been a drizzly November day, and hiking out to Kennedy hadn't been on her wish list. But once there, she'd *volunteered* to try the plane's escape slide, which was being demonstrated. Always the heroine, she now mused. Always out in front of the pack.

A gust of wind caught the slide and spilled her out. She

3

took a thirty-foot plunge to the tarmac, landing on her face. She couldn't remember anything else, except the opening strain of a dull thud.

Now she again lay in Burgess Hospital, once more wrapped in bandages. Laval had completed her third and, she hoped, last operation forty-eight hours before, and was ready to remove the dressings. The change would be dramatic. This operation had rebuilt Carly's nose and re-shaped part of her left cheekbone. She felt her heart pounding. She'd be able to face the world again. She'd be alive for the first time in a year. What would people say? What would old friends say? Would they stare? Would they give compliments, or would they be afraid that compliments were out of place? After all, this was "reconstructive" surgery, plastic surgery for the desperate.

"Are you ready?" Laval asked.

"Am I ready," Carly said, as if the question were redundant. Her speech was clear, despite a lingering stiffness from her repaired jaw.

"Remember," Laval told her, "there'll be discoloration around the eyes, and the nose won't have its precise, final shape. But you'll get a good idea. It'll be wann-der-ful, simply grand."

"I don't care if I look like the loser in *Rocky IV* today," Carly said. "It's two weeks down the line that I care about."

"Fantastic attitude," Laval intoned. "Just the spirit I expected from you, Ms. Randall."

Carly sensed Laval above her—the towering figure, the graceful hands, the monumental ego, the international reputation that she could almost feel every time he touched her. And she sensed that, at this moment, he cared only about her. It was part of his gift as a doctor to make a patient feel this way.

"I begin," he said.

He started cutting away the gauze. Carly felt her chest pound with each metallic snip of the scissors. It was a mystery, an adventure story. She'd known for some time that Laval could not restore her face as it had been. She'd seen computer projections of what she'd probably look like, but she yearned to see the real thing . . .in the mirror, the mirror that had caused her so much anguish since the day of "the mess," as she called it.

Snip.

"How long?" she asked eagerly.

"About three minutes," Laval replied.

So Carly waited, for what seemed like an eternity, and inevitably aspects of her life passed before her. She was thirty-two now, about five-one, with brown eyes and dark brown hair that was kept short because of her surgery. The last year had made her feel older, almost out of society altogether, living in the shadows. This, she mused, must be what getting released from prison is like.

She felt so alone now, as Laval continued snipping away. She wanted to share the moment with someone close, but there was no one. She was an only child. Her mother had died when she was twenty. Her father, himself a doctor, had walked out of their Cleveland home when she was fourteen, and was never heard from again.

How different to have Laval standing above her instead of her father—that hostile, drugged-up surgeon who'd yelled at her, threatened her, and occasionally beat her, until he finally abandoned his family. With Laval, Carly felt confident and secure. He was bringing her into a new world, and he was doing it with a kindness and concern uncommon in modern medicine.

Snip.

He continued cutting, and Carly could begin to feel the skin around her scalp and head start to breathe as the bandages loosened.

"About a minute," Laval finally announced. "Oh, this'll be lovely, so very lovely." Okay, so he had that artsy way of talking, Carly thought. Some people laughed at him, and made the usual snide remarks about his manliness. But what did it matter? Only his skill mattered.

Then, without saying a word, Laval removed the last bandage, giving each movement the elegance of a ballet. Carly's eyes were suddenly uncovered. The light glared for a few moments, like dozens of flashbulbs going off at once, but she quickly got used to it.

Laval's handsome face came into focus, a face that had benefited from the occasional services of another skilled plastic surgeon. Carly watched as Laval studied her, his blue eyes shifting from her mouth to her nose to her cheeks, examining every detail, scrutinizing every curve. She could see the satisfaction within him, especially when his lips turned up in a decided smile. "How is it?" she asked softly.

"I'm satisfied," Laval replied.

Carly knew that, coming from Laval, "satisfied" was the equivalent of "bravo." Now Carly smiled painfully—any twist of a facial muscle produced raw pain. She sat there, her head slowly turning toward a hand mirror that Laval had placed beside her. It was his style to let the patient decide when to look. It was an emotional moment, not to be rushed. Deliberately, she reached for the mirror, raised it slightly, then hesitated, finally lifting it up, and looking. At first she winced, put off by the swellings and marks that Laval had warned about. Yes, she thought, she did look like the loser in *Rocky IV*. But then she studied the details and could make out what was to be, once the healing was complete.

"My God," she gasped.

"I assume you're pleased," Laval said.

"Pleased?" Carly asked. "Beyond my dreams." Then she turned to Laval. "I've said it before, but thank you. Thank you so much."

Laval simply nodded. He knew how good he'd been. "As you know," he said, "I like to leave the patient alone at a time like this. You have a lot to look at." He smiled benevolently at Carly, then turned and walked to the door—the great physician, the equally great actor, making his exit at the instant of triumph. "I'll be back fairly soon," he said.

Carly was used to the style. After three operations she'd become a pro, a regular at Burgess, a veritable student of the Laval method. And, yes, she did enjoy being left alone. She *did* have a lot to look at, a new face to get to know.

Now she stared into the mirror, again trying to envision what she'd be in that magical two weeks. And what she'd be, she realized, was a woman with an exquisitely sculptured face, precisely as Laval had promised. The man was more than a doctor. He was an artist, a sculptor with flesh and bone, someone who could create an entirely new person with a gilt-edged future.

She tilted her head slightly, showing herself at a different angle. "Hello beautiful," she whispered, almost ashamed at the little touch of vanity . . . but not really. Then she giggled softly. But the giggle was cut short by more pain.

André Laval walked through the jammed corridors of Burgess, heading for his office, more than a city block away. He nodded occasionally, responding to the reverent greetings of students and staff members. He was the nation's leading plastic surgeon, knew it, and wanted everyone else to know it—and they did.

Yet, inside he was laughing. They all wanted something, he knew. They all curried favor with the great man in hopes of getting some letter of recommendation, some better position in the hospital. He wondered how they'd act if they actually got to know André Laval, got to know him and his true, inner thoughts. How would they react to the person behind the image, behind the myriad of magazine articles and cover stories? How would they react to the mind, and what was deep inside it?

He arrived at his office complex, the largest in the hospital, whisked past two receptionists, and went immediately to his office, sliding quickly behind his desk.

The office, on the hospital's eighth floor, mirrored the man—a mammoth, four-thousand-dollar oak desk in the middle, sunk into white pile carpeting that was shampooed once a week. The lighting was indirect, highlighting the photographs of patients, some of them famous, that decorated the walls. There was one of America's greatest actors, and three of his ex-wives, each one of whom had been

given a facelift as part of her divorce settlement. There
was the CEO of the Fortune 500 company who'd ordered a
more assertive nose when he began to feel he was losing
authority. And there was the chairman of a powerful Sen-
ate committee, who was convinced that his new, bagless
eyes had won him the under-25 vote. There was also a
smattering of commoners, just to make B-level patients
feel at home.

There was a time, Laval liked to recall, when people
were ashamed to have cosmetic surgery. Now they wanted
to show off the results, to be memorialized in the office of
their physician.

A sculptured bust, in bronze, of Laval himself, finished
the major architecture in the office. Laval had commis-
sioned it three years earlier. He'd believed it would im-
press his patients, and it had. People just assume that a
statue is a certificate of greatness. No one had to know
who'd paid for it.

He'd told all three of his secretaries to hold his calls.
Now, he slid his oversized black leather chair forward,
slipped on his frameless, blue-tinted glasses, and opened
Carly's folder. He pulled out a sketch that he had made of
her as she was to look after the final surgery. Had his work
measured up to the picture? He studied the sketch, looking
at it with a practiced eye, from different angles.

"Lovely," he whispered. "A work of art." The whispering was a nervous habit. He wasn't even aware of it. "I
think we've got it," he went on, now smiling at the
sketch, and at pictures of Carly as she'd looked before the
final major surgery. He turned the sketch over and wrote
on the back, "Carly—New York." Then he returned it to
the folder and locked the folder away.

Laval snapped on his intercom. "Elyse," he ordered,
"please get me Maude Cromwell at *Lustre*."

He waited—it was no more than fifteen seconds—and
the red, Danish-designed round phone on his desk buzzed.
He picked it up. "Maude, dahling. André Laval. How are
you, my love?"

He listened, bored, while one of the journalistic arbiters

of beauty described her back problem at insufferable length. Occasionally he tossed in some medical hint or expression of deepest concern. "So sorry, love. You must rest. You're running around too much being beautiful. Oh, I mean it truly."

And then, at the opportune moment, he got to the point. "Maude, you must hear something, dear. I think I have the face of the nineties. And it's a miracle, a wonderful story. A young woman who had an accident. I've remade her. You'll love the face, Maude. She'll be famous, and you'll be the one who discovered her."

He listened to some oozing at the other end, then answered a question. "No, you can't meet her yet—not until all is perfect. I'm not teasing you, dearest. When I feel she's ready, I'll make the introduction. And by the way, won't I see you at the library benefit Thursday?"

The conversation drifted off into even smaller talk and then concluded, but Laval had made his point.

Laval informed his secretaries that he wished to work before the camera. This wasn't particularly unusual because he made many television tapes for use by plastic surgeons around the world. He'd even developed an entire course in plastic surgery that could be taught almost entirely by videotape. It was a way to spread the Laval name, to strengthen his credentials as the supreme teacher of the art, and to establish him as a personality at home in front of a TV camera.

He walked from his office to the private television studio that the hospital had constructed for his use. He knew how to operate the equipment and often made the tapes without help simply by standing in a ruled-off area before the one camera.

He flipped on the lights. Then, he returned to the door and bolted it shut. He had no fear of being overheard, since the studio was completely soundproofed.

On today's schedule: a lecture on advanced dermabrasion, a technique in which unsightly marks are literally sanded from a patient's skin. One of Laval's medical assistants had already typed up the lecture notes.

But Laval had no intention of making that tape. Instead, he would make one infinitely more vital.

He warmed up the equipment—a Minolta video camera mounted on a tripod, and a JVC video recorder. He snapped a blank TDK Pro tape into the recorder and was ready to begin his performance. He took a deep breath, realizing his heart was pounding, sensing his own tension and excitement.

He checked himself in a mirror, brushing back those unruly strands of hair that always seemed to mar his image of self-perfection. Then he started the recorder and stepped before the camera.

"Ladies and gentlemen," he said, without a trace of the affectation that normally marked his speaking, "this is Dr. André Laval. This tape is not part of my regular instructional series, although I consider it the most critical lesson I will ever give. You may well be watching this after my passing. In fact, that is my intention. I intend to make a series of special tapes and leave them in a vault, with instructions that they be seen only after I'm gone.

"I will reveal certain actions I have taken to advance the art and science of plastic surgery. Some of these may make you uneasy. But pioneering work in any field can involve unorthodox methods. We must not be constrained by childish, simpleminded notions of right and wrong."

Laval tried to relax a bit before going on, even placing his right hand in his pants pocket.

"I want to tell you about a medical miracle. Her name is Carly Randall, and I predict that her face, a face that I have created, will become the face of the nineties. It will appear on magazine covers and in films. It will be idolized and worshiped like Monroe or Garbo. I have shown that a plastic surgeon can equal the work of Michelangelo, and make one face immortal . . ."

As Laval's tape rolled, an attractive woman in her early fifties lingered outside Burgess Hospital, occasionally star-

ing up at Laval's office suite. There seemed to be a yearning in her eyes, as if someone in that hospital held the answer to some deep, intensely personal secret. After a time her eyes swept down to ground level, and she focused on the hospital's main entrance. She kept watching the door, almost mesmerized, as if searching for one particular face that would change her life.

But no one came.

2

Laval visited Carly again only an hour after completing his tape. She had absolutely no idea of the plans he had for her, and he knew it was premature to let on. He recalled that even *he* had had some early difficulty adjusting to fame and publicity, and wanted to ease Carly into it gently. He was the Svengali, she his protégé. The relationship had to be nurtured.

Laval entered Carly's room with a deep smile. His green hospital gown had been replaced with a gray worsted suit and red silk tie, matching handkerchief in the breast pocket. Carly looked up at him with a gaze that bordered on reverence. Every strand of hair, including the patches of silver around the temples, was blow-dried and molded in place. Laval was tall, and looked a little older than his forty-one years; with his style in clothes and his demeanor, he could easily have been an investment banker, Wall Street lawyer, or corporation president. As he glided into the room he flashed his lordly smile—God is here to make you beautiful—and looked admiringly at his patient. "Ah, and how are we feeling?" he crooned.

"Fine," Carly replied. "I'm surprised to see you so soon."

"I had to return to the area," Laval said, "and thought I'd drop in to see my favorite patient. If there's any problem at all, please tell me."

"Only the rawness in my face," Carly said. "How could anything else be wrong? I look in the mirror . . . it's a miracle."

Laval turned to look at Carly's face in the mirror as well. "Yes, it is," he agreed. "I'm just amazed sometimes at what we can do. We've come so far in plastic surgery. Of course, I had great teachers."

"I think your reputation is due to more than good teachers," Carly said, trying to smile. "You're an artist."

"Thank you. I do appreciate that," Laval replied, trying to overpower his ego and appear gracious. "I won't deny that the individual surgeon plays his role. You know, the father of modern American plastic surgery was actually a dentist."

"Oh?"

"Yes, he developed a number of the procedures to help wounded soldiers in World War I. Then he came back and went to medical school. It shows what one individual can contribute."

"I'll use that in my article," Carly said.

"Article?"

"When I get all repaired, I'm writing about this for *Allure*."

"Oh," Laval said, almost nonchalant. But inwardly he was thrilled. The lady will give herself a send-off, an autobiography of plastic surgery.

"I hope you don't mind," Carly said.

"Not at all. Feel free to ask questions."

"I assure you, I will."

Laval approached Carly and placed two fingers of his right hand gently on her face, evidently able to tell by touch how well it was healing. "The rawness will continue for a time," he said. "But, as I've told you, we can tell from past bruises how well a patient's skin will heal. Yours heals easily. You'll look wann-der-ful. I'll hang your picture on my wall."

"At least my skin is a plus," Carly said, now trying to concentrate on her article. Every moment with Laval was an education, she knew. Usually, her mind would be flooded with questions. But in Laval's presence she became a bit flustered, slightly intimidated. It was the effect he had on her, the sheer power of his intellect and presence.

It was remarkable that she could feel this way about *any* doctor, considering the abuse her family had taken from her father before he ran off, and the botched surgery, years later, that had resulted in the death of her mother. Carly's life had not been filled with medical heroes, and it took a Laval to overcome her gut resentment of his entire profession.

"You know," she said, "I never asked you—how do you decide what kind of face to give someone?"

"The patient decides," Laval answered, now studying a small scar behind Carly's left ear. "But of course, I advise . . . and most of my patients follow my advice. After all, it's a question of experience, of knowing what's possible. Remember how we used the computer imager, and discussed things? We'll be using it again in a few moments. It's part of the postoperative procedure."

And indeed, a few minutes later a skinny orderly in a white hospital gown appeared at the door and rolled in a cart bearing Laval's computer system, with TV monitor, made by Face Systems, Inc., of New York. "This should excite you," Laval said. "Over here," he told the orderly, gesturing toward a space near the side of Carly's bed. The orderly complied, the wheels of the cart screeching against the yellow tile floors. Laval smiled broadly, anticipating the display he was about to put on.

"Plug it in there, please," he ordered the attendant, pointing to a socket at the head of the bed. The attendant plugged in the computer, then Laval snapped on the switch. Despite the clatter from the halls, Carly could hear the cooling fan inside the unit start up. The attendant left, Laval not acknowledging him.

Carly pressed the button to raise the head section of the bed almost to a sitting position. She looked at the monitor, her mind flushed with memories of the times she'd seen it before. It had been in Laval's office when he was outlining precisely what he'd planned for her. He'd been able to show a photo of her on the left of the screen, as she looked after her accident. The picture was duplicated on the right. Then he'd held a small electronic "stylus" to a board

attached to the computer, "drawing" with it and changing
the image on the right, demonstrating what Carly would
look like after surgery. But he'd cautioned that the projected image on the screen could only be an estimate.

"Ready?" Laval now asked, and Carly's mind snapped
back to the present.

"Yes," she replied.

Laval operated the machine. Almost instantly a picture
of Carly appeared on the left. She winced, and turned
away.

"I know. It's hard to look at what's been," Laval said.
But Carly did turn back for an instant, viewing her damaged face, with its scars, shattered cheek, and broken
nose. "That was hell," she whispered. She remembered
thinking, more than once, that only suicide would solve
her problem. It was only faith in Laval that had kept her
from a five-story leap.

"Now observe," Laval went on. He worked at the
keyboard again, and generated a picture on the right—the
"new" face he'd shown Carly before surgery.

Now Carly looked carefully at the screen, still amazed
at this modern wizardry, and then she looked in the mirror.
The "new" face on the screen and the actual face Laval
had given her were remarkably similar.

"Incredible," she whispered.

"We may have some further work," Laval said, with
uncharacteristic modesty. "Minor things. It's quite common."

"Whatever you say," Carly replied, still staring at the
monitor, still amazed at what had been created from flesh
and bone.

"I don't think anything basic should be changed," Laval
went on. "I hope you agree."

"Oh, yes, I do. Of course I do."

While Carly admired, Laval studied. He saw nothing in
this first postoperative examination to contradict what he'd
felt earlier—that with this face he'd achieved a new level
of plastic surgery, the very creation of classic beauty,
rising out of a tragedy. He *had* come remarkably close to
the computer projection—closer than ever before. And as

the world would applaud this new beauty, this magnificent face, so too would it applaud its creator.

Laval shut off the computer, the glow fading slowly from the monitor. Then he walked closer to Carly's bed, towering over it, his powerful frame and large head literally blocking the ceiling light. He would not sit down on the bed like some doctors Carly had known. That would be too common, too egalitarian. Laval knew his place, and the patients knew theirs.

"I'm going to prescribe some medication," he said. "It will aid in healing, and reduce some of that rawness. And I think it would be wise for you to have some sessions with a therapist."

"A psychiatrist?" Carly was startled.

"It would be wise."

"Why? Is there something wrong with me?"

"Of course not. I prescribe it in eighty percent of my cases. You'll be returning to work, and there'll be a transition period back to the outside world. Some of it may be difficult. A therapist could help."

Carly stared at him. She'd never been to a psychiatrist before, although she knew quite a few through her work. Was Laval covering up something? Other doctors, the kind who'd treated her mother, always seemed so devious. Was Laval trying gently to tell her that she was acting strange? She felt a sudden resistance, as if a psychiatrist would intrude on her newfound happiness. "I'm sure I could make it on my own," she said.

"Of course you can. But remember, the world of attractive people isn't the same as the world of unattractive people. You're coming—because of your accident—from the world of unattractive people. You're joining that other world. How people look affects their ability to adjust. You'll do well because you're attractive again. But mentally, you may still be in that unattractive world for a time. I recommend the therapy."

It was typical of Laval, Carly thought, a thoroughly reasoned, absolutely informed argument. It was impossible to resist the guy. He just knew too much. "All right, I'll do it," Carly said. "I've never thought of it as two worlds."

"Ah yes, but it is," Laval said. "Let me give you an example. And you can use this in your article. We've actually found that unattractive ex-convicts have a higher rate of recidivism than attractive ones. I've done work in prisons to improve the appearance of inmates, mostly correcting jutting jaws and hooked noses. They're less aggressive after the surgery because others view them with less suspicion. Looks *can* kill, and there *are* two worlds, the attractive, and the unattractive."

Carly was fascinated that Laval had worked in prisons. It seemed so out of character for the most elegant society doctor in New York. Was it medical slumming? A chance to try new techniques?

Laval gave Carly the names of three psychiatrists, one of whom she knew personally. Then, having put on a pretty good show, he glanced at his watch, mentioned that he had to see another patient, and started edging toward the door. "I'm encouraged," he said. "The world will love you to death, and I'll see you in the morning."

He left, and Carly leaned back on her pillow. "The world will love me to death," she murmured to herself. But would there be *one* person? That one person could be more than the world. Would it be Mike? Her heart leaped.

She began dozing off. But she just had this feeling, a feeling that she had almost abandoned after the accident, that wonderful things were about to happen to her, that Laval had opened a door that could never again be closed.

The world, or someone, would love her to death.

The woman who'd waited outside the hospital as Laval made his tape continued to wait. But the security guards ignored her, for it was common for people to wait outside hospitals. She could have been a relative, or friend, of someone seriously ill. Or she could have been a survivor, returning to the scene of a loved one's death. People lingered at hospitals, the guards knew.

3

Carly was alone only half an hour when she heard a ring tapping at her door. She looked up. She'd seen that smile a thousand times before. It was both warm and cynical, both approving and chastising, both naïve and scheming, as if belonging to some male Mona Lisa.

"Mike, am I glad to see you!"

And she meant it, more than the man knew.

Mike Moran didn't enter immediately. Instead he leaned against the door and stared at Carly. He was forty-five, and looked like Gene Kelly, although a little slimmer. Now his smile was fixed and his head was nodding a grudging approval. "Nice work," he said. "Yeah, very nice work. I approve."

"Well thank you," Carly replied with a needle in her voice. "I didn't know you went for swellings and black eyes."

Still, Moran didn't move. "They turn me on. No kidding. How much?"

"Mike, come on!"

"How much?"

"That's what you're asking? I just had my whole above-the-neck chassis remodeled, my life is reborn, I'm a saved woman, and you're talking price?"

"I hear a facelift goes for $7,750 in New York. How much?"

"This wasn't cosmetic, Mike. It was serious stuff."

"You got it free."

18

"Mike, come in. You're embarrassing me, not to mention yourself."

Now Moran just laughed and strolled in, as if he owned the room and its occupant. He didn't kiss Carly—he knew enough not to do that yet—but he did squeeze her hand and beam even more broadly. "Hey, it *is* nice work. You're gonna look terrific, kid. You've got everything going for you."

"Thanks, Mike," Carly said. "I feel great."

"Uh, get you anything? A Coke or sandwich?"

"No, Michael, they've got me on a hospital diet. Poison and motor oil."

"Well, if you decide to cheat, slip me a note. I'll bring something in a plain paper bag."

Mike Moran was editor-in-chief of *Allure*, and he didn't seem right for the part. A magazine that reported on trendy New York should, it would seem, have a trendy New Yorker at the helm. Moran, though, was a transplanted Californian who'd grown up in Los Angeles politics as the son of a Democratic state senator. He'd gotten into journalism as a reporter for the *Los Angeles Herald Examiner*, hoping to learn much and run for Congress. He'd learned much, run for Congress, got buried in Nixon's 1972 landslide, and stayed in journalism.

He lived in a brownstone in Brooklyn Heights and went home promptly at six, avoiding the after-hours nightlife of trendy journalism. He took buses, sometimes even the subways. He ate Milky Way candy bars and stuffed the wrappers into his pockets. He didn't even dress right. The suits came from outlets, the fit imprecise. The shoes were usually scuffed and his shirts were wash-and-wear. Some of the staff at *Allure* were embarrassed by him, but he had a perfect sense of what his readers wanted, and gave it to them. Besides, he was a thirty-five-percent owner. He'd raised the cash for his stock purchase from the very same people who'd financed his 1972 Congressional campaign. Those who were sold on Mike Moran were *completely* sold.

Carly herself saw beneath his glib talk and who-cares-about-tomorrow manner. She knew that Moran, educated at Berkeley, troubled by the decline of liberalism in the mid-eighties, cared most about those who couldn't afford his magazine, or the products it advertised. She once noticed that his Visa card came from a labor bank. That told his story better than his daily act. And she knew, because she'd been tipped off by one of his friends, that he often spent holidays working in soup kitchens.

Moran pulled up a chair and sat down. "A lot of your friends see you yet?" he asked.

"You're the first, Mike."

"Hey, I'm honored. It's like being at the unveiling of a statue."

"Yeah, really."

"Well, it is. Oh, everyone at the office sends their best."

"Oh, that's terrific. Send mine to them, would you?"

"Now they'll see you and get jealous. Watch the knives in the back."

Carly groaned. "You got any more good news?"

"It's NYC, Carly. It's *Allure* magazine, where we employ only the brightest and the bitchiest. Say, when are they letting you out of the beauty parlor?"

"About a week."

"Good. We'll have a party. And have I got assignments for you."

"Fine," Carly said. "I can't wait to get back. And you *know* what I want to do, assignment or no."

"Do I know? Does a punching bag feel abused? You've only been telling me for weeks. You want to use our valuable editorial space for an endless love letter to André Laval."

"You're sounding negative, Mike."

"Me? Negative. No way. I think it's a great idea. In fact, I think it's so great that I've contacted movie and book people."

Carly was completely thrown. She'd labored for *Allure* as a worthy reporter, but never had Mike Moran gone out of his way to promote any of her pieces. In truth, he never seemed to notice much of what she wrote. "You're kidding," she said.

"Would I kid?" Moran asked. "Have you ever known me to tell a lie or even a mild half-truth?"

"No, Mike, you're a real Boy Scout," Carly said, inwardly wishing he wouldn't be.

"People are interested, Carlykins," Mike said. "You've got a great story, not only in Laval, but in yourself. I don't think you realize that. You've been yapping on the phone with me about what a great guy this is, the fella next to God, maybe God himself, maybe better than God—God please forgive me—but you know what I mean."

"So what do you want me to do?" Carly asked.

"When you get paroled from this place, I want you to do a whole series on your experiences, a kind of guide to everyone else on what it's like. Then, if it's good enough, you turn it into a book. And maybe a miniseries. Who knows?"

"All right, I'll do it," Carly said. "But, Mike, it's got to be sensitive. This hasn't been fun."

Moran sort of winced, realizing that he might have sounded a little too enthusiastic, too much the editor after a terrific story. "I'm sorry, Carlykins," he said, in a rare apology. "I didn't mean to suggest . . ."

"It's okay," Carly said.

"I know what you've been through," Mike went on, that soft side coming out. "I . . . I always thought about you being here," Moran struggled. Kindness there was. Words there weren't. He always had trouble getting the feelings past the lips.

"Mike, you don't have to say anything," Carly told him.

"You're right, I don't," Moran said, reverting to form. "So tell me, this Laval, is he pretty?"

"Pretty?"

"They're all pretty. They get other surgeons to work on them."

"I don't believe that."

"Check it out. A plastic surgeon once told me. So I ask again, is he cute?"

"He's a good-looking man."

"Wife? Kids?"

"I think he's single."

"The mouth waters," Moran answered. "A single doctor. Successful. World famous. Mothers of daughters will love it. How about *his* mother? Did she scrub floors to send him through medical school?"

"Mike," Carly replied, "I really don't know." And then she paused, a thoughtful, pensive look coming over her still puffy and marked face. "In fact, I really don't know much about him at all. I just asked the people who knew who the best plastic surgeon was."

"That's all you had to know, Carlykins," Moran said.

"It's funny," Carly mused, "I've spent more time with Laval than with most men I've known. He's had more of an effect on me than almost anyone. And yet we never discussed anything but the medical problem. I mean, he knows about *my* history. It's in my file. But I guess you just don't ask a doctor about his."

"It's no problem," Moran replied. "I'll put a researcher on it. You'll know all the basics by the time you get started on the story."

"I'd appreciate that," Carly said.

"And we'll plan everything carefully. We'll have to, uh, get together after you're out of here and go over it. Maybe lunch."

"Sure," Carly said. "Lunch." Was this the way Moran asked for a date?

Mike Moran sat with Carly for more than an hour, engaging in a kind of affectionate sparring. She wondered when, if ever, Moran would make a move. And, frankly, so did he. No one could ever figure out why he was so socially inhibited, hiding his feelings behind that glib, irreverent exterior. It didn't seem right for a man who'd been in politics, whose world seemed to thrive on people, but it was Mike Moran. He now became the second man in Carly's life to imagine great plans for her. André Laval saw her as his greatest accomplishment, his ticket to medical immortality. He would have her on magazine covers and in films, a demonstration of a woman's rebirth. Mike Moran saw Carly's story as intensely personal—a battle to return from hell, a battle fought by someone for whom he cared deeply, although the feeling remained muffled inside him.

Mike left late that afternoon. As he swung out the door of Burgess Hospital, he accidentally brushed the fiftyish woman who'd lingered around the grounds. He excused himself, she smiled weakly, he moved on to hail a cab. And again she took up a position near the front door, with those searching eyes that seemed to fall on everyone who came or went. At one point, in despair, she took out her wallet, flipped the little plastic pages and stopped at a picture. She stared at it, as if for an eternity. It was a face, smiling back, happy and content.

The face was everything in this woman's life.

4

Carly saw Laval eight times during the remainder of he
hospital stay. She felt an urge to probe into his back
ground, to ask the kind of personal questions that Mike'
research could probably not answer. Anything juicy abou
Laval, she knew, would enhance her story, and her book
and her movie. The dreams were flowing.

But she asked him nothing. It wasn't the right time o
the right circumstance. He might be offended. He migh
even feel that she was exploiting him. So she acted like ar
ordinary patient—obsessed with her new face, toying wit
it, teasing with it, peppering Laval with questions on how
to preserve her new look, what hairdo to order, eve
what makeup to wear. She'd met enough vain wome
through *Allure* to put on a convincing act, even flooding
Laval with compliments . . . which were returned every
time.

And Laval was effusive. He brought in young plastic
surgeons to meet her, knowing they would ooh and aah
like country club groupies. Every one of them courted the
favor of the master, for he held the key to their advancement in plastic surgery, the fastest-growing field in American medicine.

Laval enjoyed watching his disciples gush over Carly
He wanted her to believe she was something special, tha
her face was beyond pretty, that it was the ticket to a
brighter future, a future of glamour and riches. She wa
his instrument, and he wanted her to be psychologically

24

prepared for her role, even though he would not yet reveal it to her.

It was a Tuesday afternoon when Laval waltzed into Carly's room with Adrienne, who had broken ground by becoming one of the few female hairstylists to be accepted by New York's elegant set. Adrienne, whose French accent was developed in Miami Beach, had long, jet-black hair, giving her a striking presence befitting a great star. Her nose and chin had both been by Laval, and she wore clothes lent to her—for the publicity value—by the great designers. Today she was wearing a flowing red dress topped by a blue scarf.

"In-cred-ee-ble," Adrienne remarked, as soon as she saw Carly. "André, this is your finest art, no?" Carly had met Adrienne a few times while on assignment for *Allure*, was intimidated by the woman's sheer acting ability, but respected her judgment in washing and cutting. She could never have afforded Adrienne's prices, but Laval was paying for this job—part of the "finishing" he insisted on for his more important patients. "My faces must be properly framed," he told Carly, and Carly wasn't about to arouse Laval's ire with any kind of protest. Besides, it was sort of chic to have one's hair done in a hospital room.

Proper framing meant that Laval, not Adrienne, would prescribe the hairdo. He dictated a short but frizzy arrangement, complementing Carly's newly sharpened features. Laval left, letting Adrienne work. The whole job took almost two hours, during which Carly was turned away from the only mirror in her room. But when Adrienne finished, she held a hand mirror up to Carly's face so the patient could render the usual compliments to the artist.

Carly looked, moving her head from side to side.

"So?" Adrienne asked.

"I love it," Carly replied, "I just love it. I've never looked better."

"Of course," Adrienne said. "You have my exclusive style."

It wasn't long before Laval returned, anxious to see the results of Adrienne's work. "Wann-der-ful," he said, examining Carly from every angle. "Another triumph. This is exactly what I had in mind."

Carly felt herself almost glowing. She'd become a modern-day Cinderella, and she could not deny that she liked the attention. She'd gotten little of it since her accident, and she'd always craved the spotlight she'd missed as a child after her father ran off. The fact that it now came from a man from the same profession as her father simply made it even sweeter. It was as if Laval, in his quaint and theatrical way, was turning back the clock and giving Carly the fatherly applause she'd always wanted.

And the woman still waited outside the hospital, occasionally glancing at the picture in her wallet, the picture with the frizzy hair. She was becoming discouraged, yet she knew this was a chance worth taking, for a human life was involved.

But where was she? Where was the person she yearned to see? Why wasn't she coming through the front door of Burgess Hospital?

Who was she trying to avoid? And why? Why would anyone do such a thing?

"You can see how far she's come," Laval said, speaking to the television camera in his studio, making the second of his tapes on Carly Randall, the second tape that glorified this self-proclaimed medical miracle. He held up two four-by-five Polaroid pictures that a hospital photographer had taken of Carly just after Adrienne had done her thing. He brought the photos close to the autofocusing lens of the camera. "The face is healing well, and the new hair style advances us another step in creating perfection," Laval said. "I have no reason to believe that she suspects the kind of experiment that I am conducting. Like all of them, she's so in love with her new face that she thinks of nothing else. But it's important that you, my successors, know each detail of what's been done.

"To review, I set out to create the face of the nineties, the perfect face for a new decade, a face that would excite.

I've done a vast amount of research to determine exactly how that face should look. But, you would surely ask, how does a plastic surgeon go about creating a face, rather than simply rebuilding what is already there, on the frame of the patient? How is perfection actually achieved? How much failure is permitted? These are legitimate questions. And I begin to answer them by showing you another picture.''

And Laval took an eight-by-ten glossy from a brown envelope, and held it up to the camera.

Mike Moran visited every second day, each time bringing a lavish bouquet of roses. They were the only flowers Carly received. Others weren't sure whether you sent flowers to a plastic surgery patient. It wasn't, after all, a *disease,* and she hadn't exactly been at death's door. Carly did receive some funny cards expressing the wish that she'd get back to work soon. "Get well" also didn't seem quite right. And there were some free makeup samples— graciously supplied by companies who illicitly bought lists of plastic surgery patients from clerks in the ward. One maker even advertised a cream that would cover the "telltale scars." Another said "the new you should be *completely* new." An insurance company even sent a circular on "facelift" insurance, guaranteeing the results of any facelift performed by a board-certified plastic surgeon for three years. No sag, no pay.

Toward the end of Carly's time at the hospital, Moran appeared at the door with the flowers and his old, beaten briefcase—something he rarely carried home. He tapped on the door before coming in, wearing a topcoat he'd originally bought for his 1972 Congressional race, and which hadn't been cleaned more than twice in the intervening years. He also needed a haircut, a need that faded into insignificance beside the coat and briefcase.

"Want any Fuller brushes, lady?" he asked.

"Sure, come in and show me what you've got," Carly replied, flipping a copy of *The New York Times Magazine* onto a side table as Moran entered. It struck her that Mike could never begin a conversation by just saying hello. He always started with some wisecrack, a line that obviously had been scripted in advance. Carly sensed that there was a basic fear inside the man, something that required a kind of buffer between him and the world. But she liked him, more and more. He paid attention to her. He never acted like the boss visiting an employee. Was it that decency that she was beginning to find so attractive? Or was it a feeling that he was lonely, that he needed someone, and that he had an absolutely awful time trying to express it?

"Nice haircut," he said. "Fancy, but nice."

"Does that complete the assessment?" Carly asked.

"Assessment completed." Mike dropped his briefcase, letting it flip over on its side. Then he placed the new bouquet in a vase that had been emptied that morning. "A little more cheer," he said. "Always helps."

"Thanks, Mike," Carly replied. "You really shouldn't be bringing me flowers every time. It's expensive."

"Comes out of the office budget," Moran replied.

There it was again—the flip remark. And Carly knew it wasn't true. Moran was a stickler for separating business and personal expenses and would never charge flowers to the office, but he had to say it. It was so hard for him just to play it straight.

"There," he went on, arranging the red bouquet in the vase. "If they start to wilt, call the nurse and ask for oxygen."

"Right. They'll put me in the psycho ward."

"Hey, you'll meet the best people," Moran said. "Some of my former writers. Give 'em my regards." Then he sat down next to Carly's bed, gently squeezing her hand. He *could* kiss her, she thought. People *do* that, and she was healing well. But Mike Moran was the kind who needed a printed invitation.

"You've got your briefcase," Carly said. "Carrying a bomb?"

"I don't know. Maybe I am."

Carly looked curious. "What does that mean?"

"I'll get to that in a minute. How you feeling, kid? You have an okay day?"

"Yeah," Carly replied. "Things get better all the time."

"You have everything you need?"

"Sure. I just can't wait to get out, though. Three more days of listening to doctor calls on the PA."

"Wait'll you get your first complaint from someone you misquoted. You'll miss the doctor calls."

"Yeah," Carly laughed. "No doubt."

There was an awkward silence as Mike gazed at Carly. Yes, she looked terrific with that new hair style. Did she look this good before, or hadn't he noticed? Or had Laval performed so brilliantly that she was in fact a new person? Mike's eyes kept coming back to the hair, how perfectly it framed the new face. "Uh, how'd you pick out that style?" he finally asked.

"I didn't. Laval did."

"Laval?"

"He insisted. It's a package deal."

"Why'd he give you that one?"

"Mine is not to reason why," Carly answered. "The master knows."

"You're convinced he's the master?"

"Look at me. Aren't you?"

Moran hesitated before answering, then seemed to sigh. "Yeah, he's the master all right, Carlykins. No question about it. He's also a lot of other things."

A quizzical look formed in Carly's eyes. "Come again?"

"We did some research on the good doctor for your piece. It's fascinating. Absolutely fascinating. We're talking first-class copy, maybe Pulitzer Prize in a medium year. Your doctor is a hell of a lot more interesting than you ever dreamed. This is no brilliant kid from college who studied hard, whizzed through med school, and made Mommy proud. This is a guy with a past a mile long."

"Mike, I'm not following," Carly said. "As far as I know, Laval is the world's most respected plastic surgeon. What are you telling me? Is anything bad?"

"Let's say the guy's human," Moran answered. "Let's

say he hasn't thrown a spotlight on some of the things he's done. Let's say he's created an image from scrap, and let's also say that my hat is off to him. He's done it himself and the guy does do nice work. There's just more to him than a scalpel and funny talking, that's all.''

''I want to hear this,'' Carly told him.

Without another word, Moran reached over for his brief-case, which he hoisted to his lap. He snapped open the top zipper and pulled out a raft of four-by-six cards, with red ballpoint scribblings. He smoothed out the pile, the way someone would straighten a deck of playing cards. Then he rearranged a few.

Carly, who had been leaning on a pillow, now sat up, anticipating the fruits of Moran's research.

''Subject,'' Moran began, suddenly sounding very offi-cial, ''Arnie Lemke.''

''Lemke?'' Carly asked. ''What's a Lemke?''

''A Lemke is a kid who grows up in Philadelphia and becomes a plastic surgeon. A Lemke's father was a grocer.''

''A grocer? A *grocer*? I mean, there's nothing wrong with being a grocer. But, Jesus, the way he talks, I thought he came from the royal palace.''

''The palace, ace reporter, was a three-room apartment in a changing neighborhood with an icebox that really used ice. All his education beyond high school was on scholar-ship. And here's something you'll like: he started out as an artist—I mean, with paints.''

''You're kidding.''

''He won some art contests in high school and got a scholarship to an art college. He went over to sculpture, but it didn't click. They threw him out.''

''Why?''

''They thought he was doing lousy work. I had one of our people interview some old-timers at the school. They flunked him. A no-talent guy, they thought. He was pretty bitter about it, too. He wrote some letters to the school president, and threatened to sue. There's a picture of him in a Philly newspaper. It shows him picketing the school.

He put some small sculpture pieces he'd done right outside the main building while he picketed.''

"But they never let him back in?"

"No. The picketing made it worse. They claimed he made some threats."

"What happened then?"

"He joined the army. Enlisted for three years. Can you beat that? An artistic kid enlisting in the army? I mean, they don't usually go in for the . . . sensitive type, if you know what I mean. I'm guessing," Mike went on, "that he wanted to get away from it all, and didn't want to spring for Club Med."

"Where'd they send him?"

"Alaska. Basic infantryman, 111 we used to call 'em. That's the military designation for all sweat and no luck. A bright guy like that. It was like self-punishment."

Carly thought for a moment, then smiled ironically, as if some journalistic gem were glistening in her mind.

"What's the grin for?" Moran asked.

"It may have been punishment, but it's almost romantic," she said.

Moran shot her one of his "your screws are loose" looks.

"No," she insisted. "Think about it. He failed as an artist and joined the army. Then later he took a French name, almost as if he'd run away to the French Foreign Legion. It's all very Continental."

"Yeah," Moran answered, "now that you put it that way. It is very Continental. Or very romantic. Or very crazy. I mean, Hitler was a failed artist who joined the army."

The reference sent a sharp chill rocketing up Carly's spine. She could hardly conceive of Laval as a modern-day Hitler, and Moran's use of the name was almost offensive. "Look," she said, "it isn't the standard medical background, although . . ."

"Although what?"

"I remember that the first American woman to become a plastic surgeon was also a sculptor."

"Did she spend three years wandering around Alaska with a rifle slung over her shoulder?"

"I doubt it."

"Did she get thrown out of art school?"

"Not that I know of."

"And did she ever get arrested?"

"Arrested?" Carly swung her legs around to sit on the side of the bed, too wound up now to rest like a good little patient. "Mike, what are you talking about?"

"I'm talking about a juicy story," Moran replied, flipping through his cards, getting to the one he wanted, dropping the others into his lap. "After the army, Laval got into one of those six-year medical programs—you know, two years of college, four of medical school."

"I'm surprised he got in, after being thrown out of an art school."

"He never mentioned the art school on his record. He lied."

"I see."

"And it isn't all wann-der-ful," Moran told her. "He got in, based on his high school grades and test scores. But he continued sculpting on the side. He entered his stuff in a sidewalk art show in Baltimore, where he was going to school. Someone passed by and said something—I guess one of those instant critiques. They had a scrape. Laval threw some punches, and got nailed on an assault charge."

"And this is a guy whose hands are insured for a million dollars," Carly said.

"He spent two years on probation and got suspended from school for a month. But he finally graduated—not very high in his class. He got his plastic surgery training in South America somewhere, and started to practice. That's as far as my research goes. I didn't get up to how he got his name or learned to talk funny."

Now Carly did lean back, trying to absorb the small mine of information that Mike had brought. Her opinion of Laval as a physician did not change. She had seen in her own case the quality of the man's work, of his art. But the background wasn't what she'd expected. It was awfully hard to think of André Laval as Arnie Lemke with a tumultuous past, although she wasn't sure how much that past actually mattered.

"How did he get away with this?" she asked Mike Moran.

"Get away with what?"

"None of this has ever been exposed publicly."

Moran shrugged, then raised his hands over his head, almost in a surrendering gesture. "No one dug," he replied. "*We* didn't dig. No one asked questions. Just like no one asked questions about the rockets on the *Challenger*. Laval's office, or Lemke's or whatever his name is—they give out a standard bio saying he came from Philadelphia, went to Johns Hopkins, is the world's greatest plastic surgeon and gave God a facelift. The art school's not there, the army's not there, the arrest is missing. Look, no one ever had reason to question the guy's record."

"And we still don't," Carly said. "It's all fascinating, Mike, but the man is a great doctor."

"Of course. That's what *makes* it fascinating. I'd love you to interview him at some point and throw some of this stuff at him. The man has got to have depth. The background is bizarre, but bizarre isn't against the law."

At that moment there was a tap at the door. Carly knew the tap and rolled her eyes. "Right on cue," she said quietly to Moran. "Come in!"

The door opened slowly. André Laval, né Arnie Lemke, stood in the opening, wearing a newly pressed green hospital gown, looking benevolent, cutting the image of the tall, dedicated doctor come to look after his patient. "Ah," he said, "I didn't know you had a guest, Ms. Randall."

"Dr. Laval," Carly answered, "I'd like you to meet Michael Moran, editor of *Allure*."

Moran could see the glow in Laval's eyes. It was remarkable that they hadn't met before, considering the status of *Allure* in the New York magazine market. But Moran just hadn't made the right social rounds.

"Mr. Moran," Laval said, entering and extending his right hand, "your magazine is wann-der-ful. Simply grand. It's a pleasure."

"The pleasure's mine," Mike answered, getting up, but still holding the four-by-six cards. He and Laval shook hands, then Moran casually slid the cards back into his briefcase. "In fact, Carly and I were just going over some new assignments."

"Ah, yes. Well, she'll be ready for the world pretty soon," Laval said, looking down at Carly as if he were talking about a child. "The question is, will the world be ready for her? For that face? She's smashing, don't you think?"

"Oh, yes," Moran said. "Carly looks terrific. You're a genius, doctor."

"Oh no, not a genius. Just a man who enjoys his work." He turned to Carly. "I enjoy it even more when the results are this lovely."

My God, Moran thought, the guy lays it on as thick as mustard on a ballpark hot dog. He'd heard Laval speak on television—always interviewed in connection with the latest breakthrough in cosmetic surgery—but this was the first time he'd gotten the treatment firsthand.

"Maybe I'd better leave," Moran said.

"Oh no, please stay," Laval replied, with a sweep of his Rolexed left hand. "I'm just here to ask Ms. Randall how she feels, and to check over the healing. Oh, you had a marvelous article about Monaco in your last issue."

"Thanks," Moran said.

"I've been there many times. I've always felt so terrible about Princess Grace. I have prominent patients in Monaco. Fine people."

"Oh, I'm sure the finest," Moran answered. He was watching Laval's great blue eyes, and realized the surgeon was assessing him—the raincoat, the worn shoes, the general pig style. But Laval didn't reveal his contempt. Moran was an editor, a route to publicity. Contempt had to be restrained.

"After we chat today," Laval said to Carly, "I want to recommend a fashion consultant."

"A what?" Moran asked, not hesitating to intrude on Carly's business.

"A fashion consultant. Plastic surgery can be compromised if the patient doesn't, as one might say, dress it well. The look, the color, everything, complements the new face. Look at Ms. Randall's hair. Isn't it chic?"

"Yeah," Moran replied. "Very chic."

"Yes, of course," Laval said, now brushing back a strand of hair that had dared wander down over his artificially tanned face. "With your coloring, Ms. Randall, I prefer that you emphasize the greens."

"That sounds right," Carly said. And it was right. She still could not imagine this man as Arnie Lemke, and knew she never would. Whatever turmoil had occurred in his life, his presence was overwhelming, her gratitude for his miracles was complete.

Laval left a few minutes later and returned to his office. He had an important call to make, a call critical to the advancement of his career. This call he made himself, not going through one of his secretaries. He'd memorized the number, for he didn't want it written anywhere. And he made the call on a phone behind his desk, equipped with a device that flashed if the line were being tapped. Laval had heard a rumor that the hospital tapped the lines of doctors to check on activities that might embarrass the medical center.

He dialed area code 312—Chicago. The phone rang three times. Then he heard a tired, bored woman's voice answering. "Yeah? Hello?"

"Marcia?"

"Yeah. Who's this?"

"This is Dr. Laval."

"Oh, yeah. Hi."

Marcia Lane took another sip of Scotch and put the glass down on an end table, easing onto a worn couch to talk to Laval. She lived in a first-floor, one-room apartment in a seedy section of Chicago, with two bars across the street and a stream of derelicts parading past her window. That was life for a part-time waitress who still couldn't keep a job for more than two weeks. The hairdo was homemade and mussed, and the flowered dress was secondhand polyester. The face was hidden behind huge sunglasses—Marcia wore them inside to conceal her bloodshot eyes.

"How are you feeling today, Marcia?" Laval continued, condescension in his voice.

"Oh, fine, I guess," Marcia answered, eying the Scotch, but resisting while talking with Laval.

"Well, that's good, dear, I'm sure the men are going crazy over you."

"I get my share."

"Yes. Yes, of course. Now, Marcia, I called because I'm going to be in Chicago, and I think I should check you."

"You think somethin's screwed up?" Marcia asked, now grabbing a loose cigarette from the end table and lighting it.

"No. I'm sure everything is fine. But the work should be checked periodically—you know, now and then."

"Yeah, okay."

"I'll come to you, dear."

Marcia was startled. "You wanna come *here,* to this dump?"

"I'm sure it's charming."

"Oh yeah, charming. Junkville."

"I prefer it," Laval said. "And Marcia, you know our arrangement. Because of the, well, the special nature of our relationship, please don't mention this visit. Okey dokey?"

"Yeah. I know the story."

Laval and Marcia spoke for a few more minutes, Laval not once wincing or showing any annoyance with his skid-row patient. She was special to him, more special than the stars and princesses who glided through his office each week.

"I'll be looking forward to seeing you, Marcia," Laval concluded, after making a tentative date with her. "We'll talk things over. Maybe I can help you get better work."

"Okay," Marcia replied, still eying that Scotch. She appreciated what Laval had done for her, but her world didn't get too excited about special guests. The conversation ended, and she picked up her Scotch.

The woman outside the hospital was tiring, as she did every afternoon, but she had to endure until nightfall. After a time, everything seemed to become a blur. But she knew what sight would alert her, wake her from her stupor. Some flash of green, any flash of green. And a glimpse of reddish hair. There'd been so many false alarms since she began her vigil. Maybe they'd all be false alarms. Maybe the right woman would never come through those front doors. But maybe she would.

5

Carly was released on October 2.

Mike Moran was out of town on business, but had offered to send a car to pick her up. Carly, however, had refused. Better to be independent, to hail a cab in the usual manner, and go home without looking like an invalid. Hospital rules, of course, required that she be wheeled down to the front entrance, her little suitcase on her lap. She got out of the chair, helped by an orderly, said her good-byes to some staff members, and walked through the revolving door into a brisk fall day, getting her first whiff of sophisticated air pollution in more than three weeks. The fumes were magnificent, as fine a scent as Carly Randall had ever experienced.

She didn't notice the woman standing across the street. She didn't notice the sudden shock in her face, the sudden animation in her hands, her sudden frenzy. Carly was concentrating only on getting a ride home.

Fortunately, there were some yellow cabs waiting in the circular driveway that led up to the hospital. Carly signaled for one to pull up. The driver did, slamming on his questionable brakes right at the front door. But he didn't get out to help her in—not that she expected it—so she eased herself into the back seat, her case beside her.

"Eighty-sixth and Columbus, please," she said. The driver, a Russian immigrant with a little beard, simply nodded and threw the flag on the meter. Then he lurched off, sending Carly squarely against the back seat. She felt

a sudden tug on the right side of her face, and realized that
the jolt had strained some skin that hadn't healed. "Slow
down!" she ordered the driver, who turned around and
smiled, a little embarrassed, but showed no inclination to
follow her direction. He spun out into traffic and headed
south, snaking around cars as if he were racing *to* rather
than from a hospital.

Carly watched the dirtyish stone buildings of the West
Side melt from one neighborhood into another. The streets
teemed with the conglomeration of the races, mixed in
some places, separated in others, all linked by one common piece of technology—the shoulder-borne ghetto blast-
ers whose distorted thumping exceeded even the rattle of
the taxicab.

When the driver was absolutely compelled to stop for
traffic lights, Carly noticed something she'd never noticed
before. Men looking into her cab kept looking. They were
looking at her, at her face, at her hair, at everything André
Laval had done. A few winked, a sign of the free-spiritedness
that still prevailed in the area, and she felt compelled to
wink back. She couldn't deny that it felt good. It made her
feel still more grateful to Dr. Laval, more determined to
write her story about him, determined to learn how a man
with his strange background had achieved such greatness.

"Snow?" the driver suddenly blurted out, breaking her
train of thought. Carly looked up at the gray sky, and
knew the temperature was only in the high thirties, below
the norm. "No," she replied, "I don't think so. Not this
early."

The driver shrugged. "In Russia it snow," he said, then
laughed. "All time."

"Yes, I understand," Carly answered.

"I own cab," the driver said, turning around and smiling again, while hurtling past a bus. "And another one."

Great, Carly thought. Here comes a Horatio Algerski
story. She smiled politely but kept silent.

After they had passed the red brick buildings of Columbia University, the tone of the neighborhood began to
change. The faces now were becoming decidedly white,

with a lower percentage of smiles and a much lower percentage of the shoulder symphonies.

As she cruised farther down the West Side, Carly suddenly felt strangely uncomfortable. She'd glanced into the right sideview mirror early in the trip and had noticed a cab behind hers, following close, with a woman in the back seat. Now she glanced again and saw the same cab, with the same woman. Every time her car changed lanes, the other cab changed as well. It was following her. That was beyond question.

But why?

Carly restrained herself from turning around and looking back. Why let on that she knew? Maybe the two cab drivers knew each other. Maybe there was some kind of grudge. Or maybe this was a type of street game. It was baffling and disconcerting. The cab behind her turned and followed as her cab drove down her block. It slowed as her cab slowed.

Carly reached her building at Columbus and Eighty-sixth. Still trying not to glance back, she paid the $5.80 plus tip and got out.

Suddenly, the other cab screeched up.

The rear door flew open.

A woman in her early fifties bolted out.

Yes, Carly now recognized her as a woman who'd been across the street when she'd left Burgess Hospital.

"Please!" the woman shouted at Carly. "Don't run away from me. Stop!"

Startled, Carly froze in her tracks, staring at the woman, wondering if she were some kind of mental case. The woman ran toward her. "Kitty!" she shouted. "My Kitty!" She slammed against Carly, embracing her while breaking down in tears. "Kitty, baby, where did you go? Why did you leave us? Your father, Kitty. Did you hear about your father?"

Carly was dumbfounded, for a moment immobile in time and space. "Kitty, talk to me!" the woman screamed, sobbing hysterically. "I've waited more than a year. I waited outside that hospital. I knew you'd go back there, where he was."

Gently, sensing some horrible mix-up, Carly edged away from the woman. "Ma'am," she said quietly, "I think there's a mistake. Please, ma'am."

"Stop that!" the woman begged. "You're my Kathleen. Don't play jokes on me."

"I'm not playing jokes," Carly said. "My name is Carly Randall."

"No, no, no," the woman wailed. "Don't you think I know my own daughter? Why are you doing this, Kathleen?"

"I'm not Kathleen. Look, come into the building. Sit down in the lobby. Let's talk."

Carly's voice was soothing. She felt sorry for this woman. She put her arm around her and led her to the door of her old apartment building. Carly opened the front door with her pass key, and they walked into the lobby, sitting down on a worn, fabric-covered bench.

Stay calm, Carly told herself. This is a grieving mother, obviously. Try to understand what she's going through, that this is probably a case of mistaken identity, or wishful thinking, or both. "Now, Ma'am," Carly said, "why don't you—"

"Don't call me ma'am, Kathleen," the mother said, her hands quivering as she absorbed the trauma of the moment. "You always called me Momma. Call me that."

"I don't want to disappoint you," Carly said. "I must look just like Kathleen. I'm sure that's it. But I'm not her. If you listen, you'll probably realize I don't even sound like her."

The mother began to look frightened, as if Carly was speaking a quiet truth.

"I can prove I'm not your daughter," Carly went on. "It'll come out in medical records. I'll even take a lie-detector test."

Now the mother got up from the bench and began to back away, a look of sheer horror crossing her face, the horror of disappointment, the horror of a terrible cruelty played on her by fate. "You're lying," she whispered, desperate to hang on to the illusion. "You're a sick girl."

"No, I'm a very well girl," Carly replied. "I want to help you find Kathleen too."

The mother gazed at her, the hurt flowing from every quivering pore. "Open your mouth," she said.

Carly quickly understood what the mother was getting at. She opened her mouth.

"Wider."

She opened it wider.

The mother stepped forward, fearful, and looked in. "Turn to the light," she said.

And Carly did.

The mother looked, then dropped her head to her chest. Slowly, she walked back to the bench and sat down. "She's not Kathleen," she said, as if to no one in particular. "My girl had a tooth missing, on the bottom. My baby's still gone."

Again, Carly placed her arm around the crushed woman. "I told you," she said. "Now, please tell me what this is all about."

The mother turned toward Carly, staring into her eyes, still not quite believing what was happening. "It's painful," she said.

"I'm sure. Did your daughter run away? You mentioned that you were certain she'd go back to Burgess Hospital, where someone worked. Who was that?"

The mother took a deep breath. "Laval," she said.

The name hit Carly like a thunderbolt. Somehow, instinctively, in a fraction of a second, she knew that something had exploded, that her world had been invaded, that everything would change. The name, the confusion of faces, even Moran's report on Laval's odd past—all these came together on the point of a pin that jabbed into her brain. "What about Laval?" she asked, her voice beginning to quiver almost as much as the mother's.

"He was Kathleen's plastic surgeon," the mother answered. "Kathleen Shirmer. We're from Burbank, California. My name is Margaret. Please call me that."

"I will."

"Two years ago my daughter had a car accident. Her

face was . . . badly hurt. She needed a miracle. She worked at a television company in Burbank, and one of the producers there had interviewed this plastic surgeon from New York who also worked at one of our Los Angeles hospitals, this Laval. He was supposed to be renowned or something." Margaret caught her breath before continuing, brushing back some of her gray-streaked hair. "He did a wonderful job. Kathleen's face was repaired, and entirely changed. She was beautiful. Here, let me show you."

Margaret dug deep into her black vinyl pocketbook, digging out her wallet. She flipped to a picture of Kathleen and turned it around to Carly.

Carly gazed down at the photo. "Oh my God," she gasped. "It's . . ."

"You," Margaret said.

"Someone who looks very much like me," Carly conceded. "I can't understand it. I didn't say so, but . . . Laval was my surgeon too. I also had an accident. My face was also rebuilt. I thought I had an exclusive. What is he doing?"

"That's what I'd like to know," Margaret said.

"Tell me more about Kathleen," Carly urged.

"She was finished with her surgery," Margaret went on, "but she still had to go to her follow-up appointments whenever this Laval came to LA. Then one day she told me she found out something about Laval. She snuck a look at some of her medical records. I don't remember exactly how she found out. But she said it upset her."

"What was it?"

"She wouldn't say. I've got this heart condition. She didn't like to get me excited. So look at me now."

"She gave no hint?"

"No, but she kept seeing Laval. And then, one day, she was missing."

"She just disappeared?"

"Yes. Actually, it was at night. She left work. No one ever saw her again. They found her car in a parking lot. The police have been on it."

"And Laval?" Carly asked.

"I have to say, he's been wonderful. He came and visited as soon as he heard Kitty was missing. He offered a reward. He stays in touch. He gave me advice . . . and told me not to do any publicity."

Carly winced. "Why not?"

"He said, if Kitty's picture was circulated or it was on TV, only the cranks would call."

"I see," Carly said. "Well, I can't deny the truth of that. What else happened?"

"Nothing. It's been horrible. The police look all the time. They get leads. They all go cold. My husand—rest in peace—he spent so many hours going up Los Angeles streets looking for Kitty, it killed him. A young man. Only fifty-four years old, and it gave him a heart attack at the wheel."

"I'm so sorry," Carly said.

Once again Margaret stared at Carly, then let her eyes rove, looking Carly up and down. "So much like you. She did her hair like this because Laval told her to. And she also wore a lot of green."

Another chill traveled up Carly's spine. Was she a clone of Kathleen? Why had Laval made two faces so nearly identical? Was he duplicating women? And what did happen to Kathleen?

"I know this is difficult," Carly said, "but do you have any theories on what happened to your daughter?"

"No," Margaret sighed. "Dr. Laval told me she might have run away. He said sometimes women who go through all that surgery just want a new life. But it isn't like Kitty. She was so close to us. She even lived with us. We joked that she was already working, and wouldn't move out. That's how close this family was. But I keep thinking—maybe she's just confused. That's why I came here."

"Oh?"

"It's the anniversary of her surgery. I thought, maybe she'd want to hang around Burgess Hospital, where Laval worked. Maybe she'd try to contact him. I came to New York, just to be near Laval and the hospital. Maybe I'd see my Kitty. I didn't. I know most people think the worst happened to her. I can't think it.''

''I understand,'' Carly said.

''You probably think I'm crazy.''

''No, I think you're a very good mother. Look, I live in this building. Please come upstairs. Have some coffee. Rest a while. And we can talk.''

''I don't know,'' Margaret said. ''It's too . . . strange to me.''

''I know,'' Carly told her. ''But we're related in a way. We're related through André Laval. Something is wrong here, Margaret. Something is very wrong, and I'm going to find out what it is.''

''I'll help you,'' Margaret said. ''We are related. I feel like you're . . . almost Kathleen. Maybe you can come to Burbank. Go through Kitty's things. Her notes from work. You've been to Laval. Maybe you'll recognize something.''

''That's a wonderful idea. I'll go to Burbank. Now come upstairs, please.''

''No,'' Margaret said. ''I've had enough for one day. I'm tired. Look, I'm going back to California. I'll give you my number. Come as soon as you can. But I want to go home.''

Yes, of course it was strange, Carly thought. But she tried to place herself in Margaret's position. The woman had been through hell. She'd actually thought she'd found her daughter, and had been crushed by disappointment. She needed time alone, time to confront her fate. Carly decided not to pressure her. ''I understand how you feel,'' she said. ''Please leave me that number. I'll be in touch. But one important thing . . .''

''What is that?'' Margaret asked.

''Say nothing to Laval. Have no contact with him. If he finds out we've met, and he's hiding something, it'll make things worse, much, much worse.''

Margaret nodded, signaling that she would do what Carly asked.

*   *   *

Margaret left as quickly as she'd arrived, hailing a cab herself and disappearing into the traffic. Carly now realized how shaken she was. Margaret had been a commando attack, a terror raid. The trip back from Burgess, planned as a quiet, uneventful homecoming, had descended into a nightmare and had plunged her into her worst personal crisis since the accident. The physician who had been her hero now loomed as a possible monster, a manipulator, someone whose bizarre past might be more relevant than Carly had dared imagine.

It had happened in a matter of minutes, and now Carly Randall had to react. She sensed, as she recalled the story of Kathleen Shirmer, that her life might depend on it.

6

Carly took the self-service elevator to her apartment on the third floor. It was a twelve-by-twenty-two-foot studio—the size of the living room of her mother's house, with a rent three times what her mother had paid each month on her mortgage. Carly was paying about a third of her salary just to rent the place, and she expected a rent increase any month. She had a sign on the wall: WELCOME TO MILLIONAIRES' ROW.

The apartment was decorated in white modern, relatively inexpensive furniture bought largely at Workbench, a local chain. The carpeting was blue wall-to-wall—it came with the apartment—and a raft of windows, behind blinds, looked out on Eighty-sixth Street, a two-way thoroughfare lined with apartment buildings.

The street noise could be oppressive. No one in the building called it "the rhythm of the city."

Carly set her suitcase down. The apartment was immaculate, just as she had left it, and the four green plants, watered by a neighbor, looked healthy. Carly knew all her back mail would be delivered the next day. A full day without bills.

Her answering machine wasn't even flashing. People had been considerate. Only the young woman living above her wasn't considerate. She was still blasting the soap operas.

But there was no time to rest, no time to enjoy being home. Margaret had made that impossible. Yet, Carly wasn't sure exactly what to do. She couldn't call the police. She had no evidence of a crime having been committed. She surely wasn't going to call Laval and confront him, not based simply on the testimony of a distraught mother. She couldn't write about the situation yet. She hadn't enough facts.

She wanted to talk to Mike. Yes, Mike could be trusted. But wasn't it odd to think that way? No, not really. Carly knew that deep inside her was a suspicion of men that grew out of the awful experiences with her father. It had taken her years to overcome that feeling, that suspicion that all men would eventually betray her. But Mike wouldn't. She knew it. She *felt* it. As for Laval, she knew she shouldn't rush to judgment. Don't convict him simply because he, like her father, was a doctor. Don't convict him because of Margaret's revelations. Get the information first. Go out and dig. As she dialed *Allure*'s number, Carly fought to restrain herself, to keep her objectivity, to treat Laval like any journalistic subject. She knew how hard the fight would be.

Mike was in Philadelphia, she realized, but could always be reached. He subscribed to a beeper service, wore the little device on his belt, and was beeped several times during any day away from his office.

Carly told the *Allure* operator that the matter was urgent. She was instructed to hang up and wait by her phone.

The phone rang only four minutes later.

"Carlykins?"

Carly could hear, by the traffic noises, that Mike was in a phone booth. "Mike, am I glad to hear from you."

"That's good news, Carlykins," Mike said. "I hear this is urgent stuff. What's wrong?"

"You won't believe it."

"Probably not, but . . . Hey, you didn't have an accident, did you?"

"No, I'm fine."

"You sure?" Mike saw that a passerby was waiting to use the booth, and waved him away. "You positive, Carly?"

"I'm okay. I'm at home, in the apartment."

"So what's wrong?"

"Mike, I think André Laval gave me the face of another woman."

"What did you just say?"

"Listen carefully. When I left the hospital, I was followed by an older woman. She confronted me. She thought I was her daughter. Her daughter had *also* been in an accident, also had her face rebuilt by Laval. This mother showed me a picture. It was *me*, Mike."

"You're hallucinating," Mike said, not really meaning it.

"No, I certainly am not. Mike, I *saw* the picture."

"Carly, are you on medication?"

"No. Absolutely no."

"Must've been a similarity," Moran said.

"If you'd been there, you wouldn't be saying these things, Michael. Laval gave my face to another woman."

"Where is this other lady?"

"She's missing."

"Jesus."

"Now it gets serious, doesn't it?"

"I'm not passing judgments," Moran said. "The whole thing sounds crazy. I've seen reporters misled by similarities before, Carly. Not you, though. I've never seen you misled. Look, hit me with all the details."

Carly then filled Mike in on her conversation with Margaret. He listened, said little, ventured no opinion, having heard no absolute proof. When Carly finished, there was a long pause as Moran gathered up his thoughts. "Carlykins," he finally said, "either Laval has committed one of the great horrors in medical history, or you've been hit by the mightiest snow job since Cain said 'trust me' to Abel."

"I don't think it's a snow job, Mike," Carly said. "I think I know the genuine article."

"It's some story," Moran replied, thoughts of the Pulitzer Prize dancing in his head, as they did regularly.

"You're thinking about a *story?*" Carly protested.

"What kind of an editor would I be if I wasn't? Look,

my first concern is you, obviously. But it *is* some story—if it's true. I mean, Laval, this godlike doctor, mass-producing faces?''

"Yes. Yes it is some story," Carly agreed, "and I know it's true."

"I don't want it spread around," Moran said. "It's too . . . impossible. It's not the kind of thing you discuss around a magazine office. It would stay inside those four walls precisely two minutes. So it'll be business as usual around *Allure*. Please remember that. Now look, Carlykins, it *still* sounds crazy to me, but we'll work on it. We'll track it down. We'll find out exactly what's going on. . . .or not going on. I promise."

"Thank you, Mike."

They both hung up. Carly had sensed the skepticism in Mike's voice, and yet she respected it. It *was* an impossible story, and impossible stories sometimes didn't pan out. But this was far more than a story to Carly Randall, and she knew she'd be driven until the truth was finally known.

She couldn't wait.

She had to get started immediately. It was only eleven A.M. on her black Braun alarm clock. Why wait? Trails could go cold. Sources could dry up.

Carly was about to ask the most important question of her journalistic career. Who really was André Laval, and what was he up to?

Was she in danger? She didn't feel she was. Strangely, the idea of danger never crossed her mind. How dangerous could a plastic surgeon be?

She grabbed her little leather phone book, worn at the edges. Levin, she thought. Scott Levin. Plastic surgeon. She'd gone to college with him. Interviewed him for *Allure* many times. She'd have gone to him for her plastic surgery, but she never liked to do business with friends. And Laval was the best, the highest recommended. She found the number. Levin's nurse put her through.

Carly was in luck. Levin was only doing office work and could see her immediately. She cabbed across Manhat-

tan to a white brick townhouse on East Sixty-eighth Street,
where Levin had his office. It was an excellent location for
a plastic surgeon, in the midst of Manhattan's chic, well-
heeled, and medically insured upper crust, an area where
faces were changed as often as doormats—and people did
get younger every day.

Scott Levin, though, was not the slick magazine image
of a plastic surgeon, certainly not the image of the Laval
school of plastic surgery. Short and pudgy, largely bald
since twenty-three, he'd had a hard time building a practice, succeeding only because of medical excellence and a
warm personality that occasionally overcame his looks.
He'd had the good sense to work at several hospitals
around the city, and got most of his referrals from Queens,
where a plastic surgeon still did not have to look as if he'd
had his own services.

"Terrific," Levin said in that taut, high-pitched voice
as Carly came into his office. "Carly, you look great.
Really, I mean smashing. André outdid himself." Then he
laughed, that nervous little laugh he'd had since college.
As they shook hands, Carly felt the pudginess of Levin's
grip. "Thanks, I feel great," she replied routinely, then
requested that they meet privately, behind closed doors.

Levin saw immediately that something was wrong. Carly
was minus the bounce and smile that were her two trademarks, and she didn't do the small talk that she'd perfected
as a staff member of *Allure*. He ushered her into a small,
oak-paneled office and shut the door. "You've got a problem," he said. "I can tell."

"I don't know," Carly answered, slumping into a visitor's chair. "It's more of a question than a problem. I
thought I'd come to you, Scotty. I don't want to impose,
but . . ."

"You're never imposing. I was just doing my corporate
taxes. I'm incorporated, you know."

"Yes, I'm sure."

"This is a medical question, I guess."

"Sort of. I hope it is."

Then Levin grimaced, his double chins giving birth to

triplets. "I can't believe you're having a problem with Laval. He did magnificent work. I look at it with pure admiration."

"Scotty," Carly asked, "what do you know about Laval?"

The grimace continued. "What do I *know* about him?" Suddenly Levin looked defensive. "Hey, if you've got the kind of problem that needs a lawyer, maybe we shouldn't . . ."

"I'm not suing him for malpractice."

Levin relaxed. All but two chins melted away. "Oh. Well, I hope not. You know, we doctors get nutso about that. But, if you're not . . ."

"No, I'm not. Honest, Scotty."

"What do I know about him. He's the best. He's an artist. Yeah, I know all about the personality." Again, that nervous little laugh. "But you've got to look beyond that."

"What do you know about his background?"

"Johns Hopkins. Thriving pactice. On the staff of a half dozen hospitals around the country. I don't know him socially. I'm not sure anyone does . . . except maybe the president."

"Have you ever heard rumors about him?"

"Rumors? Hey Carly, what are you getting at?"

"Scotty, I can't tell you everything," Carly replied. "Not yet. You'll know why eventually. But, okay, you don't know anything . . . negative . . . about Laval?"

"No. He's a snob. And he makes more than most of us. But that's all."

"All right, a theoretical question." Carly turned in her chair. The sun was coming in the window behind Levin and highlighted her wavy hairdo and the chiseled lines of her new, exquisite face, right down to the elegant, almost pointed nose. "Speaking as a plastic surgeon, would you ever use the same face twice?"

Levin smiled, a bit of a condescending smile, then shook his head in the negative. "Carly, Carly. What a silly question. You can't mass-produce these things."

"But you can come close."

"Sure, close, but . . . yeah, I would."

Carly turned red, so red that the blood rushing to her face highlighted the fading scars. "You *would?*"

"If I thought a look was nice . . ."

"How close would you make it?"

Levin thought for a few moments. "I may not be making myself clear," he said. "I don't think you get a face and try to copy it. It's features y'see. I've done the same features over and over. Here, let me show you."

Carly experienced a strange mixture of feelings. In a way, she wished the question could be answered here, and in some manner that exonerated Laval. It would be so easy, and she could be content with her new self. But in another way, she couldn't believe it could be this easy, that what Laval had done was routine. She almost *wanted* something sinister to emerge.

Levin pulled a sketch from his drawer. It showed a human face, with little lines and measurements written all over it. "Now I know this looks like a face designed by engineers," he said, "with all the numbers written on it. But it's actually something based on research. Surveys have been done to find out precisely what characteristics are regarded as attractive in a female face. For example, we find that chin length, to be ideal, should be one-fifth the height of the face. The nose should cover less than five percent of the face. The height of the eyeball should be one-fourteenth—"

"I don't believe this," Carly snapped. "You can actually measure?"

"It's all based on a survey," Levin replied. "Of course this was done in the United States. It might be different in other countries."

"It's the flesh market," Carly shot back.

"Well, in a way . . ."

"In a way? I mean, are we cars or furniture, or what?"

"Carly," Levin exclaimed, the chins multiplying again in a put-down smile, "I didn't know you were such a hot feminist."

"Right now I'm a hot-angry patient," Carly answered. "This really turns me off."

"I'm not sure you follow this," Levin explained. "This was just some research on what young men thought. But by applying it we can give our patients more of what they want. I mean, we know *how* to alter a part of the face to make it attractive. In . . . your kind of surgery, more can sometimes be done. You've got to realize that people see other people in terms of their attractiveness. Any patient will tell you that people react differently to them once they've had plastic surgery."

Carly was calmer now, listening intently. "I can testify to that," she conceded.

"There, you see. So don't knock this. It's only research."

"So," Carly asked, "a surgeon might select a feature that research showed was attractive, at least to men."

"Yes. As long as that feature fit the rest of the face."

"He might select this over and over."

"Why not?"

"And he might select others as well? What I'm getting at is—do some surgeons have a trademark face?"

Levin shrugged. "We all have our preferences."

"You're not answering."

"Goddammit, Carly, this isn't a courtroom." Then Levin narrowed his eyes, which filled with the suspicion of a man who thought he was being had. "Hey, come clean. Why are you asking all this?"

"I told you. I can't say." Now Carly squirmed in her chair, seeing that Levin was becoming agitated. Maybe she'd gone too far.

"I've seen trademark features," Levin finally answered. "I mean, I saw a pair of ears and said to myself, 'Those are Allison ears.' You know, Fred Allison, the plastic surgeon." Again he paused. "This has to do with Laval, obviously. I wish you'd tell me, Carly. I might be able to help."

Carly sensed that maybe Levin *would* help. She'd always known him to be trustworthy, not the kind to break a confidence, especially when an old friend was involved.

And Carly had always been a risk taker. She gazed at Levin, assuring herself that she saw sincerity in that roundish, almost cherubic face. In an instant, she convinced herself that he wouldn't want to be known as someone who went back on his word. Maybe, she knew, she was convincing herself because now she *wanted* to tell him, to go all the way with this discussion.

"Scotty," she said, "I have reason to believe that Laval tries to duplicate faces."

"What's the reason?"

He saw Carly balking at that. He sensed, rightly, that she would have to reveal something embarrassing to answer the question. "All right, don't tell me that," he said. "You think he's used your face before."

"You hit it."

"Well, frankly, Carly, it's a nice face. The features are . . . no offense . . . not that unusual. He's probably done similar faces."

"Almost exact," Carly said.

"You met the ladies?"

"Lady. The answer is no."

"You saw a picture?"

Carly didn't answer, hesitant to reveal too much about Margaret. Levin made his assumptions. "If it's too close, I'd say he's done something wrong, but not really unethical. Maybe he got a little lazy. Or maybe the other patient lives far away, and he said to himself, 'What the hell.' "

"You wouldn't think it was serious, then?"

"No, and you shouldn't either. Look, the guy's an egotist. Who knows what he's doing? Hey Carly, you happy with your face?"

"Of course."

"Guys are looking?"

"Yes," Carly laughed.

"So what are you worried about?" He giggled again, and this time seemed to jiggle in his chair, as if enjoying giving his old friend some advice. "In fact, to show you how *un*concerned I am, I'm kicking you out. It's the best thing. I don't want to see you worry over nothing. You're in super hands."

But Carly didn't budge. "Scotty," she asked, almost solemnly, "have you ever heard of anything similar to this? I mean, that face was twin-close. Have you ever heard of such a thing?"

"Frankly, no. But I haven't got Laval's talent either."

"My magazine will want me to investigate."

Levin froze in his chair. "What do you mean?"

"Find the other woman."

Levin remained frozen. "You can't quote me, Carly."

"Oh Scotty, I wouldn't—"

"I didn't think this was journalistic. I *thought* it was medical."

Carly knew Levin was suddenly getting angry, extremely angry, and she could understand it. The press, especially a magazine like *Allure*, was still not trusted, not regarded as quite serious. Levin felt used, even though that was the farthest thing from Carly's mind. "It *is* medical," she told him. "The story is separate, Scotty. Please don't misunderstand. I'd never get you involved."

Levin's face relaxed, although a face that round always looks as if it's ready to explode. "Don't make a fool of yourself, Carly," he said sternly. "Don't hurt a very great doctor."

Carly left Levin's office, disturbed and somewhat disoriented, his last words echoing in her ears. She thought she understood what she'd seen in Kathleen's picture, but did she? First Mike Moran, now a plastic surgeon himself, had raised the specter that she was exaggerating—inadvertently, of course—but exaggerating nonetheless. All right, maybe Laval did copy some features. Maybe he did use all that research on "attractiveness" to develop some favorite noses or chins and use them over and over. Maybe those faces looked alike in the pictures, but would show marked differences in real life. The camera lies. The camera tells tales.

Yes, there was Margaret, and her vigil outside Burgess

Hospital, her pursuit back to Columbus and Eighty-sixth. But maybe Margaret was a kook, a nut. What proof did Carly actually have that Kathleen had disappeared? Maybe she'd just gotten disgusted with her mother and left.

But Carly instinctively trusted Margaret. And Margaret did have that picture, that lookalike picture. And no, Carly had enough good sense to realize that no camera could lie *that* much.

On her way home Carly stopped at a small supermarket to pick up some groceries, then returned to the apartment. Now the green message light on her Code-a-phone answering machine was flashing. She pressed the PLAY button and heard Mike Moran's voice. He was just checking to see that she was all right. And he asked her to prepare a memo on how she would proceed with her investigation of Laval. Carly knew she was in deep. She *did* run the risk of ruining a great man, or making a fool of herself.

But in the end, she *had* to know. And she remained determined, despite Levin's words, to go ahead.

She spent the weekend writing the memo for Moran, and decided that Los Angeles would be her first target—at Margaret's invitation. She needed a starting point. She needed more contact with the one woman who had some link to this mystery.

She checked United Airlines. She could get a round trip to LA for $318, as long as she spent one Saturday night there. She checked Hertz. With her Visa discount, she'd have a Toyota for $152 a week, plus tax and insurance. The figures would please Mike Moran.

As for the hotel—Moran's edict for staff trips was no more than $80 a night, and at that Carly balked. She liked the Beverly Hilton because it was only five blocks from Rodeo Drive, where any editor from *Allure* could always find a story. But that would cost $110 a night, so Carly would have to dig into her own pocket. She was willing. She made the calls. Everything was set up.

Then, Sunday, at nine P.M., just as she was turning on cable to watch the news on CNN, the phone rang. Carly picked up, expecting to hear another friend, or maybe Mike Moran.

"Ms. Randall?"

There was no question about that voice. "Ms. Randall, this is Dr. Laval."

Carly's heart pounded. She felt she'd spent two days plotting against him, even discussing him with a colleague.

"Doctor," she replied, "how nice to hear from you."

"Well, I knew you were going home and I wanted to check your progress."

"Oh, I'm fine."

"No pain from the cold air?"

"No, not at all."

"That's wann-der-ful. I'm sure you're getting admiring glances."

There he was, fishing for compliments again. "Yes, I've had many."

"Wann-der-ful, wann-der-ful. Now I want you to take your medication, and call my office tomorrow to set up an appointment for a post-surgical check. And please, don't be influenced by the fashion magazines. If you want to change your hairdo or makeup, consult with me. We have a great deal of experience here."

"I will, Doctor," Carly said.

The conversation ended, and Carly felt almost sleazy. Her mind flashed back to her father, to his obsession with his appearance, to how he inspected his children each day, to his constant use of "good-looking" as one of the highest compliments, almost the way Willy Loman used "well-liked." Father would have blessed Laval for saving his daughter's appearance, for making her good-looking again. He would have forgiven any strange activities, any pictures.

Carly wasn't the same way, and as she looked into a bedroom mirror hung over her dresser, she somehow regretted it. Father had been shallow, but he knew when to be thankful.

Carly brought her wall calendar up to date. She'd always liked October in New York—its crispness and light. And, despite her suspicions of Laval, she felt this October had still brought a special blessing—a new face, and new life.

Trouble was, the face wasn't an exclusive.

And the woman who had the original had disappeared from the face of the Earth.

7

Allure had its offices in a glass tower on Third Avenue, a thoroughfare filled with publishing companies and other media firms. The setup was pretty standard. You got off the elevator, saw a sign with an arrow saying *Allure*, and followed the sign around two bends to a large blue door. Inside was a vestibule lined with blown-up *Allure* covers—the usual celebrities, fashion models, power brokers, and politicians. At a desk was a twenty-three-year-old receptionist with the required look of boredom and who-the-hell-do-you-think-you-are-coming-in-here snottiness. Visitors loved it. A rude receptionist was a sure sign that the magazine was important, exclusive, and in the black.

Carly rode up in the elevator on Monday morning, a knot forming in her stomach. These people hadn't seen her yet. She knew they must be gossiping about her. They might be wondering if she'd be competition for them now. Moran must've told them something, and maybe it was a glowing report on Laval's work—although Mike usually avoided the glow. But some might now resent her.

She'd never really gotten too close to the staff. Most of her time was spent on assignment, and her friends generally weren't in journalism. Also, Moran's obvious attention to her didn't get her any medals for team spirit. Warmth was not the prevailing feeling in high-gloss New York journalism. It was another chilly spot in an icy city.

She wore, under Laval's orders, a mint-green dress, and

she had to admit that the green, against her reddish hair, was perfect. She knew she'd never looked better.

As she approached the *Allure* headquarters, Carly's mind suddenly flashed back to her childhood. She really didn't understand why those early years came roaring by. Maybe it was the similar situation she'd faced then—trying to overcome her father's abandonment of her family, just as she now had to overcome the accident, the plastic surgery, the totally changed appearance. Her mother had been an English teacher, so at least there'd been some income when her father left just after Carly's fourteenth birthday. But she could never completely shake the embarrassment of her father's actions, explaining to friends, to other relatives, knowing that people would gossip. They stared then. They would stare now. The conditions were different, but stares always seemed to look the same. The years of struggle with her mother had given her that reporter's resilience that she needed now so much.

Carly approached *Allure's* front desk.

"Hi!" shrieked Merle the receptionist, employing un-used muscles to break out in a smile. "Is that . . . I mean, is that *you?*"

Carly nodded.

"I mean, you look *gor*-jus. Amazing. I never saw such a miracle!"

Success, Carly thought, as she graciously acknowledged the high-pitched hello from someone who'd always ignored her. Merle stared for a few more moments, then went back to her romance novel, but not before thinking that she too might benefit from a little chiseling here and tucking there.

Carly wandered into the main editorial room, a clutter of desks, coffeemakers, bulletin boards and stacks of fashion photographers' transparencies in protective sleeves. It was hardly the look of glamour, but, under Moran's architectural guidance, the most was squeezed into the least amount of space. Funny, Carly thought, but no one was there. Must be in an editorial meeting, probably some crisis discovered over the weekend by Mike Moran. She went to her desk to check for messages, finding a bundle of pink slips announcing who had called, what they said they wanted, and what Merle thought they really wanted. Most were from public relations firms pushing stories on the latest luxury car or ten-thousand-dollar watch. Two were from men whom Carly didn't particularly want to see.

Suddenly, she heard some shuffling. Then, a back door leading to a stairway swung open. Other employees from the magazine swarmed out.

"SURPRISE!"

Carly was stunned. It had never happened at *Allure* before. She had such collective gaiety at the magazine since a lead designer came through with free gifts and wet kisses. Carly was moved, not quite to tears, but moved just the same.

The others rushed toward her. She was kissed and patted and flooded with compliments. Yes, what they'd heard from Mike Moran was true. Laval's work had been superb. And Carly did sense some warmth, perhaps more than she'd really thought was there. Maybe she'd been a little too wary of the staff, a little too conscious of competition.

And there was Moran, amidst the chattering group, pointing to himself and mouthing, "It wasn't my idea," like a journalistic Woody Allen denying blame for some fiasco. Of course it was his idea, Carly knew. No one else could authorize the use of time or space. And she caught Mike beaming at her, the way he'd never beamed before. All right, maybe it was the new face that was doing it. All right, maybe beauty was only skin deep. But beaming was better than no beaming, and this was no time for introspection on the deeper meaning of lifelong relationships.

"All rested up?" Mike asked, as several writers and editors drifted to some coffee and cake that had now been brought out.

"Yeah," Carly replied, brushing back some hair that had been dislodged in the rush of affection. "I had an easy weekend—but I've got your outline. Every detail."

"Terrific. I don't like paying sick leave. I want you to get started pronto. Oh, I invited Laval."

"You . . .what?"

"I invited the genius doctor to this party. Hey, what's wrong with that, lady? I want to get to know the fella. I may be in court against him someday."

"You probably will. He coming?"

"No. He's got surgery. But he sent . . . uh . . ." Mike pointed to a photographer who had just whizzed past Merle the receptionist, and Carly immediately recognized him. "Jesus," she said, "he even clones the photographers."

Mr. Philippe shook a few hands around the office, his red beret the object of some minor admiration. He was tiny—almost jockeylike in size—and had a little beard that he liked to stroke for effect. He'd been a staff photographer for the New York City Department of Sanitation before deciding to cash in on the chic craze in the city and change his image. He learned a few tricks about fashion photography, set up a studio in a building owned by his brother, and became "in." He only waved to Moran—Mr. Philippe did not feel moved to speak with the boss—and whipped his Hasselblad from a camera bag. He seemed to know who Carly was, and started snapping.

"Smile," Mike said to her, "you're on *Candid Camera*."

"I wonder why he sent him," Carly mused.

"For effect," Mike replied, in a whisper, so Philippe would not hear him. "He wants pictures of his prize patient. It looks impressive. It looks big-time. With what we now know about the guy, you so surprised?"

"Not really," Carly answered, also softly. "I hope Philippe does as good a job on me as he did on garbage trucks."

One by one, staff members came up to Carly again, complimenting her on her face, on Laval's genius, and hoping to get into the pictures. The chatter was becoming a din, with even the ringing phones having trouble being heard. Marge Gruen, six-foot-one, the magazine's fashion editor and arguably the most intimidating woman in New York journalism, strode over and assessed Carly for a full ten seconds before commenting. "Dear," she finally said in a voice deep enough to be labeled baritone, "I've seen jobs and I've seen jobs. That is the face that can lunch a thousand men."

"Thanks, Marge," Carly said coyly. She'd always been frightened of her.

"It's a funny thing," Marge droned on. "André—I know him, love—well, André called last week and told me to be *sure*, utterly sure, to take a good look at you when you returned. He told me—and this is official—that *this*, you, are the face of the nineties. I mean that, dearest. This man, who's seen every decent face in the universe, believes your new face will set a trend. That's the real reason Philippe is here."

Carly stood there dumbfounded. And Moran had his mouth at half mast as well. Laval had never mentioned this to Carly before. He'd never even intimated it.

"Is that all he said, Margie?" Mike asked, wincing a little, wondering whether he'd heard it right.

"Do you need more?" Marge answered, bellowing above the stir. "The man is simply the world's greatest plastic surgeon. He knows. When he says something like that, take note . . . and invest."

"What did he *mean*?" Carly asked.

"He meant he thinks you could be . . . larger than what you are." A sneer crossed Margie's face, denoting what she thought Carly was.

"This is sedition," Moran insisted. "What does he want her to do, become Cheryl Tiegs?"

"Uh huh," Marge answered, looking down on both of them, a bleached-blonde Statue of Liberty. "Or Kathleen Turner. Either would do."

Moran turned to Carly, with a slight wink. "Don't ask for a raise. You won't get it."

"I don't get *any* of it," Carly said. The three drifted into a corner, where the din was lessened, Marge leaning against a wall and taking an inch or so off her height. "Laval has always taken a personal interest in his patients," Marge explained. "When he works on a model,

he calls me afterward . . . and a few other editors, I admit.
He tells what he's done, and how it could help us. Look,
it's marketing. He's a self-promoter. So what. Carly, my
little love, listen to him. The face is great. So is your
story—I mean, the traaa—gedy and the rebirth. Gawd, it's
good copy. You don't have to write feature pieces all your
life. Tra-la."

Without another word, Marge sauntered off, her head
barely clearing a low-hanging fixture, her shoes clomping
along the floor, above the din. She disappeared into her
office to write a piece on Calvin Klein, leaving Mike
Moran and Carly Randall with the latest Laval bombshell.

"In there," Mike said, gesturing toward his office.
They walked that way, Carly accepting more compliments
from secretaries and a few regular visitors as she and Mike
maneuvered around desks and filing cabinets.

His office was plain—a wooden desk, two visitors'
chairs, some *Allure* covers on the wall, and a picture of
him as a young man with John F. Kennedy during the
1960 presidential campaign. Mike and Carly entered, Mike
slamming the frosted glass door behind them.

"I'm suddenly not liking this any more than you,"
Moran said, slouching down in a worn leather chair that
creaked and rattled behind his desk. He looked back, down
at Third Avenue, staring into the window of the Barnes &
Noble bookstore. "Sure," he said, "the great physician
would love to see your remodeled mug—"

"Mike, please!"

Moran turned red. He hadn't meant it that way. "Gee,
I'm sorry, Carlykins. I got excited. I mean, this doctor
would love to see your face on some book in that window
down there. But calling editors even without your permission . . ."

"I'll play devil's advocate," Carly responded, slipping into one of the chairs. "Maybe he thought I'd be flattered . . .
considering where I work."

"Are you?" Moran asked. There was a toughness, a
kind of challenge in his voice, although his face broke out
in a grin.

"Yes," Carly said firmly. "It won't affect my attitude toward him. But any woman would be flattered."

"Yeah, I guess," Moran replied, now flipping his legs up to his desk, revealing holes in his soles. "By the way, what *is* your attitude toward him, currentwise?"

"*Currentwise?*" Carly teased. "You mean, what changes have occurred in the last three days? None. I still wonder what he's up to. *Not* playing devil's advocate, his calling Marge just increases my suspicions. I know he's called her before about other patients, but they were models or actresses. That's what she said. And I don't know if he duplicated their faces. I'm not looking for publicity. I'm not a public figure. There's something wrong."

"I second that," Moran said. "But he's a good doctor. He set you up nicely."

It was a compliment, Carly knew. Mike was trying. It was his way of saying she looked great. "Thanks," she said.

"Now Carly, I want to look at your outline. And I want you on the road pronto. Get to the bottom of this. I want you to find that woman in LA if it's possible. Or find out what Laval did to her, or with her. Bring her back here if you can. Find out if the guy's been involved in any scandals we don't know about. Don't come back without a Pulitzer. And don't spend too much on phone calls."

"How much time do I have?" Carly asked.

"As much as you need . . . as long as you're making progress."

"I'll go to LA tomorrow."

"Good. Uh . . ."

Carly didn't like the sound of that "Uh . . ." She'd heard it before, and it usually meant that Moran had something unpleasant to say. "Out with it, Mike," she said.

"Uh . . . I was wondering. Do you want someone with you?"

"You?" Carly wondered.

"No, I've got to be here, Carly. You know that."

He'd never asked her to team up before, and she was

becoming less than pleased. "Why would I want some-one?" she asked.

"Oh, look, Carly, I don't doubt your ability. Hey, I mean, you know, you're the best. But, uh, you're in-volved in this. It's your face. You've just come through all this surgery, this tragedy. Now you dive right into the story."

Carly knew that Moran had a point. She still couldn't believe the transition she'd made from damaged goods to woman reborn to woman determined to get at the truth about her plastic surgeon. In a way, she frightened herself. How could she even pursue this story and maintain her sanity? Was she running away from the reality of her new face, from the new social world it would lead her into? Was there a silent self-loathing here, a feeling that plastic surgery was silly, that it diminished her standing as a "journalist," and that therefore she had to hunt down her surgeon? She really didn't know. She only knew that unraveling the mystery of André Laval—whom she re-vered as a doctor—was becoming an obsession, and obses-sions were dangerous for journalists.

"You think I can't be objective," she said.

"It's a worry—sure."

"Why don't you try me first," she replied firmly. "It's a medical story. I've done a truckload of those, Mike."

Moran grinned—Carly didn't know whether it was conde-scension or confidence. "All right, let's try it solo," he said. "But if you get twisted around in this, call for help. When you get back from LA, show me your copy. We'll discuss it."

Not in the office, Carly hoped.

On one side of that office, an Associated Press ticker was banging out the story of a young Boston woman found murdered and partially dismembered. No one at *Allure* would much notice the story. It wasn't in their line.

André Laval's mind wasn't on his work. He stood over his patient, a fifty-five-year-old school principal from Yon-kers, New York, who was having a facelift to improve her image and chances of advancement. It was a subtle face-lift, the first of three planned procedures. Change a little at a time, Laval had urged her, and no one would notice.

Laval was tired, having driven back to New York in the middle of the previous night.

This was what Laval called his Monday-morning audience. He was conducting the procedure in an operating theater before a group of twenty-four selected plastic surgeons who sat, behind glass, in a raised, round seating area surrounding the surgical floor. They were at Burgess to attend a conference led by Laval in the latest advancements. All were certified by the American Board of Plastic Surgery, which meant they'd done an internship in the specialty and passed a stiff examination. Laval always insisted that his Monday audience be composed of "board-certified" practitioners. And these were eager practitioners, determined to learn as much as they could from Laval—their idol—so they could work the gold mine that plastic surgery had become. Each knew that procedures had increased sixty-one percent in a three-year period in the early eighties. They knew that "aesthetic" surgery—what the profession preferred to call cosmetic surgery—was hot, especially among the yuppified of New York and Los Angeles. They knew that men were a new mine to be dug. Once a minute percentage of plastic surgery patients, men now made up fifteen percent of the national practice.

The disciples watched as the world's greatest plastic surgeon performed an SMAS-Platysma facelift. In this procedure he would not only tighten the skin, but the underlying muscles and tissues as well, producing a result that should last longer than a facelift in which only the skin was tightened. The patient would pay six thousand dollars, about two thousand less than Laval would ordinarily charge. It was part of his public relations genius to give generous discounts to "public servants," like teachers and school administrators.

But Laval wasn't thinking of his patient. After all, you could get only so much mileage out of a Yonkers school official. He was thinking of Carly. He couldn't wait to see the pictures that Philippe would bring back. More and more, he was convinced that his future and Carly's were inextricably linked. He suspected that Marge would mention his call to Carly, and that had been his intent in speaking with Marge in the first place. Let Carly know there was excitement building. Let her know what was in his mind, but let it come from someone in her field. People could refuse almost anything, Laval was sure, except immortality. No one ever refused immortality.

"Ladies and gentlemen," he announced, as he was finishing the procedure. "I expect to have this patient back at work in a week. That would be wann-der-ful, and I know she'll look forward to it. But I stress—such rapid healing can only be possible with a strict regimen. The patient must be a nonsmoker, or give up smoking before the surgery. You all know that smoking restricts the flow of blood to the skin, and impedes healing. I have my exercise program, and my prescription of vitamins and nutrients. For this evening's seminar I want you to study what I prescribe. Nurse Willingham has copies. Everything must be done to increase blood flow to the skin."

And there was Marcia in Chicago. Laval was thinking of her too. She was a hindrance to his experiments, and he had to settle the problem. He worried that she would disappear, even with an appointment. She *was* a poor choice, as he'd realized earlier. He'd based it all on facial structure, and hadn't considered her background sufficiently. After all, he'd found her in a prison. He'd been doing volunteer work. She'd been doing time for armed robbery.

He hated when he made a mistake. He hated to admit it to himself. Failure had played too great a part in his early life for him to take it lightly. And now he worried about this mistake, far more than he worried about the obscure patient beneath him. "As we all know," he told the assembled doctors, "this procedure would have been preferable about ten years earlier, despite the misgivings of the straitlaced."

They all knew what he was talking about. Plastic surgeons preferred to work with young skin, which is more flexible and yields a better result. But some in the field recoiled against facelifts in young women, fearing it was carrying vanity to an extreme. Laval did facelifts for actresses and models in their early thirties, and had no such qualms. He'd once told a magazine interviewer that he'd seen teenagers who could use some tightening.

Laval operated for four hours, speaking intermittently to his audience, which eventually grew weary. A few nursing students who sneaked into the gallery to watch left after a few minutes, sickened by the reality of plastic surgery—the cutting of the face, the temporary distortion of human appearance. There was nothing pretty about the process.

Laval ended with his usual pep talk, a serenade to plastic surgery in which he talked about the specialty's contribution to the inner peace and sense of self-worth of its patients. Listening to him, one would think that heart surgery was a minor sideline and neurology the specialty of plumbers.

And his last line, whenever he spoke to colleagues, was, "Remember, you are artists." The line pained him. He almost felt physical hurt in his abdomen every time he spoke it, recalling his early days, how the art world had turned on him, how he had been rejected. But he believed he was an artist. He had shown it, with a scalpel. The art crowd had been wrong. He knew that.

Now, as always, his audience applauded and stood as the world's greatest plastic surgeon left the operating theater.

Laval rushed back to his office.

Pictures were waiting.

Mr. Philippe had rush-developed some of the photos he'd taken of Carly and had them messengered to Laval, who found them on his desk. He took them out of the brown envelope and studied them carefully, even examining some with a magnifier. Each one revealed Carly in a different pose—some smiling, some laughing, some with no expression at all. Philippe had known what Laval wanted, a set of pictures that would tell instantly whether Carly had "it," that vague quality that could be merchandised around the world.

"It" was what she had. The pictures reinforced everything Laval felt about Carly. Laval knew that he had created a thing of beauty. The world would thank him. The world ultimately paid tribute to its great artists.

But he wanted the world—at least the world that would exist after his death—to know exactly what he was doing. He realized that revealing the entire nature of his "experiment" might be part of a death wish, or might expose the same self-destructiveness in his nature that had created so many problems for him early in life. But he also knew that the story itself would ensure his immortality, as would the creation of Carly Randall's face.

Laval went once more to the television studio adjoining his office. And once more he prepared to make a videotape of himself. As usual, no one else would be present. And, as usual, the tape would be stored in a vault to which only Laval had the combination.

All his tapes were special, but this one was decisive. He had already made several tapes in which he discussed the work he'd done on Kathleen Shirmer of Los Angeles, whose mother had eventually confronted Carly. Now, Laval would make the last tape about Kathleen, completing the saga that had begun when she stepped into his visiting doctor's office at a Los Angeles hospital.

Laval turned on his equipment and flipped on the studio lights. Then he went to an unlocked cabinet and took out a wood box about ten inches square. He placed it on a table, then stood next to the table to begin his presentation.

He cleared his throat and looked directly into the Minolta camera, which he now operated by a new remote control switch.

"Ladies and gentlemen," he began, "this will be a somewhat difficult tape to make. During the last two sessions I've reviewed the work I did on Kathleen Shirmer of Los Angeles. You'll recall how enthusiastic I was when her initial surgery was completed. You'll also recall how difficulties began to develop in the case as skin did not tighten as I had projected, and some muscle stretched in an unanticipated manner. At the end of the last tape, I commented that Kathleen had become unacceptable. Yes, the face was there, and it was magnificent. I've shown you pictures to demonstrate that. But the face was also flawed.

"It became obvious that this was not the face I could reveal to the world as perfect, as the highest expression of the plastic surgeon's art, as the face of the nineties. But I wanted to duplicate the essentials of that face. That presented problems, though. What to do with Kathleen? Would there be two women with the same face?

"Ladies and gentlemen," he continued, in a subdued, artificially sincere voice, "we all know that sacrifices have to be made for science. We in medicine see this every day. New drugs that produce disastrous results. New surgical procedures that yield a high death rate before they're perfected.

"It was obvious to me that the perfect face I had set out to create had to be exclusive. It could be like no other. And so, I made the difficult but inevitable decision to terminate Kathleen Shirmer so I could be free to duplicate and perfect her face on some other woman. I ended her life on a ride in the California hills. She was sacrificed to a higher medical purpose.

"And yet, I didn't want to lose her as a research subject entirely. The surgeon can always learn, even from his imperfections."

At that moment, Laval turned to the small box on the table. Slowly, his graceful hands undid a small brass latch holding it shut. He swung open the hinged front cover.

Inside was a human skull.

"Ladies and gentlemen," Laval said, "may I present Kathleen Shirmer."

8

"I love Los Angeles," Carly said.

"Oh dear God," the plump lady in the seat next to her gasped, as United Airlines Flight 5 passed over Kansas. Carly was sure the woman was going to faint, her head sinking into the worn Kafka paperback that she was reading.

"I loathe it," the woman said. "I'm from New York."

"So am I," Carly explained.

"I can't see anyone from New York liking Los Angeles. It's so, so . . ."

"Phony?"

"Yes."

"Un-intellectual?"

"Yes, both those things."

"Everyone running around doing deals?"

"And that too," the woman said.

Carly turned to her challengingly. "You describing Manhattan or Los Angeles?"

The woman glared back. Carly was beneath contempt. She liked LA and admitted it to a New Yorker. There was no hope for sinners.

The Boeing 767 landed at 12:35 P.M., flying right into the Los Angeles smog, which blanketed the city. Carly visited LA at least once a year, usually to cover the motion-picture industry. And she *did* like Los Angeles. She liked the Spanish influence, the unashamed glamour, the sheer glitz. There had to be something terribly gutsy about people who would live in air they could see, and in a city that could vanish in an instant if the earth cracked the right way.

It took United forty-five minutes to dump Carly's two suitcases on the baggage carousel. As usual, she got edged out of her place on line by an army of children who thought pulling a thirty-pound bag from a moving belt was the living end. She finally got her luggage, picked up her Hertz contract, and rode one of the free Hertz vans to her rented car. Instantly, she felt more mellow in the California sun. The sight of palm trees added to the effect, even if the sight was regularly blocked by overweight men in printed Hawaiian shirts looking for the next flight to Vegas.

A thought began to nudge the back of Carly's mind: What were the odds of Laval finding out what she was doing? She'd thought of it before, of course, but it had more immediacy now that she was actually in LA, actually about to plunge into the investigation. There was always the chance that someone she met, or questioned, would alert Laval. It was a risk she had to take, she realized. What could happen? So Laval would be angry. Maybe resentful. What would he do? Sue her?

Carly drove up the San Diego Freeway, heading for Beverly Hills in her rented Toyota Camry. She snapped on one of the all-news radio stations, always good for a listing of the local murders and a rush of car ads, each one more spectacular than the last. One dealer was offering a day's lesson in defensive driving—to resist kidnappers—if you bought a Chevrolet from his showroom. Carly wondered why anyone would kidnap the driver of a Chevy.

She pulled up to the entrance of the Beverly Hilton, at the intersection of Santa Monica and Wilshire Boulevards. The entrance was in the rear, and attendants immediately took charge of her car and luggage. The hotel was big-chain nondescript, with a bustling lobby and a bunch of restaurants and meeting rooms that always seemed booked by local religious and civic groups. This was the hotel where the big Academy Award party was held each year, but Carly never bothered to visit the ballroom where it occurred. Her favorite place in the hotel was the coffee

shop, something of a secret, where she could get a soothing turkey dinner along with her favorite dish—a hot fudge
sundae—for under eight bucks.

She unpacked in her room quickly and stole only a brief
glance out the window at the store tops of Wilshire Boule-
vard and Rodeo Drive. She couldn't quite make out the
Van Cleef and Arpels jewelry shop, where a major hostage
drama had been played out in June of 1986, but she knew it
was within six blocks. It was 2:35, and she had no intention of lingering at the hotel or observing rooftops. This
trip was business—her own business.

She left the hotel and got back into her Toyota, now
heading north and east to Burbank. Soon she would see
Margaret Shirmer again, and would have a chance to
examine some of Kathleen's effects. Carly wasn't optimis-
tic about finding anything useful, but the trip would give
her a chance to question Margaret more closely and get a
sense of the atmosphere in which her surgically arranged
look-alike lived.

Carly zipped from the San Diego Freeway to the Ven-
tura Freeway and on into the Burbank area. She'd visited
Burbank every time she'd come on business to LA. Once
ridiculed as a town of retirees or as "beautiful downtown
Burbank" on the old *Laugh-In* television program, Burbank had grown to become one of the most important
media centers in the country. It was home to a number of
motion picture companies, as well as to NBC, whose large
headquarters sign had become a landmark on Alameda
Avenue.

Carly saw that the Toyota, which was supposed to have
had a full tank of gas when she rented it, was actually
running close to empty. So, after muttering some quiet
curses at the rental agency, she pulled into an Exxon station
in Burbank, got out of the air-conditioned car into the
melting sun, and started filling up at the self-service pump.

Carly never noticed another customer staring at her. She
never saw him leave his own Buick at a pump, run to a
mechanic, carry on a hurried conversation, then rush to a
phone.

Carly topped off and paid the bill in cash. She got back into the Toyota and drove off, trying to remember the map she'd studied in order to find Margaret Shirmer's house. She had been riding only a few minutes when, discreetly, a Burbank police car pulled into the lane behind her. The cop on the passenger side, a young, blond California beach type with peach fuzz for a beard, checked her license number from behind Porsche sunglasses which reflected the big NBC sign in their polished lenses. He nodded to his partner behind the wheel, a burly, slightly overweight patrolman with a bushy mustache.

Suddenly the driver swung out into the left lane, accelerated, and pulled even with Carly. His partner yelled to her. "Would you pull over, ma'am?" Then the police car rocketed forward to get ahead of Carly.

Carly was disoriented, but not frightened. Okay, maybe they'd made a mistake. She wasn't speeding or weaving. Maybe her brake light wasn't working. Or maybe the rental agency didn't have a legal tag on the car. She pulled over to the side of the street and remained behind the wheel as the two officers got out of their car and walked toward her.

"Ma'am," the beachcomber inquired, "could we have a word with you?"

"Sure," Carly replied. "What's wrong?"

"I think you know what's wrong."

Now Carly's heart started beating faster. She didn't like the sound of that. "No," she said, "I don't."

"Are you Kathleen Shirmer?"

Now Carly froze, and both cops noted her sudden edginess. "No," she answered, "I'm not. but I can explain. It's understandable that you . . ."

"Come along, ma'am," the heavy cop said, as he opened her car door.

"No, you're making a mistake!" Carly protested, pushing one officer's hand away. "Just call her mother. I *look* like Kathleen. But I'm not her. I'm visiting Mrs. Shirmer."

"Right," Beachcomber said. "And I look like Robert

Redford and I'm seein' his dad tonight. Just come along, ma'am. You're a missing person.''

"No I'm not."

"We're here to help you."

"I don't need help. If you'd let me explain . . ."

But they wouldn't listen. They grabbed Carly and started forcing her out of her car. They undoubtedly thought she was some kind of lunatic, someone who didn't know her own identity. "Are you arresting me?" she asked loudly. "I'm a reporter."

"Good. You can write a story."

Carly struggled to get her ID out of her purse, but both cops pinned her hands to her sides and hustled her toward their own car.

"Stop!" she screamed, almost shrieking. "You're making a mistake! I *look* like Kathleen, that's all!"

They wouldn't even answer any longer. They simply forced Carly into their car and sped off, some people on the street staring, as if a dangerous criminal had just been apprehended.

Carly sat in the back seat with Beachcomber. "If you'd just talk to me," she protested, knowing it was futile. "I have ID."

They wouldn't answer.

"We're taking you to the station," Beachcomber finally said, almost whispering softly into her ear. "It's gonna be okay. We'll get a doctor."

"I don't need a doctor!"

The driver turned around a bit, grinned at his partner and rolled his eyes.

Within minutes they pulled into the parking lot of the Burbank police department. Immediately, Carly spotted a medical van from a local hospital and saw two attendants outside, both clad in white, one carrying a straitjacket. She stiffened in the back seat of the car, trying to figure how she could convince the cops to let her call Margaret Shirmer.

The officers took her out of their car and started escorting her into the station house, while the ambulance attendants waited.

Inside, Carly confronted a mass of commotion, with policemen staring at her and a desk sergeant preparing a bunch of forms that would get her sent to the nearest psychiatric hospital.

"Please sit down, ma'am," Beachcomber said, pointing to a plain metal chair.

Carly sat. She wasn't going to argue amidst the bedlam. She heard her police driver go over to one of the other patrolmen and utter the words "Nut case," just loud enough for her to hear. She let it roll off.

Funny, she mused, but in all her time in journalism she'd never been inside a police station. She hadn't come up through that route. After attending Ohio State, she'd come right to New York and gotten a research job on *Newsweek*. She never had done the kind of daily reporting that was typical of the newspaper writer.

She saw that the sergeant was just about finished going through his forms. But then, suddenly, the main oak door of the station house swung open. The glare of the sunlight blinded Carly momentarily, but her eyes adjusted and she saw, rushing in . . . Margaret Shirmer.

Carly stood.

The two faced each other.

Margaret smiled, an embarrassed smile, as if she'd put Carly through all this.

"Well," Beachcomber said to Carly, "aren't you going to kiss your mother?"

The two embraced.

And then Margaret Shirmer explained it all to them.

9

Margaret Shirmer's house on North Fredric in Burbank was a three-bedroom ranch on a street of similar homes. The house was immaculate, kept that way by a mother who wanted her daughter to find a decent place when she finally came home. A color photograph of Kathleen—after plastic surgery—rested on a living-room table, and instantly gave Carly the chills. She was looking at *herself*—the face, the hair style, everything that Laval had prescribed. What had the man had in mind for Kathleen? And why did Kathleen—with that beautiful new face—suddenly disappear?

"Would you like something?" Margaret asked, as the two sat down in the living room. "You must be very hungry after that bout of mistaken identity."

"Yes, the second bout," Carly laughed, referring to her earlier confrontation with Margaret in New York City. "Maybe a cold drink. Anything you've got."

Margaret went to the kitchen, and Carly could hear the refrigerator door open, then close. She gazed around the living room, her eyes finally settling on another picture, this one of a man apparently in his fifties. She guessed this was Kathleen's father, now deceased, a victim of his daughter's disappearance. Then her eye caught something else—a small sampling of women's magazines, one with a photograph of Kathleen's new face glued to the cover. Why? Was this Margaret's dream, or Kathleen's? Margaret had said nothing about Kathleen wanting to be a model.

Margaret returned with a glass of Diet Coke for Carly.

"I noticed that magazine," Carly said. "Did your daughter model?"

"No," Margaret sighed, her face haggard after her ordeal of months. "It never really was in her mind. But this doctor told her, after the surgery, that she could model if she wanted to, or be an actress."

"I see." Carly's mind flashed back to the calls that Laval had made to Marge at *Allure*. Same line. But why? Was it just self-promotion, as Marge had assumed? Or was there something else involved, something related to the duplication of faces?

"Has Laval been in contact since we met?" Carly asked.

"Yes he has," Margaret replied, "but he does that. I did what you wanted. I didn't tell him I ran into you. He called just to keep contact, as he said. And to reassure me."

"Reassure you?"

"Like I told you in New York," Margaret sighed, "Laval said that women who have plastic surgery sometimes try to change their lives and go away . . . but that they almost always return. He keeps telling me that."

"Maybe he's right."

Margaret didn't respond. She just stared into space. She really didn't think Laval was right, and the encouragement had long since ceased to be soothing.

"You mentioned," Carly said, trying to be as gentle as possible in her probing, "that Kathleen had discovered something about Laval when she got into her medical folder in his office. You said you didn't know what it was."

"No, she never told me."

"It would almost have to be negative."

"Well, that's what I think," Margaret agreed. "But how negative is negative? Maybe Kitty was exaggerating. Sometimes she got a little dramatic. I mean, don't we all? How would I know?"

"The police have no theories?"

"They really weren't interested in that stuff. They treated it like a routine missing person. Not a big deal."

"I'd like to see the things that Kathleen left behind, if it's okay," Carly said.

"Of course. I prepared it all," Margaret explained, "and I went through it again. I just don't think you'll find anything."

"Let me try."

"Come with me."

Margaret led Carly into Kathleen's bedroom, the same bedroom she'd occupied since the age of three. The idea of going into a bedroom occupied by an "adult child" of the household was no longer unusual for Carly. Many of her friends in New York still lived with their parents well into their twenties, sometimes their thirties. The high cost of housing was just too high.

The room was modest, painted white, with red striped curtains. There was a single Hollywood bed decorated with the stuffed animals from Kathleen's childhood. There were some pictures of friends, and a few prints and posters of famous movies.

"This is the room," Margaret said with a sigh, "exactly as Kathleen left it—except that I straightened up a bit. You can look through her drawers if you like. In the top drawer of the dresser you'll find a brown envelope. I stuffed some of her things in there—little notes, letters from a vacation, phone messages . . . things like that. Her address book is in the night table over there."

"I'll be very careful with all this," Carly said.

"I know you will. I'll let you alone."

Then, just as she had left Carly in New York, Margaret slipped away, this time to go to her own room and wait. She really didn't know what she was waiting for. She was sure there was nothing in Kathleen's room that could possibly provide a clue to the young woman's disappearance. The police had combed it. She had. And she'd even asked a retired detective to go through it as well. All had come up empty-handed.

Inevitably, Carly felt a kind of eeriness as she started looking around the room. Here had slept the duplicate face, Laval's other work of art. Now Carly felt strangely like a twin sister . . . a surviving twin looking after the effects of the departed. It was a thought she tried to shake, but it lingered on the fringes of her mind.

On the surface, she saw nothing that could help her. It was a common room, that's all. There didn't seem to be any hidden messages in the wall posters, and the pictures of friends on the dresser appeared routine and bland. So Carly started searching through the dresser. Here again, what she found was uninteresting—the normal clothes of any young California woman.

And then she opened the brown envelope that Margaret had told her about. She read each letter that Kathleen had sent home from a vacation in Colorado and postcards she'd sent from a northern California resort when she was recuperating from her plastic surgery. None of them gave any clues to her eventual disappearance. Indeed, none of them even mentioned André Laval. As she leafed through more papers, and phone messages, Carly began to come to the same conclusion that the police had arrived at—that there was nothing there.

She started through Kathleen's little red address book. It was meticulous, with names, addresses, phone numbers, new phone numbers, alternate phone numbers where people could be reached at all times. Carly had the distinct impression that Kathleen was extremely careful, well organized, a keeper of records. And yet there was no record of what she'd found so disturbing in her medical file. Maybe she didn't want to put it in writing. Maybe she'd been afraid Margaret would find it, and that it would upset her.

Carly continued flipping through the little book.

And then she saw something.

She passed it at first, then went back. It was only two words, separated by a dash. A woman's first name. A city.

Why?

Why would this meticulous person Kathleen Shirmer, simply jot down so vague a reference. It wasn't like her. It didn't conform. It didn't fit. It was the only incomplete reference in the book. And the construction, with the dash in the middle, was odd. Why were there no other notes?

Carly knew she might be grasping at straws. After all, the police hadn't questioned the entry, and they investigated things like this all the time. But hunches had worked for Carly before, and now she had a strong hunch that this little notation, and the way it was written down, meant something.

She had to find out what those two words meant.

She would pursue it.

She had to. She had nothing else.

Mike Moran was in his underwear—the conservative white kind—sitting on the living room rug of his Brooklyn brownstone. Spread out around him were more than two hundred 35-mm transparencies shot by freelance photographers for upcoming *Allure* features. Moran was staring into a light box on the floor, examining eight slides for a feature on a new Mercedes Benz. He leaned over to study each Kodachrome through a magnifying glass, settling on one that showed the car's new instrument panel and another that showed it "full-figure," parked outside the Waldorf-Astoria. Mike Moran owned a Ford, and was perfectly pleased with it. But Fords didn't make it in *Allure*.

The living room was Moran elegance—he'd bought the red rug second hand on the Lower East Side, and picked up the furniture at Brooklyn tag sales. There was no particular style—only a stimulating mixture of functional pieces, dominated by an overstuffed sofa with a flower pattern. The furniture wasn't important, though, because it was rarely seen—back issues of *The New York Times*, *Smithsonian* magazine, and investment newsletters filled the room, providing a protective coating against dust. The walls were decorated with *Allure* covers, supplied, with frames, at no cost by the magazine's printer.

It was 10:36 P.M. when the phone rang. Moran, his right leg having fallen asleep by now, managed to creak to his feet and saunter over to the telephone, which he kept on an old roll-top desk. He picked up. "Moran—whether you want him or not."

"I want him," came Carly's voice, perfectly clear on the discount MCI line.

"Hey Car-lot," Moran replied, flipping his magnifier onto a soft chair. "You calling with news, or are you lost on the Yellow Brick Road?"

"I'm lost," Carly replied, lying on her bed at the Hilton. "I'm in the middle of a jungle, with only one phone and occasional room service."

"Very funny," Moran said. "Thanks for calling at night. We save about fifteen percent . . ."

"That's what he's interested in," Carly moaned. "Phone bills. That's what the staff is good for."

"This is a very warm conversation," Moran countered, "and we're being charged by the minute. What've you got?"

"A request," Carly replied.

"Oh?"

"Mike, I *may* have hit on something. I don't know."

"Did you find that girl?"

"No. There's no sign of her. But I did go through her things. Mike, I want you to think about something."

"Shoot."

"There were two words in Kathleen Shirmer's phone book. They were out of place. They just seemed to float there. I may be off, I mean *way* off, but they may mean something."

"What were the words?"

"Fern—Washington."

"'Fern—Washington?' What the hell is so interesting about that?"

"That's what I want to find out. There didn't seem any reason for Kathleen to write that entry. I asked her mother whether she knew anyone named Fern in Washington. Mrs. Shirmer told me that Kathleen had never even *been* to Washington."

"Maybe it was someone in LA who was *going* to Washington," Moran volunteered.

"Maybe. But why write that in an address book? It would be on a note pad."

"Good thinking, Carlykins. Of course, Fern could be the name of a business, or an organization. The letters F-E-R-N could possibly stand for something."

"I hadn't thought of that," Carly said. "Look, it's possible."

"Or maybe Kathleen was planning to send a fern to someone named Washington."

"That's far out, Mike," Carly said, "but who knows? Look, that's the point, and that's the request. If you could put some researchers on this. Maybe they could figure out what 'Fern—Washington' means. Maybe it means nothing."

"I'll do that for you."

"Thanks, Mike." And then she paused. "Fern—Washington," she said once more. She'd repeat it over and over in her mind, and on the flight back to New York. It would stare out at her before she slept, and when she got up the next morning. *Fern—Washington.*

Who, what, was Fern?

10

Mike Moran collected menus, the better to choose a cheap restaurant if, God forbid, he had to take someone out. And so, when Carly returned from LA, Moran invited her to talk about her trip "out of the office," which, for Mike Moran, was a massive nosedive into the social whirl. For Carly, it was a victory of sorts—and her first dinner out with another human being since her operation.

Mike had another motive. *Fern—Washington* had been rolling over in his mind, and, with the help of his *Allure* researchers, he was able to put together a solid theory. He couldn't wait to see Carly.

Moran, crunching those numbers, chose a Chinese restaurant on Columbus Avenue in the Seventies. The area was chic enough to be respectable, the restaurant modest enough to keep its prices to Moran's pitiable level. Moran leaned toward Chinese restaurants anyway. On a price/portion basis, they were hard to beat. The only time he went to French restaurants was when he was invited, and only then if the menus were printed in English.

He met Carly at the place, she cabbing down from her apartment. They sat at a sidewalk window with a good view of the passing attaché cases swinging from eager yuppie arms. They shared a shrimp dish, some fried rice, and soup, but the main item on the menu was Carly's trip, and the question it raised: "Fern—Washington." She was tired from jet lag, having flown in that same afternoon, but it didn't show immediately. She'd become a woman obsessed with a mystery.

Moran did not make her wait long before springing his notion.

"I put the researchers on it," he told Carly. "No one named Fern showed up in Laval's life. But Washington did. It's one of the four cities outside New York in which he has an active practice. The others are Los Angeles, Chicago, and Boston."

"If that's the connection," Carly replied, not terribly surprised by the discovery, "then Fern must be a patient in Washington."

"I made the same guess," Moran said. "You told me this Kathleen sneaked a look in her medical folder. Your doctor prince might've made a note about another patient, maybe with the same problem—a patient named Fern, in Washington."

"All right," Carly said, waving away a waiter's offer of more tea, "but why did Kathleen write that in her little book?"

"Maybe it was related to what she'd discovered about Laval—the thing she wouldn't tell her mother," Moran replied.

"Maybe. And . . ." Carly stopped.

"What and?"

"And maybe there's some connection between Kathleen and that woman, or why would her name be in *Kathleen*'s medical file instead of someone else's?"

Moran knew Carly well enough to realize that her mind was zeroing in on something important, something critical. "What are you driving at?" he asked.

"Mike," Carly answered, "I've been thinking about this ever since LA, ever since the name Fern came up. If Laval made two . . . why not three?"

"Faces?" Moran asked.

"Faces," Carly replied firmly. "It all fits, Mike. What would Kathleen discover in *her* medical file that would upset her about Laval? She'd discover the same thing I found out by encountering her mother outside my building—

that Laval is running an assembly line, and you can get any model, as long as it's me.''

"Possible," Moran said. "Always possible."

But then Moran clammed up, dousing his remaining fried rice with hot Chinese mustard, nibbling at it, then washing down the nibbles with tea. Carly knew he was suddenly troubled, and she sensed it was because of her approach to the story. She knew that he'd been burned during his political days in California, burned by inaccurate press reporting, a few wild editorials, loaded questions asked by poorly trained reporters. Although housed in the world of knife-in-the-back upscale journalism, Carly knew he was eminently fair, even to those he loathed. And the word *unfair* was now all over his brow.

"I don't like the son of a bitch," he suddenly said. "I never liked him, or his kind of self-promoter. But I don't want a lynching party, either. Carly, these are all hot theories, but we haven't got any real evidence. He did this thing with faces. Okay, it was outrageous. But all this other stuff. Theory."

"Granted," Carly said. "I'm going on a hunch, but it's a good hunch."

"You've had trouble with doctors," Moran asked. "haven't you?"

Carly stiffened, and put down her fork, letting it clink against the side of her plate. She hadn't expected that question, or that kind of challenge. Moran had always kidded her, joked with her, needled her in an affectionate way. But he'd never challenged her so personally before, and she didn't know immediately what to make of it. "Explain that question," she demanded.

"You once told me about your parents," Moran replied. "Your father was a doctor . . .''

"My father was a doctor," Carly said matter-of-factly. "He left my mother and me. And he barely provided for us."

"You mentioned once that another relative had trouble with doctors . . ."

"Maybe you'd like my whole life story," Carly snapped.

"I'm sorry, Carly," Moran told her. "I don't mean to get personal. Look, I'm trying to protect you. If you've got a bad thing about doctors . . ."

"I suspect them, okay?" Carly replied. "I'm not a great fan of them, okay? But I'm not a nut either. My father was a doctor who didn't want to support his family. My mother died because a doctor screwed up. I haven't been lucky with MDs. But I'm out for facts, and either you trust me or you don't, Mike."

Moran held up his hand to stop her. He'd seen her like this in tense moments on controversial stories. Carly Randall was intense if nothing else, and went into everything full throttle. It was one of her strongest points, and one of her weakest. Right now, Moran didn't need another one of her ritual offers of resignation. "Trust you," he said, without a beat. "I *told* you that before."

"Apology accepted," Carly said.

Moran broke out laughing. He didn't recall apologizing.

His laugh broke the tension of the moment, but did nothing to distance the two from the reality they confronted. Both Moran and Carly toyed with the idea of contacting the police, if only to get some advice. Both rejected the notion. They still had no *actual* evidence of a crime, and Kathleen's disappearance from Burbank was already the subject of a formal police investigation.

There was another reality they confronted, one that neither wished to tackle head-on. *If* Laval was involved in Kathleen's disappearance, and learned that Carly was probing, he could react against *her*. What would he do? What *could* he do?

"When do you see Laval again?" Moran asked.

"Tomorrow," Carly replied. "A follow-up appointment."

"Be careful what you say."

André Laval looked gorgeous.

He always looked wann-der-ful, but this night he was almost ravishing. It was one of the great dinner parties of the year, thrown by one of Fifth Avenue's wealthiest women, someone possessed of officially certified old money.

In her case, of course, the ancient funds came from nineteenth-century drug running, but they'd been laundered and bleached in the decades since, and everyone thought the grande dame had actually gotten it from auto stocks and an insurance company.

There were only eighteen people invited to the twelve-room triplex overlooking Central Park, and there were exactly the same number of servants to take care of them and, after the party, to ridicule them. This was a party for the elite of the elite. A politician could get an invitation if he'd served in a "high" cabinet position, a Wall Street lawyer only if he'd been a *senior* partner for more than ten years. Doctors were considered beneath the group unless they were internationally famous and part of the social scene, qualifications that Laval possessed. There were, however, several journalists—rabble by most social standards, but rabble to be courted because they provided that most precious gift of all, favorable publicity.

And Laval did look gorgeous—in a two-thousand-dollar dark blue suit, custom white shirt and tie, and Gucci loafers. Inside the suit pocket was a set of photographs, for these parties were for business, as everyone really knew, and Laval came prepared.

He circulated amidst the bejeweled, listening to the nasal tones of the upper crust as they bemoaned the twentieth century. His target was across a forty-foot living room, a tiny woman of about sixty, in a bright red dress, being fawned over by a high-fashion designer and his wife. Laval started making his move, exchanging a few words with guests as he slowly moved toward his objective, passing a buffet piled with food and drink. He knew the trip wouldn't go without incident, a fear confirmed as he was intercepted by a man he thought he knew.

"André," the man said. In these circles, no one was called "doctor."

"Oh yes," Laval replied. "So glad to see you. Really grand." Laval didn't recognize him. The man was about fifty-five, medium height, with a haggard face that yearned for Laval's services.

"You know, André," he said, "my wife thinks I should make an appointment to see you. You did such a great job on her."

"She's a lovely lady," Laval replied. "One of my favorite patients—of all time."

"Oh, I know. I could tell that. But as for me . . . what do you think?"

Laval had one eye on the haggard face, the other on his objective across the room. He feared she'd be surrounded by more fawners if the haggard face kept him too long. "Awfully hard to say," Laval replied. "The light in here is difficult. Why don't we chat in my office. I could do things properly there."

"Sure. I like that, André. Let me take you to my wife. She's dying to talk to you."

"Oh not now," Laval replied. "I've got to answer someone's question, and I want to devote *plenty* of time to your wife. That's the conversation I'm looking forward to. Give me a few minutes."

"I like that. Shasta can't wait."

Thank God he mentioned the name of his wife, Laval thought, as he eased away. And then he remembered that Shasta Crane, heiress to a copper fortune, was a thirty-eight-thousand-dollar job, a complete makeover that did nothing to change her colorless personality. He caught a glimpse of her in a far corner, talking to a financier, possibly her next husband, but probably the one after that.

Laval moved on, waving coyly at two women who'd been his patients, mouthing words like *lovely* or *delectable* to express his approval of his own work. No one who'd been "done" by him hesitated to admit it. Plastic surgery in the eighties had come out of the closet and fallen into the dining room, a proper subject of dinner conversation.

Finally, Laval reached his destination. Olympia Gould was the most influential gossip columnist in New York, having written the "Olympia After Dark" column for thirty-six years. A mention in her daily report could make a fashion designer, ruin an actor, or start divorce proceedings in the state supreme court of New York or a number of other coastal commonwealths. And yet Olympia Gould was a remarkably straight shooter, for all the fawning she was due, and the power she'd accumulated. Maybe it was the background as daughter of a Midwestern minister, or her husband's death in combat in World War II. But her speech was sanitized of *dahling* and the other trademarks of the terminally affected. Laval knew to cool his extravagant prose in her presence, lest he offend her sense of propriety.

"Olympia," he said, controlling himself, as he drew near, "I haven't seen you in months."

"Oh, hello, Doctor," Olympia Gould replied. She was the only one at the party who insisted on the title. "Got any good medical gossip for me?"

Laval knew she'd ask that right off the bat, for Olympia Gould was all professional, and parties like this were good for two columns. He came prepared. He'd even rehearsed his comments in front of a mirror, practicing the combination of sincerity, excitement, and professional concern. This was part of the business, too.

"I don't know if it's gossip, Olympia . . ."

"Not interested."

"I've got the face of the nineties."

"Interested."

"Ah, Olympia, you never let me down."

"Where's the face?"

With a sweeping gesture, Laval reached into his jacket breast pocket, then looked around to make sure no one else was watching. "Maybe we'd better . . ." And he led the diminutive woman toward a couple of chairs in a small sitting room.

They both sat down and Laval pulled out the pictures. "I'm doing some exciting research, Olympia," Laval said. "Let me show you something." He took out a picture that looked like three faces superimposed to make one.

"She's very nice," Olympia said. "Is that the nineties face?"

"No not yet," Laval replied. "That's where I got the

idea. Look, we plastic surgeons know that the perfect face changes from generation to generation.''

"Yes," Olympia said. "The girls of the fifties aren't like today."

"Precisely, Olympia. You're very perceptive." Laval caught himself, knowing that Gould hated gratuitous compliments. "The picture I'm showing you now is a composite of some of the great actress and model faces of the forties. I put them together to show what was beautiful then."

"Kind of the Rita Hayworth type," Gould said.

"She's one of the faces, that's right." It was also right that Laval, whose lack of artistic imagination had been detected in school, was simply borrowing this technique from a New York City artist, who'd combined photography with computer science to create the composites. Laval never gave credit where it was due, for, in his mind, it was due only one man. "Now," he said, pulling out another picture, "here's a composite of the ideal faces of the fifties. The Grace Kelly look, you might call it."

"Yes, that was the look. Doctor, you're building something, and I think it's a column."

A full column—Laval was entranced. "Notice, Olympia," he said, "how the look of the fifties reflected the era. The ideal face was roundish, almost motherly, even in young women. It was full, conservative, and soft."

"And I liked it," Olympia said. "But I'm not old-fashioned. I like the present, too." Now Olympia was protecting herself, realizing that being behind the times was cause for retiring a gossip columnist.

"If you like the present," Laval said, "look at this." He took out still another picture, about four inches by six, and placed it in Gould's tiny hands. "This is a composite of ideal faces of today. Christie Brinkley, Kathleen Turner, a few others."

Gould studied the picture, then compared it to the ideal of the fifties. "Hah," she said, "it's amazing. I never saw this in pictures." She saw that the ideal female face of the eighties was stronger, more intense than the fifties model.

Less motherly, more go-getter. The jaw was sharp, rather than round, reflecting women's new assertiveness.

"Now," Laval said, "the last picture." He placed another photograph in Gould's hands. This wasn't a composite. It was a real photo of a real woman. But it bore a striking resemblance to the ideal face of the eighties, with a slight modification. A more relaxed look, a balance between old and new—modern, without being brash. It was the face of Carly Randall.

"Very pretty," Gould said. "Very pretty indeed. An actress?"

"Actually, she works on a magazine," Laval replied. "But I won't tell you where. She's a patient, Olympia."

"What did you do to her?"

"She was in an accident. I reconstructed her face. The basic bone structure was there—a bone structure I believe will be seen as ideal within three years. I added what had to be added."

"*Very* nice," Gould said. She held the picture closer to her tired eyes and studied it, utterly fascinated by what Laval had done. And Laval realized he'd had the intended effect, building toward this picture with the three composites that went before. *No* other plastic surgeon did this, he knew.

"She needs a little more work," Laval went on. "But she's a lovely girl, really lovely, Olympia. And that face will be known the world over."

The claim, like Babe Ruth pointing to the center-field stands before hitting a home run, sent a chill up Olympia Gould's narrow spine. Discovering new talent, a new look, was the cream of the gossip's business. "Doctor, you may be right. I can't take my eyes off that face." Then she thrust the picture back at Laval. "Let's get to the bottom line. When do I meet her?"

"Soon," Laval said. "Very soon, Olympia. As long as her recovery continues normally."

"I want the first interview. I don't care about the first pictures. We're not good on pictures. Let someone else publish color photos. I want the interview."

"And you shall have it."

"Doctor, we're making history."

Laval was in ecstasy. He'd known Olympia Gould would be easy—primarily because she was a good newswoman and this was first-class stuff. But her sheer enthusiasm was a bonus, a bonanza that would translate into Laval's ultimate goal—establishing him as the man who created the look of an entire decade. He would do with surgery what he could never do as a sculptor. He would become the first plastic surgeon to be immortalized as an artist, not just as a doctor. And anything he did to this end was, in his mind, legitimate.

It was even legitimate to "sell" Olympia Gould while still realizing that Carly might not work out. If her face didn't heal properly, if she had to be disposed of, a story was easy to make up. In the meantime, he could probe and test . . . and Olympia's reaction was exactly what he'd wanted.

The image of Kathleen Shirmer suddenly flashed before him.

It was legitimate.

He told it to himself over and over.

It was perfectly legitimate.

He knew, though, that he had some hurdles to overcome. He had to convince Carly to give up her profession and make her face, literally, her fortune. But it was a small hurdle, he was sure. Who wouldn't want the riches, the fame of a great modeling or screen career? And she owed him. She owed him everything. He'd saved her from a life in the shadows. André Laval was a godlike figure, and he felt it in his talented bones.

And then there was the problem of Marcia, in Chicago. He hadn't yet been out to see her, to do what was necessary. But he had to, no matter how unpleasant it was to travel through her neighborhood.

It was legitimate.

It was all legitimate.

11

It happened as Carly was getting into a cab, just outside her apartment building. She hadn't described the prior episodes to Mike Moran or any of her friends, lest word get out and affect her career, or her personal reputation. Laval knew, although it wasn't his medical area, and her neurologist knew, but said the episodes would probably go away in time.

Carly got into the cab, and went completely blank. She couldn't remember where she wanted to go, or what day it was, or even *where* she was.

"Where to?" the driver asked, with the interest of a block of stone.

Carly just stared at him as he looked back.

"Where to?" he repeated.

"Uh . . ."

"Where you wanna go?" he asked, having had six years of experience dealing with confused passengers, mostly foreign.

"I want to . . ." Carly stopped. Everything was a haze.

"You speak English?" the driver asked, glancing at his watch and counting the lost seconds.

"English?" Carly replied.

"Erright, Español?" In New York, that was always a good guess.

"English," Carly said.

"Then tell me where you want to go, lady, or get out.

96

There's a fella over there who wants a cab. I got airport calls. Come on.''

"I want to go . . . uh . . ."

"You had a big night last night. Come on. Get out.'' Now the burly driver jumped from his cab and flung open the rear door, his menacing shape blocking out the sun. He reached his thick, hairy right arm inside and started jabbing at Carly's shoulder.

"Stop!'' she snapped.

"Want me to call the cops?'' the driver asked.

Frightened, Carly flipped the handle on the other side and bailed out of the cab.

"You learn to hold your booze!'' the driver shouted after her as she hurried away, still dazed, her mind not yet focused. Heads of passers-by turned her way, and she was embarrassed. As the cab lurched past her, she leaned against her building, holding her head, trying to recover. People walked by, and, aside from staring, didn't bother to stop. One teenager eyed her purse, but decided it was too risky to snatch it with all the people around, so he gave up the commercial opportunity.

Carly's mind began to clear, but she shook with fright. She'd had these brief lapses since her accident, but tests showed nothing permanently wrong. The lapses were part of the post-accident trauma, she'd been assured, part of the healing process, and wouldn't last. Now she pulled herself together and hailed another cab. Her memory snapped back. She'd told Mike Moran she was seeing Laval, which was true, but, out of a feeling of awkwardness, hadn't told him whom she was seeing *before* Laval. She had an appointment with Dr. Gordon Slesar, clinical psychiatrist, authority in treating accident victims, and she was already a few minutes late.

Slesar had been one of the psychiatrists recommended by Laval when he insisted that Carly, like all his patients, receive some post-surgical therapy. Carly chose him because she'd interviewed him for an *Allure* series on New York's most outstanding young doctors. She'd been deeply impressed by his intelligence and sensitivity, and she knew his reputation was beyond reproach.

She was able to get another cab, and then she became completely lucid, recalling Slesar's exact address, and even a description of his building. The cab ride took just under twelve minutes.

Gordon Slesar's office was in a brownstone near Columbia University, where he often conducted seminars for doctoral students in sociology and psychology. A bachelor, Slesar lived on the second floor of his modest duplex, devoting the first floor to office space. Patients coming in had no sense of being in a medical office. His waiting room was the former living room, and decorated like one. His receptionist sat at a small antique desk that would have fit in well in any traditional home.

Slesar greeted Carly with that wonderful smile for which he was, in psychiatric circles, literally famous. It was one of those smiles that lit up a room and everyone in it, and told you that this was a genuinely nice guy. He was thirty-three, with a roundish face, medium height and fashionably slim, and always wore precisely the same uniform to work—dark gray suit, blue shirt, maroon tie. He was balding prematurely, but on him it looked good, and, besides, the smile drew attention away from all possible defects.

"Come in, Ms. Randall," he said, his voice almost breaking out in the warmth of song. You couldn't dislike him. You *wanted* to tell him your troubles. Gordon Slesar was born to be a shrink.

Carly entered the examining room, a thickly carpeted den paneled in oak, featuring Slesar's desk and a comfortable black leather couch. "Please, please sit down," Slesar said, picking up Carly's file from his desk and reviewing it briefly. "If it's too warm in here, just tell me," Slesar said. "Sometimes I forget." He flashed the teeth.

"It's fine," Carly said.

"Oh good. Now, you were referred by Dr. Laval, who thinks very highly of you."

"Oh, that's very nice," Carly replied.

"Yes, and I see you told my receptionist that you interviewed me. Of *course* I remember. You work for *Allure*. I have many copies of the article."

"You *do* remember."

"Every question. It was a good interview. Very intelligent. I can see why André thinks the world of you."

"He's a good surgeon," Carly said.

"Oh, the best. He's done a wonderful job with you. So sorry about your accident. But you're as good as new, and we just want to chat about any adjustment problems."

"I'm getting along pretty well," Carly said.

"Oh, I'm sure. I'd imagine you'd have very few problems. But why don't you just make yourself comfortable and let's talk. And, hey, don't hesitate to bring up anything at all. You know, your life has been changed twice in a very short time—first by that accident, and now by the surgery. If something seems to be spinning you around, let's hear about it." And again he flashed that smile.

Carly leaned back, with full confidence in Slesar. She knew that his nice, easygoing manner and personal warmth hid his brilliance—he'd graduated first in his class from medical school and had lecture invitations from all over the world. She also knew she was lucky to get an appointment with him immediately. Those without referrals from Laval had to wait at least two months.

"Now," Slesar began, "why don't we start by learning a little about you. I'd love you to give me a little autobiography, and I may interrupt with a question here and there. Want something to drink?"

"Oh no, I'm fine."

"Sure. That's great. Why don't we just begin. Hey?"

Slesar sat down in a rolling chair and placed a yellow pad in his lap. Carly started, and spoke about herself for close to half an hour, and every time she looked up she saw that Slesar was listening intently. She was pleased by this because she'd always wondered whether psychiatrists' minds drifted. Slesar did interrupt occasionally with a comment, but it was mostly Carly's show. Slesar's main contribution, aside from listening and making notes, was smiling his encouragement.

But then, after the half hour, Slesar started leading Carly with questions, fairly routine questions that he asked anyone who'd had extensive plastic surgery. For example, "Do you resent people who stare at you now?"

"No, not really," Carly answered. "I'm aware of them, but it's flattering."

"What about friends? Obviously they see a profound difference."

"Sure, but this wasn't cosmetic surgery. It was an accident. I don't think they see you the same way."

"Very perceptive. Do you have any confusion about identity? Do you look in the mirror and wonder who you are?"

"No, that hasn't happened to me. In fact, the only abnormal things are the memory lapses."

"Yes. That's on your medical record. They'll go away, but why don't we gab about them. Are they bothering you?"

"Well," Carly answered, squirming around on the couch and moving a leg that was starting to fall asleep, "they're usually very quick. Five or six seconds. This morning I had a longer one. The longest was about twenty seconds."

"When it happens," Slesar said, "and you're with people, you can just say you feel faint and want to sit down. People understand. I wouldn't discuss these episodes with anyone outside medicine, because wrong impressions are created."

"Yes, that's good," Carly said.

"Now, I believe you're back at work . . ."

"That's right. At *Allure*."

"One problem many patients have is that co-workers begin to feel jealous. You're looking great and they're feeling tired, and if you get a promotion, there may be problems. They may think your looks got you the job." He smiled.

"So far, nothing," Carly said.

"If it happens, you must tell yourself that you've earned

what you've gotten. Good looks are part of your person. They're an ingredient. If they help, they help. No one can take that away from you.''

"That's the way I would feel," Carly said. She was intrigued by the points Slesar was making, but, inevitably, there was one item that kept flashing through her mind, the thing she cared about most, the subject that obsessed her. But could she bring it up? Could she discuss one doctor with another? She knew how they protected one another. She'd heard, even from her father's old friends, about the code of silence that, in some places at least, makes it virtually impossible for one doctor to comment negatively about a colleague. She'd seen it in action when she wrote about "slip-ups" at hospitals.

"Do you have any guilt feelings over your surgery?" Slesar asked.

"Guilt feelings?"

"I'll explain it this way: Sometimes, in war, a man feels guilty if his buddy is killed and he survives. In your case, you were repaired by a great doctor. Yet, I'm sure you know that many people have had similar accidents . . . and live the rest of their lives in the shadows."

"I'll always feel for others who've been disfigured," Carly said, suddenly sinking into a sullen mood. "I saw some in the plastic surgery ward. Very little could be done for them. I know what they're going through."

"I'm sure you do," Slesar said. "Now tell me what you're holding back."

Carly turned suddenly toward him. "What?"

"Tell me what you're holding back. Come on. Everyone holds back something."

"Not me."

"Everyone."

What did he see? Did Slesar actually see something in her behavior, or was this one of those sweeping, vacuum-cleaner questions designed to catch anything that had been missed?

"Let me think," she answered, stretching for time.

"Please do," Slesar said, glancing at his watch to remind Carly that his cheerfulness did not free him from an appointment schedule.

Now Carly debated with herself. Tell him about Laval, one side said. Bring it out. See what he says. Surely other patients have had suspicions about doctors, and have discussed them with psychiatrists. He's sworn to secrecy, isn't he? He might be able to help.

But the other side balked. This could be a criminal case. No doctor would want to get involved with that. And maybe he'd become afraid of her, afraid that she was one of those people who went after doctors, who sued on impulse. Bring it up, and "malpractice" would flash before his mind like a stop sign.

"Well?" Slesar finally asked.

"Let me ask you a question," Carly replied.

"Sure."

"When a patient feels . . . uncomfortable with a doctor, is that something you'd discuss?"

Slesar laughed, and the smile actually became wider. "Of course," he replied. "Look, we doctors aren't as uptight as we used to be about that. We understand people have problems with physicians. Sometimes they're psychological, sometimes not. But never hesitate to bring up a concern. I'll try to help."

"But if *you* know that doctor personally, wouldn't you feel loyal to . . .?"

Carly looked toward Slesar, and saw the smile melt from his face, replaced by a near-frown, a disapproving frown, as if she'd insulted him, maybe insulted Sigmund Freud and the whole committee. This was a man who, according to reputation, took his professionalism seriously and didn't like it questioned. Carly realized immediately that she'd questioned it.

"Look," Slesar said, still sounding gentle despite his obvious upset, "I'm a doctor. We take an oath. Privacy is part of it. I would *never* reveal anything you said to me to any other doctor, unless I had your express permission. What you say stops inside these walls, and these walls are pretty thick."

"Even if I said something horrible about that doctor?"

"No matter what you said. I've heard everything. Some of my colleagues don't win popularity contests. I'm aware we have bad doctors, and rude doctors, and doctors who sometimes botch things. Hey, I'm aware."

Somehow, Slesar's comments reassured Carly and tipped the scales in her mind. She simply had to talk to someone who knew medicine, someone other than Mike Moran, and someone who, unlike Scott Levin, wouldn't automatically defend a plastic surgeon.

"Something's happened," she said, almost dramatically.

"All right," Slesar replied. "Please tell me." The smile returned, glowing and reassuring, sucking the patient into Slesar's psychiatric grasp.

"I respect Dr. Laval's ability . . ."

"But you can't stand his personality." Slesar laughed. "I get that all the time. He is a little bit godlike. I—"

"That's not it."

"Oh?"

How much do you tell him? How much do you reveal without feeling embarrassed, without damaging a man who might be quite innocent? "Uh, I respect his ability," Carly went on, with obvious hesitation, "but I discovered that . . . I discovered that he'd given a face just like mine . . . I mean, *really* like mine . . . to another patient."

There was a chill silence. Carly didn't know what to make of it. She glanced over to Slesar and watched him flash the grin once more. "I don't understand," he said.

"A woman confronted me outside my apartment," Carly explained. "She thought I was her daughter, who'd disappeared. I assured her I wasn't, but she showed me a picture. Her daughter and I . . . were virtually identical. And both of us had our faces rebuilt by André Laval."

"I see," Slesar said. He looked skeptical. "I haven't heard that one, but I'll withhold judgment. Continue."

"The woman was from Burbank, in California. So I went out there to track this down. Would you believe the local police stopped me? They thought I was this woman, Kathleen Shirmer."

"You said she was missing," Slesar interrupted.

"Yes. She just disappeared. But the police action, and the pictures I saw—they showed how close our faces are. And the same doctor."

"Well," Slesar shrugged, "these similarities . . ."

"If you saw the pictures," Carly said firmly, "you wouldn't be that casual about it."

Slesar realized just how deadly serious, and deadly convinced, Carly was. He quickly jotted some ideas. "You're disturbed then," he said, "because another woman looks like you. Is that it?"

"I'm disturbed that Dr. Laval would give the same face to two women. I don't think that's right, do you?"

"It's not something I would've done," Slesar answered.

"And I'm disturbed because she's missing. It wasn't in her character just to disappear. And I have some other suspicions."

"Like what?"

"Something in my bones. Look, I'm feeling my way around here. But I think Laval gave this face to more women as well."

"You have evidence?"

"I'd rather not go into that just yet," Carly replied. "I'm still tracking it down. But Laval is doing something funny, and it may be worse than funny. That much I think I know."

Now Slesar took a deep breath, let it out slowly, and placed his pad beside him. "Wow," he said. "This is pretty heavy stuff. Look, it's awfully hard for me to assess what you say . . ."

"I understand that," Carly said.

"And I'm not going to defend what Dr. Laval did. But . . . is it possible . . . consider this for a moment . . . is it possible you're not seeing this quite the way you might see it? Dr. Laval could have his motives."

"Maybe he does," Carly said firmly, hearing the echo of Scott Levin, "but they can't be honorable, they couldn't be anything medicine would accept. No doctor has the right to duplicate faces."

"Agreed," Slesar told her. "I'm catching your drift and it's gotten me upset too. You're right. He shouldn't have done it. I'm stunned. I really am. This isn't the André Laval I know."

"So what do I do?"

"I'm not sure. I certainly wouldn't go to the state medical board. You haven't got enough evidence."

"Agreed," Carly said.

Slesar rubbed his chin, appearing to consider a variety of solutions. "This isn't really in my line," he said. "I treat psychiatric symptoms. But you might want to contact Laval himself and discuss it. Confront him."

"I couldn't do that," Carly countered.

"Well, you could, but I understand why you wouldn't. Okay, what did *you* intend to do . . . before you came in here today?"

"I intended to pursue the story, as I'd pursue any other."

"Well, I'd probably do the same," Slesar said, "but I'm concerned that it could affect your mental equilibrium. You know, even great doctors do things they might not be proud of. Taking the worst case—that Laval duplicated faces to prove he could do it, or because he wanted some trademark—it hasn't really affected you, has it?"

"It upsets me."

"That's not enough. And I think you may be frustrated in pursuing it. You had a lucky break and learned about this other woman. You may not be so lucky next time. This has all the possibilities of becoming an obsession. Obsessions destroy people."

"You're asking me to give it up," Carly said.

"In a way, yes. Ms. Randall, you don't have enough evidence to press any charges against Dr. Laval. You haven't been directly hurt. You're happy with his work. Your life has improved . . ."

"I want to find out why he did this."

Slesar shrugged his shoulders. "I can only advise you," he said, "I can't stop you."

"I *won't* be stopped," Carly said, summoning her journalistic militancy.

"I see that," Slesar observed. "But I'll make this request . . ."

"Yes?"

"I want you to continue to discuss this with me. Whatever you find, tell me. I'll be happy to help you, in confidence of course, but I'm going to be very rough on you if the obsession sign flashes. Use me as a sounding board, okay?"

"Okay," Carly said. "For how long?"

"As long as this is bothering you. Since it's my request, I'll keep the fees down. I'm always interested in a patient's interaction with a physician. In your case, you've had family problems with doctors . . ."

Carly groaned, then slammed her right arm angrily into the couch, startling Slesar who stared at her quizzically. "My boss brought that up, too," she said, more than a touch of biting anger in her voice. "That's not influencing me."

"We'll see," Slesar said. "Sometimes we don't know what influences us. But I suspect you're right. I don't think your past is influencing you either. But there are other things here as well, things that—"

"Like what?"

"Those memory lapses."

"What does that have to do with Laval's assembly line?"

Slesar smiled, then laughed at the reference. "Assembly line, eh? Never heard of that one either. Ms. Randall, I don't know what the relationship is. But memory lapses might indicate a perception problem. We'll have to examine exactly what you're seeing."

"I know what I'm seeing."

"I accept your feelings," Slesar said.

The session ended with Slesar reassuring Carly that he would do all to help her—that his challenging comments had simply been designed to uncover any problems she might be having. He gave Carly his private number, urging her to call him at any time, especially if she discovered something new about Laval. And he muttered some vague words about doctors who embarrass their profession.

Carly felt she'd found a friend, if not an ally. She left armed with at least moral support from Gordon Slesar, and the knowledge that Mike Moran was backing her professionally. Her next appointment of the day was with André Laval, and she actually looked forward to it. She was going right to the source, returning to the scene of what appeared to be a crime.

Back in his office, Slesar slumped into his desk chair, pondering what he'd just heard from Carly Randall. He didn't smile. He didn't show any of the outward joy that ordinarily oozed all over his personality. He simply stared into space, then nervously tapped a pencil on the side of his desk. Finally, he snapped on the intercom that connected him to his receptionist. "Cancel the next two appointments," he ordered. "I'm not feeling well."

And he wasn't.

In fact, he was facing one of the worst crises of his career, and Carly Randall was right in the center of it.

12

Carly had two hours between appointments, and decided to have a leisurely lunch at an Italian restaurant on Manhattan's East Side. She was already planning her next trip—pursuing the name that she'd found in Kathleen's address book. She spent a good part of lunch going over the Metroliner schedule to Washington, and checking the location of some hotels on a map. She knew only that her target's name was Fern, and she wondered whether Fern was part of private Washington, or the public capital. Carly knew she could be tampering with a power—the wife of some prominent politician or lawyer, or someone connected with a foreign embassy.

She never noticed a green car that crept its way past the restaurant, a Toyota with MD license plates, driven by Gordon Slesar. Nor did she hear the sharp honk of the Toyota's horn as Slesar, looking tense and anxious, struggled to squeeze around a double-parked Con Edison service truck. The Toyota finally eased past the truck, turned a corner and maneuvered away, heading toward the East Seventies.

About twenty minutes later Slesar, having parked his car in a garage, walked up the steps of an elegant town house with neither a name nor a number on the door. So worldly was André Laval, so exclusive was the renowned plastic surgeon, that he felt such identification superfluous, even a bit boorish. Some people just don't need addresses, and the medical shingle was a symbol,

Laval felt, of the physician in need of a practice. People important enough to be treated at Laval's town house knew where to find him. His unlisted phone number was available through proper channels.

The town house was a vast contrast to the studied simplicity of Slesar's brownstone. Slesar entered through a glass and wrought-iron door and stepped into a reception area decorated with paintings and finished with deep pile carpeting and antique furniture. There was no waiting room, for Laval's precision allowed for no waiting.

Laval's receptionist, whom he dressed in a chic red jumpsuit, sat at a formal desk and greeted Slesar in a mechanical, practiced manner, meant to drive home the idea that Laval was more important than anyone who might enter. "Good afternoon, Dr. Slesar," she said. "I'll inform Dr. Laval that you've arrived." There was no invitation to sit down. One does not sit when one expects immediate attention.

Although Laval had known Slesar for years, he did not come out to greet his colleague. Style was everything, so the world came to André. When Laval signaled his receptionist, she pressed a button on the side of her desk and a bronze door slid open, leading to Laval's offices. "Please go in, Dr. Slesar," she said.

Slesar entered, as he had on several previous occasions, and walked down a long corridor, stopping at an examining room, where Laval was making notes based on his last examination. The plastic surgeon, dressed in a blue cashmere Burberry blazer and gray Armani slacks, looked up, but only after completing a sentence. "Gordon," he said, "come in. You're looking just grand, Gordy."

"Thanks, André. Of course you *always* look good."

"Requirement of the trade, Gordy. I'll revise my assessment, though. You could lose a few pounds, my friend."

"Yes André, I know. People tell me."

"Looks are everything, Gordy. Believe me. I've built a world of beauty. That little bulge you've got will cost you, my friend."

"Oh, I know." Slesar spotted a large book on Italian

art, lying, of all places, on an examining table. "Going to Italy?" he asked.

"Oh no," Laval replied, "but I'm brushing up on Mediterranean features. That's the trend, Gordy. Women are moving away from that Anglo-Saxon look and toward the more ethnic styles. Mediterranean is very popular. I did a wann-der-ful face just yesterday. The lady could have been a Medici from Florence."

"A real Sophia Loren, eh André?"

Laval laughed condescendingly. "Gordy, I can do better than that."

Slesar quickly adjusted to Laval's supercharged ego. "No doubt about it, André."

Laval could see that Slesar looked nervous. "Now Gordy," he said, "what's this about? When you called you said you had to see me immediately. You insisted the phone wasn't good enough. And you asked me to cancel an appointment with a major star whose last film grossed eighty-six million dollars, which I did with great reluctance. And you said this was about me. I hope it's important, Gordy."

"It's crucial." Slesar wasn't smiling, and Laval sensed that there was no exaggeration in the psychiatrist's urgent visit.

"Sit down," Laval said, suddenly very businesslike. Slesar's manner made him uncomfortable. He was not used to hearing anything but compliments from visitors.

Slesar sat in a leather chair usually reserved for patients. "André, I saw one of your patients this morning."

"Oh?"

"Carly Randall."

"Oh, yes. I referred her. Grand girl, Carly."

"I'm sure, André," Slesar said. "But something came up during my interview."

Laval suddenly frowned and leaned forward. "Is she having psychological problems, Gordy?"

"I don't know. I'll have to determine that."

"So?"

Slesar hesitated, then gazed up at a framed copy of the

Hippocratic oath, which Laval kept on the wall of each of his six examining rooms. "André," he said, "I'm not supposed to tell you this."

"Well, she authorized you, didn't she?"

"No. Just the opposite. I assured her of secrecy."

"Gordy, what are you talking about?"

"I'm talking about guilt," Slesar replied. "I'm talking about doing something I shouldn't be doing." Beads of sweat broke out on Slesar's forehead and Laval saw that he was breathing more heavily now. "I'm also talking about the fact that you saved me from a malpractice suit three years ago."

"Yes, I recall," Laval said. "The Andrews case."

"Don't remind me of her name," Slesar groaned. "But you saved me. I've got to do the same for you."

Now Laval fairly leapt out of his chair, stunned, caught off guard. "Is Carly Randall thinking of *suing* me? Why? What could be her motive? I've given her a new life, Gordy." And while Laval's act was convincing enough, inside he could feel the churning start. Something wasn't right with Carly. It was his nightmare, the potential destruction of his dream. But he didn't immediately deduce from Slesar's manner how much Carly knew. "Legal action," he went on. "I can't believe it."

"Sit down, André," Slesar said. "It's a lot worse than that."

Laval did not reply. He sank back in his chair, wondering what could possibly be worse, whether his prized patient had done something crazy, had gotten him in some kind of trouble, had besmirched his name.

"André," Slesar continued, "did you give her face to somebody else?"

Laval glared. "What the hell you talkin' about, boy?" he snapped, reverting to the language of the Philadelphia streets from which he came, language he used only when denigrating another doctor.

"She found someone in California. Burbank, I think. One of your former patients, André."

Laval's heart pounded, but he fought desperately to

prevent the shock from showing. Damage control. That was the only thing that interested him right now. She knew. If not all of it, she knew part of it. But how did she find out? Maybe someone tipped her. It had *always* been a possibility, always a high-risk experiment. Pass it off, Laval now advised himself. Remain André Laval, the master of elegance. This was a dreaded moment, but it could, like anything else, be handled. "I'm not sure I follow this," he said, his voice suddenly the essence of mellowness and calm.

"She claims," Slesar replied, "that some woman confronted her in New York and thought Carly was her daughter. The faces were identical, and you worked on the daughter too. The woman was from Burbank. The daughter is missing."

For what seemed like an eternity, Laval said nothing. Then he looked Slesar right in the eye and shrugged his shoulders ever so slightly. "That is essentially correct," he said softly, leaving Slesar absolutely flabbergasted at the instant reversal.

"It's *what?*"

"Yes, Gordy," Laval said, now smiling with an almost arrogant indifference.

"But a moment ago you . . ."

"Just establishing that I was thinking of the same case Ms. Randall was. Very sad, isn't it? I did so much for her, and now she doubts me. Selfish, I think. This poor girl in Burbank has disappeared, and Ms. Randall is obviously thinking only of herself."

"Now André," Slesar said—and the normally beaming face was utter stone—"let me get this straight. You're admitting that you duplicated this girl's face?"

Laval got up and started pacing the room, slipping his hands gracefully into his blazer pockets, the thumbs arching out over the sides. "No, no, no," he answered, "I didn't duplicate, Gordy. That's such an oversimplification; such an intrusion into our world of medical art. I did seek to perfect certain features. I've been working on a number of problems in plastic surgery, and I found solutions that I liked—"

"I was thinking that same thing, I—"

"Let me continue, would you, Gordy? I've been doing some work in mentoplasty—that's the chin implant—and I perfected a very sensuous dimple. I know that may sound foolish to you, but to many women that dimple is their identity. I gave it to these two women, Kathleen Shirmer and Carly Randall—geographically separated—as part of my research. And then cheekbones. One of my greatest challenges. You know what the biggest problem with cheekbones is, Gordy?"

"No, André, I don't."

"Skin. Women don't realize that. Now, I can create any cheekbones I want. The problem is getting the skin to look natural when reshaped over the cheeks. Very difficult, I tell you, Gordy. Skin loses elasticity as it ages. It doesn't shape well. But I perfected some new techniques, and used them on these women." He waved his right hand loosely through the air. "Look, I have likes and dislikes. I may have used the same techniques on some other patients. I'd have to check my notes."

"Admirable, André. I'm beginning to feel rotten, scaring you like this. And I'm beginning to feel like a goddamned creep too—breaking a confidence."

"Come on Gordy, get off it," Laval said. "You did it for a good reason. You weren't trying to advance yourself. You were coming to my aid. It's the strangest thing, though—this other woman finding Carly Randall. You know, you use some of these techniques several times and you *can* come out with fairly similar faces. Since this girl is missing, the mother remembered what she thought she remembered, and even read things into pictures. The faces are close, not identical. But I can understand the confusion."

"You know where she is, André?"

Laval shot a contemptuous stare in Slesar's direction. "Of course not. What kind of a man—?"

"Oh I wasn't suggesting—"

"I went out to California when I found out the girl was missing. I spent some of my own money on the case. I'll always be willing to help. She was a marvelous patient. She was wann-der-ful."

"Was?"

"As a patient."

"André," Slesar went on, "Carly Randall told me she's pursuing a suspicion."

"What suspicion?"

"She thinks you may have given that face to other women as well."

"Oh she does? Sounds more like an obsession than a suspicion."

"That's my fear."

"Well, let her pursue it. She may find some reasonably close faces. You know I've done more than thirty-five hundred facial procedures, Gordy. You put any thirty-five hundred women together, done by the same art . . . the same surgeon, and you'll find similarities."

"Sure. I know that."

"And especially with the work I've been doing—trying to perfect particular features—you'll find more. Maybe I should stop."

"Don't stop because of her, André," Slesar said. "You're too great a doctor."

"Now I have to fear that she'll go out and embarrass me. She's a reporter. They're irresponsible. You know, plastic surgery is one of those fields they love to smear. She'll say in print what she wants to say, and the lie'll be halfway around the world before the truth catches up to it. My work will be compromised. There are so many women I want to help."

"I'll talk to her, André. I think she'll calm down. I can't tell her that I've spoken to you. But I can relay some of the things you've said. I'll tell her I did research into plastic surgery, and that these little . . . similarities . . . are common."

"Tell her that, Gordy. And have her reflect on the new

life I've given her. Let her," Laval went on, a theatrical bitterness in his voice, "reflect on what her life would've been like had she not met me. And Gordy . . ."

"Yes?"

Laval got up again and started to pace, this time with his hands clasped in front of him. Slesar had seen the pose before. It usually anticipated Laval's making a request. The great man would never call it a favor, but it amounted to the same thing. "Gordy, I know how badly you feel about coming over here, violating privacy . . ."

"I still feel bad about it," Slesar said. "It's the first time."

"Well, I understand, although your motives are grand, really first-class. But Gordy, it's important that I be kept informed."

Slesar had expected that, but the request still jolted him. He was essentially a decent man, but he knew his motives in coming to Laval weren't quite as "grand" as Laval had pictured them, and he suspected Laval knew that too. Gordon Slesar was a climber, a medical politician. He was plagued by insecurity, fearing that people didn't like him, that other doctors didn't respect him. It was this very insecurity that had led him into psychiatry, part of a search for the truth about his own troubles. This insecurity had prompted him to flash that exaggerated smile and ooze that frothy warmth and goodness. And this insecurity had sent him across town to André Laval, shredding the Hippocratic oath in the process and spilling everything that Carly Randall had told him. He was doing the great plastic surgeon a *service*, the same way a minor politician did a service for the political boss, the same way a soldier in organized crime did a service for the godfather. Laval would *like* him more, would remember the service, would protect Gordon Slesar and advance him.

And now Gordon Slesar felt small. He felt small because he *was* small—a physician with the soul of a ward heeler.

"Well, Gordy?" Laval nudged.

"In my professional opinion," Slesar said, "giving you

insights into this case would help the patient. I'm prepared
to stretch the privacy rules to help her.''

What a lie, Slesar thought.

What a lie, Laval thought.

They understood one another.

13

"I will kill Carly Randall."

Laval spoke directly into the lens of the television camera in a small studio attached to his office. This wasn't as elegant as the studio in his hospital suite, but he made tapes here too.

"I regret the need," he went on, "but we have a crisis—the worst of my career. Ms. Randall found out that I gave her face to a woman in California. The experiment is in some difficulty. Something has gone wrong.

"You may wonder why I put this on tape. Wonder no more, if you will. This tape is for posterity. No one can punish me. I have told you of my experiment and I feel I must now tell you of this development. I will demonstrate how an experienced surgeon handles a crisis, and how he defeats it.

"I had hoped to decide Carly Randall's fate much later, when everything had healed. I would have judged her against my own high standard. But now her discovery of the other face has intervened. Fate has turned against me. But it must now turn against her too.

"Kill her, silence her before she does damage.

"She'll be here in a few minutes. Shall I kill her now? It's convenient. I have the opportunity. But no, I haven't planned. It would be too obvious. Slesar knows about her. He's a fool, but even he would become suspicious. I have to stage her killing in such a way that someone else gets the blame.

"But do I have the time? What if she goes to the police?"

"There *has* to be time. She's still investigating. She hasn't got any hard evidence against me. She'll continue poking around. These reporters don't like to go to the police too early and ruin their story. There has to be time . . ."

Laval snapped off the machine. He felt an enormous frustration well up inside him. Carly would be a few inches from him that afternoon, yet he could do nothing for fear of being caught. He was angry. He felt betrayed, but by whom he didn't know.

Make the appointment as normal as possible, he told himself. Reveal nothing. See what *she* does.

Everything was collapsing around André Laval. Yet he had no thought of running away to another country, of hiding. His ego wouldn't let him. He had to survive this, his profession and reputation intact.

But how?

Carly arrived for her appointment precisely at two P.M. Laval was obsessed with promptness, and his patients knew it. Arrive more than five minutes late and your appointment could easily be canceled. New York gossip columnists had buzzed not more than a year before when he had canceled an appointment with one of the five richest women in America, then dropped her as a patient when she was late again.

"Ms. Randall," Laval's receptionist said as Carly entered, "I'm Geneen, a new member of Dr. Laval's staff. I'll inform the doctor that you're here." Actually, her name was Edith, but Laval had insisted on the upgrade.

The bronze door opened and Carly entered. "Examining room three," Geneen told her. Carly had been here many times before, as Laval liked his patients to visit his offices in both the town house and Burgess Hospital. Give them a taste of medical grandeur. It helped explain the bills.

The doctor was assuming his usual busy pose, writing in a patient's folder as Carly appeared at the door. The book on Mediterranean art had been removed from the room—

Laval was in no mood for idle gossip about Mediterranean faces and their current popularity. He looked up as soon as Carly's shadow flashed across the spotless cork-tiled floor. "Ms. Randall," he said, "you are utterly ravishing. I'm absolutely shocked that you aren't trailing a squad of suitors behind you."

Carly laughed, seeing right through Laval but feigning the necessary units of embarrassment, shyness, and grace. "Thank you," she said. "It's all your fault, Dr. Laval."

"And I accept the blame."

Each was starting to maneuver, each aiming for the jugular, all under the umbrella of a routine medical visit. "I got a wann-der-ful report on you from Dr. Slesar," Laval said. "Naturally, he didn't go into detail on what you two talked about, but he found you the picture of emotional health."

"He's a very nice man," Carly responded. What else do you say?

"I've known Gordon Slesar for an eternity," Laval added, now slipping his Mont Blanc pen back inside his blazer. "He's a prince. He'll do everything he can for you, if you need it. He's very loyal."

"I'm sure," Carly said.

"Ah, come in, Ms. Randall," Laval said, realizing Carly was still at the door. "Please sit down and tell me how your life has bloomed."

Carly entered the office and sat in a leather chair next to the examining table. Although he sometimes examined patients in his oak-desked office, Laval felt the traditional examining room was more intimidating, more forbidding, more awesome. Laval never wanted his patients to forget that he was a great physician as well as a great artist.

"Well, it *has* bloomed," Carly told him. "Everyone thinks you did a terrific job. I get noticed. I don't have anything to hide any more."

"Of course not."

"And I've even heard some people at *Allure* say that I may have another career."

Now Laval threw his head back and laughed his I-told-you-so laugh, patented some years before. "Well, my lady," he said, "you're beginning to see the full extent of your wann-der-ful potential. I, uh, took the liberty of sending a photographer over there."

"Yes, Marge told me."

"Ah, Marge, I know her well. Grand girl, Marge is. So statuesque. And a superb editor. She expressed the view that your face is indeed a model's face, or an actress's. Ms. Randall, you'd be very foolish not to recognize what you now have to offer."

"Oh, I think about it," Carly said.

"Let me fetch your file." Laval walked over to a wood file cabinet and started going through it. He kept thinking about Slesar's revelations. Why wasn't Carly hinting at anything? How much did she actually know? How much damage could she do? Yes, of course, her trail could easily run cold. She could reach a dead end. But still, she already knew too much. Some things could be explained away. But who would believe André Laval's explanations?

For her part, Carly was determined not to slip anything that would reveal what she knew. She'd psyched herself for this examination, trying to push her suspicions of Laval to the back of her mind. For this, she inwardly thanked Gordon Slesar. Even in his skepticism, he'd been so understanding. He was already becoming a kind of escape valve, the very person Carly knew she needed as she maneuvered through this minefield.

"Ah," Laval said, glancing through her records, "as smooth a recovery as I've seen. How are you feeling, Ms. Randall?"

"Just fine. Oh, by the way, you really should call me Carly."

"Oh no I shouldn't," Laval said. "I appreciate that but I can't stand plastic surgeons who become too familiar with their patients. They run their practices like beauty parlors. Ms. Randall, this is a medical office. I always want to remember that you're a patient first."

"I understand," Carly said. God, she thought, the guy was a better actor than two-thirds of Hollywood.

"Now," Laval went on, "have you been taking it easy?"

"Well, I'm working, but not knocking my brains out."

"No traveling?"

Carly hesitated. She was sure the question was routine. "I did some traveling," she replied. "Nothing much."

"Oh? A vacation, I hope."

"More or less."

"Where to?"

"Los Angeles." Carly felt she had to tell the truth. Laval had contacts at *Allure,* and he might ask around.

"Interesting city," Laval said, now walking over to Carly and making a detailed inspection of her face. "I do some surgery at Unity Hospital. Grand place. Some very prominent patients."

"How am I healing?" Carly asked, trying to get Laval off that subject.

"Very well," Laval replied. "But there's a little area near where we did the right otoplasty—"

"The what?"

"The work on the ear. I'm not entirely pleased with the tightness of the skin. It's a minor repair. Let's just watch it for a short time."

"Would I have to go to the hospital?"

"Well, we'll see," Laval replied. "I know those doctors who call patients by their first names like to perform surgery in their offices—soon they'll start doing it in their cars—but I prefer the hospital. Remember our first talk?"

"I . . . think so."

"I told you that the most important thing to know about plastic surgery is that it's dangerous."

"Yes, I remember."

"And what are the great dangers in facial reconstruction, Ms. Randall?" Laval asked, as if in a classroom. "Blindness, brain damage, and infection."

"God, yes, I remember," Carly replied, wincing at the list of joys.

"Good. Never forget it. Dangerous things should be done in hospitals."

Laval was beginning to devise a plan. True, he *was* a conservative surgeon who never liked to perform "procedures" in his office and who insisted that patients understand the risks, but now he knew he would have a special reason for luring Carly back to the hospital.

People die in hospitals.

All the time.

Accidentally.

"Will you be in town should I decide to do this procedure?" Laval asked.

Carly hesitated, striking a pose that made it appear as if she were reviewing her schedule in her mind. "Hard to say," she replied. "I do have some out-of-town assignments."

"Far away?"

"Not really." Now Carly was tempted. She was finding it hard to resist her old urge to approach the edge and look over. "I may go to Washington." She glanced at Laval to see if he'd react.

But Laval didn't budge. He was completely in control, determined that Carly Randall would learn *nothing* from him. Inside, though, the juices started to stir. Why Washington? Was it just a coincidence? Going to the nation's capital was a perfectly normal thing for a journalist to do, but these circumstances weren't normal. "Lovely city," he said. "I've done some prominent people there."

"I'm sure," Carly said.

Then Laval smiled benevolently at Carly. "Well, Ms. Randall, with the exception of that little ear problem, I'll give you a clean bill of health . . . and beauty. And I'll let you know about further surgery. Questions?"

"No, I'm afraid not. I'm actually very content."

"Just glorious," Laval said. "Oh, by the way, if you do go out of town, make sure my office knows where to reach you—if we want to schedule that hospital stay."

"Sure."

"I suspect we'll have to do it, Ms. Randall. I suspect we'll have to do it—in the hospital, just to be safe."

14

A few minutes after Carly left, Laval's private line rang. Only a select group had his private number, so he knew the call had to be from someone of top rank, possibly a favored patient, a political leader, possibly the representative of a royal family, or a show-business personality. The number was discreetly changed once a year, in December, so Laval could send the new number, with a holiday card, to the favored few. For some, it was the best present they could receive.

Laval picked up. "This is André Laval."

For a moment, all he heard was someone breathing at the other end, with distorted rock 'n' roll music in the background. This wasn't the average Laval caller.

"Hello?" he repeated. He assumed someone had gotten the wrong number.

"Oh, yeah, hi Doc," said a woman's voice, the speech slurred.

Laval instantly cooled. "Oh, hello Marcia," he said. "How, uh, nice to hear from you." It was Marcia Lane. Laval had given her his private number because he wanted no one else to know of their unusual medical relationship.

Marcia was leaning against the wall of her slum apartment, sunglasses on, holding the phone in one hand, her chronic Scotch in the other. She was thirty-two; a man of about twenty-one lay on the floor beneath her, dead drunk, his clothes half off, a tattoo of a snake throbbing on an exposed left arm. Marcia stared at him as she spoke.

"I called, uh," she said, "because I got this here appointment with you."

"Ah yes," Laval said, "I'm flying out on Thursday, Marcia."

"Forget it, pal."

"I beg your pardon?"

"You don't gotta beg nothin'," Marcia said. "I just can't see you this week, Doc."

"But why?"

"I got some problems."

"Perhaps I could help."

"No. I got man problems. I don't need no help. I need a gun."

"Now, now, maybe we can talk about it," Laval oozed, in mock sympahy. "I do want to see you. I think you should be checked." God, he thought, how did he ever choose her? True, she'd deteriorated since her operation, but he should've known.

"Nope," she said. "I gotta make it another time. Maybe two weeks. Okay?"

Laval sighed deeply, not out of concern for Marcia, but out of concern for himself. "Well, if it has to be," he said, "it has to be. But I think you're jeopardizing yourself— you know, making it bad for you."

"I know what 'jeparizing' means," Marcia said.

"Of course you do, Marcia."

"Look, you gimme a call in two weeks. There won't be no jeparizing. Thanks, Doc."

"All right, Marcia, I . . ."

Marcia hung up before Laval could finish. She kicked the man beneath her, then poured her drink on him. "You dead?" she asked. He answered with a mere groan.

Laval stared into space after completing the call, then looked down at the telephone as if it contained germs from Marcia's apartment. Suddenly, his life was in a downward spin. Carly Randall was a loose cannon waiting to go off. Marcia was becoming difficult. Laval felt himself cursed. They were after him again. The same people who rejected him in his youth and threw him out of art school—they must be involved in some mysterious way. There was always someone out to get him.

The answer to the problem was the same as it had been with Kathleen Shirmer. Death. Death solved all problems.

Marcia's death.

Carly's death.

15

Carly boarded the Metroliner at Pennsylvania Station.

She loved the Metroliner, especially when it was going to Washington, DC. Her first trip on a train had been to Washington. Her mother had taken her in 1963 as an eighth birthday gift, and it remained one of Carly's fondest memories. She still recalled getting a glimpse of President Kennedy as his limousine left the White House. And she remembered, ever so vaguely, the civil rights marchers holding a weekend vigil in Lafayette Park.

She even remembered how she would look carefully at every grown man who passed, hoping to find her father, who'd been off on one of his binges. It was an obsession that stayed with her after he left for good. Even now she occasionally caught herself searching crowds when away from home, hoping to see that face that she hardly knew, knowing instinctively she'd never see it again.

But this wasn't a vacation trip.

It wasn't a search for her father.

Carly had a name to track down: Fern. *Fern—Washington.*

The train pulled into Union Station in early afternoon, two hours and fifty minutes after leaving New York. Carly grabbed her one suitcase and walked to the cab stand just outside the terminal.

There is one manner in which Washington and New York are soul sisters—the condition of their taxis. No vehicle is too dilapidated to be pressed into service, no rattle or safety defect too great to be overlooked. The

drivers in each town bathe in the charm of indifference—
only in Washington most of them speak English. But,
unlike New York, Washington uses a zone system, so the
fare does not change until the cab passes into a new zone.
For drivers this encourages a new mathematical formula
wherein the shortest distance between two points is a
grand tour of most of the city.

"You got money on the game?" Carly's driver asked as
her cab agonized away from the station.

"What game?" she inquired.

He turned around to her, stared in amazement, and
remained silent for the rest of the ride.

Carly checked into the Hampshire Hotel, one of her
favorite spots in Washington, just off DuPont Circle. It
was a tiny, European-style hotel where the rooms were
equipped with small kitchens. Carly dropped her bag in
her room, stopped long enough to munch one of the
Godiva chocolates that the hotel provided for guests, and
dashed off to begin her probe.

Kathleen was missing from Burbank, and Carly theorized that Fern—if she were a real person—might have
suffered the same fate. A list of missing persons, with
photographs, would therefore be the right starting point.
But Carly was shy about going to the police. She didn't
want to start with the authorities before she had a solid
case, and she had no legitimate reason—at least not one
she could prove—for looking through their files. So, using
her *Allure* press credentials, she got a visitor's pass to
examine the files at the *Washingion Express*, a weekly
newspaper that emphasized coverage of the city, and especially its vigorous and lively crime scene. If Fern had been
reported missing, the *Express* would have probably picked
up the story.

The *Express* was part of a chain, and was far better
financed than most weeklies. It had offices on K Street in
a building that the chain owned. Its "morgue," or library
of clippings, was computerized. A visitor could tap an

entry into a keyboard, and the desired story would appear on a TV screen, complete with photographs.

Carly decided to walk the short distance from the Hampshire to the newspaper's offices. It was one of those glass structures, with all the glass tinted dark green. And it had only eighteen stories—another one of those gloriously low Washington buildings that allowed for plenty of blue sky.

She entered the building.

The *Washington Express* was on the seventh floor, sharing offices with a small newsletter that serviced operators of pet stores. Carly rode up in the elevator, snapping on her dark glasses before reaching seven. She didn't want anyone to remember her looks. If she found a picture of Fern, and the editors at the *Express* saw the picture and her face, they would immediately link the two.

"Mr. Farmer," she told the receptionist. Roy Farmer was the librarian for the paper, in charge of the morgue. The receptionist buzzed him.

A few moments later a scholarly-looking man easily seventy years old emerged from behind the swinging doors that led to the *Express*'s innards. He wore thick glasses that distorted his eyes and made them appear too large for his face. "Roy Farmer here," he said, extending his hand.

"Carly Randall," Carly replied, extending hers. "We spoke on the phone."

"Mr. Bell's machine," Farmer replied with a little giggle. "I remember when we had to crank them up. If I recall, you wanted to look through our crime files."

"Yes, I'm doing some background research for a story."

"Always happy to help a colleague," Farmer replied, "just as I helped Ben Hecht and Ernie Pyle in their day, may their souls rest in eternal peace."

"I . . . I appreciate your help," Carly said, not knowing quite how to respond to such pious incantations. She, too, hoped that Messrs. Hecht and Pyle had found their rest, but didn't care to discuss the subject further. "Can we get started?" she asked.

"Of course," Farmer said. "Ambition is the engine of progress."

"I agree," Carly said.

"Please follow," Farmer instructed. He led Carly through the swinging doors and down a corridor lined with famous front pages from the *Express:* KILLS THREE, WOUNDS TWO was a nice one. RAPES TWO, GOES FREE was prominent at the end of the hall. "There's one I like," Farmer said, pointing to STEALS BABY, BEATS MOM. "Very poignant. Like James Agee."

They reached a small room equipped with three personal computers. No one was using it. "Here," Farmer said, "let me turn on Mr. Edison's invention." He flipped on the lights. "If I gather correctly the text of our discussion," he said, "you wanted information on missing persons."

"That's right," Carly told him. "Anything in your files for the last, say, three years."

"No problem. We have a computer record with all the stories we've run on missing persons. Exciting cases, some of them."

Farmer opened a file drawer and went through rows of computer disks, finally finding one that filled Carly's order. "Our system is equipped to show photographs on the monitor," he explained. "Do you have any particular case in mind?"

"Uh, no," Carly said. "I'm doing a general survey."

"Very fine. I'll insert the disk and show you the operation of the device. In the old days we read actual newspaper clippings. We got newsprint on our hands. It was more glamorous then. They've taken all the elegance away from us."

"Did you always work in Washington?" Carly asked, curious about the quaint little man.

"No. I worked on the old *New York Daily Mirror*. It was three cents in those days. I knew Walter Winchell personally, may his soul rest in eternal peace. We sometimes had lunch."

"I envy you," Carly said.

"At least someone does."

Farmer gave Carly a very quick course in operating the

keyboard that ran the personal computer, demonstrating how she could go forward and back, or find a particular case if she was so inclined.

"I'll leave you alone," Farmer told her. "I've got work. But if you need me, my extension is 611, on the Bell."

"Thanks," Carly said. "I know you've gone out of your way. I do appreciate it."

"Right. By the way, you'd see better if you took off those shades. Women nowadays, always wearing sunglasses. I just don't understand it."

"The light hurts my eyes," Carly explained.

"Must be doctors for that," Farmer said, to no one in particular, then walked off.

Eagerly, Carly got down to work. She closed the door and snapped off the light, working only in the glow of the monitor. Now, with no one around, she took off her sunglasses.

Of course, it wasn't true that she was simply doing background research. She wanted to jump to Fern's case—if there was a case. There was an index with a disk, and Carly quickly went down the list of missing persons, checking for anyone whose first name was Fern.

She quickly found two names.

Following Farmer's instructions, she zipped to the first case. The clipping came up on her screen. Fern Carielo, who lived on Kalmia Road in the northwest section of Washington—had disappeared November 4, 1986. But she was only nineteen, and the picture with the story clearly showed a face unlike Carly's. It had to be the other Fern, Carly assumed.

She tapped in instructions to go to that next Fern. The clipping came up. Fern Simon, of Georgetown, daughter of an oil man, had disappeared January 2, 1986. There was no picture with the story, probably because the family couldn't get one to the newspaper quickly enough.

The story said Fern was thirty-two—Carly's age.

The story also said she was single, and hoped for a break in her minor acting career.

Carly's heart began to pound. She sensed she'd hit the right case, and was amazed it had happened so soon. But she needed much more information. She needed a picture. And she had to know the outcome of the case.

Two more clippings dealt with Fern Simon. One reported that the police were pursuing leads. Fern, it seemed, had disappeared on a Saturday, after leaving her father's Georgetown home, where she lived. She hadn't told him where she was going.

The second story reported that Fern's father had put up a twenty-five-thousand-dollar reward. Carly eagerly went through the story, which was on page one. It continued on sixteen.

The story continued.

But there was something else. There was a picture.

It bore no resemblance to Carly.

Carly's heart now sank right through her stomach. Those *were* the only two Ferns, and her luck hadn't been quite as good as she'd thought only moments before. Maybe she was entirely wrong, she reasoned. Maybe there was no Fern. Or, if there were, maybe she hadn't been a patient of Laval's at all. Maybe the entry in Kathleen Shirmer's address book was entirely irrelevant. And maybe the trail had run cold, and she would return to New York defeated and empty-handed.

She was ready to turn off the monitor when she hesitated, feeling her journalistic thoroughness jabbing her in her ribs. Maybe it would be a good idea to go through the entire missing-persons disk. Maybe she should just review all the cases the *Express* had on file. There could have been a filing mistake. A name could have been confused. It was a shot in the dark, but Carly decided to stay with it. The stories of missing persons had always fascinated her anyway.

She started on the disk, almost immediately getting a sense of the tragedies that ran through each story. She knew that most "missing" persons were missing because they wanted to be—runaways, people fed up with marriages or careers, others who couldn't cope with economic responsibilities. She wondered, as she gazed at photos and read descriptions, where some of those women were, what their new lives were like, whether they would ever come home.

Carly read for almost an hour, virtually hypnotized by the glow of the screen and the soothing hum of the computer that serviced it. She flipped past clippings that looked dull, lingered for a time on others.

And then she came to a clipping whose title intrigued her: WOMAN VANISHES FROM ARCHIVES. She read on:

"A thirty-year-old woman vanished last night on the way home from doing doctoral research at the National Archives. Kristen F. Lowry, of 1717 R Street Northwest, has not been seen since saying goodnight to a librarian who'd helped her find documents on American relations with Brazil. Ms. Lowry . . ."

Carly scanned the rest.

And then . . . a phrase.

She stared at it. She blinked. No, it couldn't be true.

She read it again, then again:

"The political researcher, who had recently undergone plastic surgery . . ."

Desperately, Carly looked for a picture. There was none. She raced through the story once more. Plastic surgery. How many missing women had . . . ?

But the name. Kristen F. Lowry. It didn't work. But . . . maybe it did.

The middle initial—F.

Fern?

Maybe she didn't like her first name. Maybe she'd been named for a relative she couldn't stand, and used her middle name. Fern Lowry? Why not? It was as good as any other theory.

Carly pressed on, trying to find more on the Lowry case. What was the outcome? Where was she?

But there was only one more story. The usual follow-up, the normal second-day angle, or, in the case of the *Express*, the second-week angle. It simply said that police were interviewing friends of Ms. Lowry, as well as several people at the State Department, which had hired her to research a project on Latin American policy. There was nothing else, and there was no picture. Maybe she hadn't had pictures taken since her plastic surgery.

Or maybe this was just another blind alley, and the middle name was really Frances, or Felicia, or Francesca. Why were there no more stories?

Energized, yet frustrated, Carly snapped off the machine. She flipped on the light, removed the disk, and, slipping on her sunglasses, hurriedly walked out into the hall. She wanted to leave the disk, but had forgotten Farmer's extension. A secretary was walking by and Carly tried to stop her. "Excuse me, could you . . .?" But then she saw Farmer coming out of an office, a bunch of files under his right arm.

"Looking for me?" he asked.

"Yes," Carly replied. "I'm finished. I wanted to thank you and—"

"Could've called me on the Bell."

"I'm, I'm sorry. I forgot the number."

"Was a time when reporters made notes on a little yellow pad. Must be outdated." He finally smiled, the sour, weasel-like smile of a man who lived entirely in an era that was only memory.

"I'll remember that," Carly said. "At any rate, thank you."

"Come back any time," Farmer said. "Just sign out when you leave. We keep accurate records."

Carly left the building and zipped to a phone booth, calling Information for the number and address of Missing Persons, Washington Police Department.

Within a half hour, she found herself sitting on a plain metal chair in the "reception room" of Missing Persons. The reception room consisted of nothing more than a six-typist pool and a few extra chairs for visitors. This wasn't where ordinary "complainants" came, but Carly wasn't ordinary by police standards. She was from a magazine. She'd given only short notice, but official Washington was always ready for the press, its third industry after government and influence-peddling.

Carly waited a few minutes for Lieutenant Pete Romulo, the spokesman for Missing Persons, who himself had eleven years of experience tracing those who had vanished. Romulo rolled out of his office, a substantial chap with a bulging waistline and a forward, gung-ho manner more associated with the Marines than with a local police force. He was clothed in a flashy light gray civilian suit and a red, almost incandescent tie. "Romulo," he announced as he extended his hand to shake Carly's. "Missing Persons. And yes, I'm a Filipino, and no, I'm no relation to Carlos Romulo, former foreign minister of the Philippines and also no, I never met Cory Aquino." His broad smile lightened an oversized face, which was topped with an enormous shock of black, wavy hair. "That do it for you?"

Carly was flabbergasted. She'd never gotten a full autobiography, complete with name-dropping, in a police introduction before. "Carly Randall," she said quietly, "and I'm just a reporter for *Allure*. And I hope that does it for *you*."

"Sure does," Romulo said. "I like reporters. I like freedom of the press. It's good . . . most of the time. You know Walter Cronkite?"

"I met him once," Carly said.

"So did I. He was down here for an inauguration . . . of the president. Tell you, that was a thrill."

"The inauguration?"

"No. Meeting Walter Cronkite. Inaugurations, hell, we get 'em every four years. Same old parade. What can I do for you, Madam Reporter?"

"Uh, could we step into your office?" Carly asked, not wanting to advertise her questions before the typing pool.

"Sure. Come on in," Romulo said. "It's not much, but it's home."

He was right, Carly thought. It wasn't much. It was four walls of plaster with a desk, a desk chair, and two visitors' chairs, one of which was broken. The walls were blank. No decorations or pictures. Behind Romulo's desk was a pole bearing an old American flag, and a single window looking out on a brick wall. An olive drab filing cabinet, filled with scratches, completed the decor.

"Told you," Romulo said, as he saw Carly look around at the furniture. "Look, the FBI it isn't. Now, sit down and spill your heart out."

Carly sat in the unbroken visitor's chair, which squeaked, while Romulo slid into his desk chair, which rattled. "I'm following a case," she told Romulo.

"For your magazine?"

Carly hesitated. She had to frame her question with some finesse. It was risky enough to go to the police, which she hadn't wanted to do. She didn't want to get them involved in her investigation. "It's a case that interests me personally, but it'll find its way into a story."

"What kind of story?"

"I don't know yet."

"You don't know? I mean, is this a story on missing persons?"

"It may have a lot to do with that, if this case is linked with some others."

Suddenly Romulo turned cold. "You one of those scribes who's playin' detective?" he asked. " 'Cause if you are, you're in the wrong place. I supply information to legitimate reporters. We're not lookin' to encourage any Sherlocks here. Get the picture?"

"Uh, sure," Carly replied. "Look, I just have a few questions. I'm legitimate. You can call my boss . . ."

Romulo waved his hand in front of him. "I don't have to call," he assured her. "I like your face. I won't ask any more embarrassing questions. These are public files. You got as much right to be here as Jerry Ford, or whoever is in town. Gimme details."

"Kristen F. Lowry," Carly replied.

"Never heard of her."

"Well, I'm sure, with so many cases . . ."

"This Lowry, she disappear?" Romulo asked, placing his hands on his considerable stomach.

"Yes, on the way home from the National Archives.

She was doing something for the State Department, a research project I think.''

"The Archives.'' Romulo paused and thought for a few moments, swiveling in his chair. "Yeah, right. The Archives. Now I think I remember. Yeah. I do know that very particular case. Wasn't she the one who had some medical stuff done?''

"Plastic surgery,'' Carly said.

"Yeah, that's the one. And you want to know . . .''

"I went through some clippings, but I couldn't find the outcome of the case.''

Without a word, Romulo slipped out of his chair and walked to his filing cabinet. "I got the last few years here,'' he said. "I don't remember the very exact time. Let's see what we can do.''

"And I couldn't find a picture,'' Carly added. "I'd like to see one.''

"Hold your donkeys,'' Romulo told her. "I'll find the file and maybe we can give you everythin' your heart desires.''

Carly felt her muscles tighten as Romulo's fingers danced along the worn tops of the files, looking for the right name. "Loden,'' he said. "Lomax. Loring. I remember that one. Congressman's wife. Bad marriage, that one. And here . . . yup, here we got Lowry, Kristen F.'' He pulled out the manila file.

"Does it give her middle name?''

Romulo stared at Carly over the top of the file, closing one eye in a chastising glance. "Hey now look,'' he said, "I told you to hold your donkeys. We'll get all of this on the table.''

"I'm sorry,'' Carly replied, realizing she was antagonizing her only link to Lowry, Kristen F.

Romulo sat down again with a relieved sign and plunked the file on the desk. "Now,'' he said, "we'll take care of the name first. I've got the info sheet—y'know, what we make out. Yeah. Middle name . . .''

Carly held her breath.

"Fern.''

Carly didn't budge. Don't show emotion. Don't get him suspicious. "Yes," she replied, trying to control the quiver in her voice. "That's what I thought."

"Now," Romulo went on, "disposition of case. Oh, you wanted a photo. I think I see one back here. Yeah, yeah. A photo. Says . . . before accident. Oh, I guess that's why she had the plastic—"

"Is there one after the accident?" Carly asked. She was fighting that eagerness, that tendency to go to the edge.

"I think so," Romulo said. "Right in back of these papers I see . . ." He found a photo. He pulled it out.

He stared at the photo. Then, abruptly, he jutted his head upward, staring at Carly. His eyes narrowed as he squinted. And then he turned them down again. "Oh Jesus!" he shouted.

"What's wrong?" Carly asked.

"Oh, holy Jesus! Mary, mother of . . . ! Lady, what the hell you think I am?"

Carly was stunned. "I don't understand."

Romulo jumped up. "You don't, eh? Well, goddamn, don't you think a trained cop learns to look at a face behind sunglasses?" He charged around to the front of his desk and snapped the glasses right off Carly's head. "Don't you think I see you're her twin sister?" He took the picture and angrily thrust it right in front of Carly's nose.

Mortified, frightened that she'd blown everything, Carly recoiled, lurching back in her chair. So much for disguises, she thought. So much for forging ahead.

Then she looked at the picture, almost in resignation. Maybe she had known all along what a photo would show.

Yes, she'd found Fern.

Or at least she'd found a picture of her.

"I'm not her twin sister," she explained quietly to Romulo.

"Oh, really?" Romulo asked. "Then what are you, some clone? Maybe you're gonna tell me you're a close cousin. Or maybe you're one of them things they make in a laboratory."

"Look, Lieutenant Romulo," Carly broke in. "I'll tell

you the whole story in a little while. Let's just say both of us had plastic surgery, and there were . . . coincidences.''

"Yeah, yeah, yeah," Romulo said. "I'd love to hear that story. Yeah, yeah. Tryin' to hide the relationship. Okay, that's your sweat, not mine. I don't give a—''

"But right now," Carly said, "I want to know the outcome of Fern's case."

Romulo just stared at her, sizing her up. He could see that she was utterly serious and determined. So now, with the practiced eye of an old missing-persons hand, he went through the folder. To Carly, it seemed to take an eternity for Romulo to note each page and flip it over. Finally, he came to a pink sheet. And instantly the look of fascination melted from his face.

"What's wrong?" Carly asked.

"No wonder you didn't find out from the newspaper files," Romulo told her. "There was a newspaper strike when the case was cleared."

"Cleared? What happened to her? What happened to Fern?"

Romulo looked directly into Carly's eyes. "Ms. Randall," he replied, "Fern is dead."

Carly just sank back in her chair. "How?" she asked.

"Doesn't say here," Romulo replied. "Just found in the bush on a hillside in Maryland. Most of her."

"Most?"

Romulo flipped a picture around to Carly.

Carly gazed down. There, in an eight-by-ten police glossy, was the body of a woman . . . with nothing remaining above the neck.

16

"Tell me I'm dreaming it," Carly said. "Go ahead, just tell me."

She and Mike Moran were alone in Moran's office, long after hours. Carly had just returned from Washington.

"You're not dreaming it," Moran replied, uncharacteristically subdued. Now he was irrevocably convinced that his tantalizing idea for a feature on plastic surgery was turning into a grim investigation of a crime. "I just want you to be careful."

"Why? Am I going over the speed limit?"

"Maybe. Look, Laval duplicates faces. You've established that. Kathleen is missing. Fern winds up dead."

"Yeah, and I'm assuming Kathleen is also dead," Carly broke in.

"In journalism we assume nothing," Moran cautioned.

"The legendary editor speaks," Carly responded. "Well, what about this for assumptions? I made some friends in the administration at Burgess Hospital when I was there. I had them check the surgery schedules for the days Kathleen disappeared and Fern was murdered. Laval wasn't operating in New York either of those two days. There's no record of where he was. This is a guy who doesn't spend time on golf courses, Mike."

"You're assuming he was in Burbank and Washington."

"Look, I can't prove it. I can't even prove Kathleen is dead. But that's a *working* assumption. And if she *is* dead, who else is dead? And if Laval has all these dead patients . . . is my skull going to wind up as a bookend too?''

That stopped Moran cold. It struck him that he'd never seen Carly afraid before. Was Laval murdering or kidnaping his patients? Moran could hardly rule it out. "Look," he said, "this isn't a musical comedy. Better stay away from Laval."

"No, that's not the problem," Carly said. "Laval isn't interested in getting caught. He wouldn't kill in an obvious situation, where everyone would know about it. He must ambush these women . . . late at night. It's only a theory. But I can take care of myself around New York. I stay out of alleys."

Moran had his legs up on his cluttered desk and dropped them to the floor with a thump. "Carly," he said bluntly, "I think we should go to the police."

Carly hesitated. She knew he'd get to that. Moran never did like playing games where the law was involved. *Her* instinct was to resist, to keep the story almost as private property.

And yet, how could she really hold it back from the New York authorities? She'd developed too much information. There were civic obligations involved, even for journalists. And, for the first time, she was openly, actively confronting the reality that she might be in danger. "I can't really justify saying no," she said.

"No, I'm afraid you can't," Moran replied. "This goes a little beyond journalism, doesn't it?"

"If you have a good guy at headquarters, maybe a little talk would . . .''

"I know a guy," Moran said.

"All right, let's." Carly paused. Her mind was racing. What if the police messed it up? What if they went in heavy-handedly and alerted Laval? So many things could go wrong. "Just a second," she continued. "Let me just think about it. Maybe there's a little more I can dig up."

"I think you're pushing, Carlykins," Moran said. "There may even be a legal problem. You're *supposed* to go to the police."

"Give me a day," Carly argued.

"Why?"

"Just give me a day."

"You don't want to discuss it?"

"Mike, trust me. My instincts so far have gotten all that information. I just think in a day I could do much more."

Moran mulled it. What choice did he have? He couldn't drag Carly to the police. "A day," he said. "Exactly twenty-four hours. I'm depending on your judgment."

"Trust me," Carly said again.

Gordon Slesar was in his bathrobe when he opened his door to Carly Randall at 12:20 A.M., not long after Carly left Mike Moran. He was exhausted after what he called "a very heavy psychiatric day," but he beamed just the same. The smile was part of the uniform. "Come in, come in," he said, letting Carly by. Carly had called him and said it was urgent, that she had to see him that night. Psychiatrists were used to that. Like obstetrics, psychiatry was a twenty-four-hour job. And Slesar, knowing this might involve Laval, couldn't refuse.

"Let me take your coat," Slesar offered. "I'm really glad to see you. Really."

"Sorry to bother you this late," Carly said, dropping into the old rocking chair that Slesar kept for times when he didn't want to use the couch.

"Hey, no bother. That's my job. You look a little troubled, and I want to get right to it." Slesar grabbed a pad and pencil from his desk and sat down opposite Carly. "Let me ask you right off," he said, "does this involve Dr. Laval?"

"Yes," Carly replied.

"You've seen him?"

"No. I tracked down another one of his patients who looked exactly like me."

Slesar feigned confusion. "Exactly like you? I thought there was only one—that woman in Los Angeles who disappeared."

"I'll be completely straight with you," Carly said. "When

I was here before I didn't mention that I'd seen an entry in the address book of the missing California woman. It led me to another case . . . in Washington.''

Slesar looked blankly at her, not quite knowing what to make of it. This wasn't information that Laval had volunteered. "Why didn't you tell me this before?" he asked.

"I wanted to check everything out," Carly answered.

"I see. I understand. Hey, cool. Don't worry about it. We shrinks understand. But it does make this a little bit broader, doesn't it?"

"Yes," Carly replied, a quiver in her voice, "especially when you consider that the woman in Washington is dead.''

"She's what?"

"Found dead, with her head missing."

Slesar understood immediately where Carly was going. "That's awful. That's absolutely awful. But you're not suggesting that Dr. Laval . . .''

"I don't know what I'm suggesting. But the man gives these women the same face, and something horrible happens to both. *He* is the only link."

"He and all the people who work with him," Slesar said. "And all the people who might have had access to your file."

"Yeah, I guess so. I hadn't thought of it that way. But you'd have to agree that only Laval, because of his expertise, could have decided to give those women the same face.''

"Granted," Slesar agreed. "What are you going to do?"

"I'm not sure. But I'm thinking of going to the police."

"I see. Well, hey, that might be just the thing to do right now. But . . . maybe you should hold off.''

"Why?"

"Because you might hurt a very good man. The police like publicity about things like this, and they love to cut down big men. Dr. Laval could be irreparably damaged. Look, this may be a tragic coincidence. I know it's statistically unlikely. But it isn't as if two women were found under identical conditions. After all, one was found dead, obviously murdered. And the other is missing. All right, Laval gave them the same face. But coincidences do happen. These women could have simply both met unpleasant fates. Or, maybe the one who's missing actually *wants* to be missing. Maybe she's happy somewhere. Live and let live. Y'know?

"And, look, if there is something going on, there are all those other medical people I mentioned who might know about these women, about Dr. Laval's work. Maybe someone jealous of him . . ."

"What do *you* think I should do?" Carly asked.

Slesar thought for a moment, trying to determine a course that sounded reasonable, but which would serve his own interests. He did have this loyalty to Laval, a loyalty that, he knew, could aid his advancement in medicine. And yet he felt a growing uneasiness. Laval's duplication of faces was bizarre. The fate of those two women was even more bizarre. What was right here? Yes, there was loyalty to Laval, but there was also the fear of being sucked into something scandalous. And yet . . . Laval wouldn't do anything crazy, would he? Laval was the Rock of Gibraltar, a man at the top, secure and envied. But Carly Randall's story seemed solid. She wouldn't have made up something with that much detail, something so easily checked . . . would she?

"You haven't answered," an impatient Carly finally said.

"And that's because I'm thinking about it," Slesar replied. "You know, I'm not so sure what I'd do. But I *wouldn't* go to the police. I mean, the authorities in Burbank and Washington are involved in these cases, I'm sure . . ."

"Yes, they are."

"I'd leave it to them. You're still seeing Dr. Laval, aren't you?"

"Yes."

"Will your treatment be over soon?"

"I think so. There's some slight surgery left."

"Well have him do it. Then maybe . . . hey, I'm a

psychiatrist. This is out of my line. I shouldn't be advising you. But if you have a problem after that, and if the other police forces haven't come up with anything, then maybe contact the medical society. I'm sure, I really am, that there's probably some explanation for this. I'm trying to be rational and scientific. I don't like to see people hurt."

Carly had nothing to say. She was still convinced of Slesar's sincerity, but the man really hadn't come up with anything useful. He was right. Why would a psychiatrist know anything about this?

"Please keep me informed," Slesar went on. "And if *I* have an idea, I'll buzz away."

Carly was disappointed, but there was something else now. She noticed for the first time a certain tension in Slesar. The act was still in place, complete with the grins, but he did seem disturbed by what she'd told him. It was curious, because he didn't express any particular alarm in what she'd said. It was just something in that face, some strain, that Carly detected. It was as if he were saying one thing, and thinking something entirely different.

Carly was barely out the door when Slesar got on the phone. His hands were shaking, his palms sweaty. He suddenly looked, as he dialed the number, as if he were going to have a nervous breakdown.

"Dr. Laval," said the voice on the other end. Laval lay in bed in his apartment, clad in green silk pajamas with his initials on the pocket. The bed itself had a large *L* on the covers.

"André," Slesar said, "Gordon Slesar."

"Gordy," Laval replied, "so late? Have you got an emergency?" But he already knew that it had to be Carly Randall.

"She was here," Slesar replied. "Carly. It isn't good, André. I'll tell you what she said."

"Oh do, Gordy."

Practically blurting out the words, Slesar gave a quick summary of Carly's visit, of everything Carly had reported. As he spoke, Laval winced, his face becoming distorted. When Slesar finished, there was a long silence as Laval collected his thoughts.

"Well," Laval said, "I'm shocked, Gordy. I'm sickened. I had no idea something had happened to that patient in Washington. The one in Burbank I knew about. Yes, we'd spoken about that. Probably a psychological question. But I'm really shattered about that girl in Washington. She was a lovely person. No one informed me."

"I'm sure, André," Slesar said. "But, André, she did express concern about these other women with her face."

"Medical experiment, Gordy," Laval said. "Women widely separated by geography. We've discussed a little of this. There was no duplication to speak of. These women could never know each other." The words flowed easily from Laval's lips, as they always did, but Slesar couldn't imagine how grim Laval really was. It had gone too far. *She* had gone too far, and now she was more than dangerous. She was deadly. Sure, someone might be able to explain Kathleen and Fern as a coincidence. But what would happen if Carly discovered the evidence that was out there? "I wish she would just talk to me about it," Laval went on. "I could explain how experiments in plastic surgery are done."

"Yeah, André, but . . . she's upset about those two women—one missing, one dead."

"And so am I," Laval insisted.

Slesar was increasingly worried about something else. He knew that *he* was in possession of explosive information. And Laval knew it.

The two felt strangely alone, shadowboxing with each other, maneuvering for advantage, all the while maintaining their professional style. But then Slesar let fly with a question that threw Laval off guard. "Look, André, be straight with me. Are there any other women with that same face—Carly's face?"

"Why?" Laval asked, almost belligerently.

"Because I want to know how to respond if Carly tells me she's found them."

Laval tried to calm himself. He couldn't stonewall, not

with such a great chance of Carly uncovering the facts and presenting them to Slesar. Better to come out with it, make it appear a normal part of a great experiment. "There are two others," he finally replied, sounding almost nonchalant. "Part of my work."

"Tell me their names, André."

"Why must you know?"

"Again," Slesar replied, "Carly might think she'd discovered those names. I'd be more effective for you if I could evaluate her claim instantly."

"Yes, very reasonable," Laval said. Go along with Slesar, he told himself. Lure him in. Make him a co-conspirator. "Well," he continued, "there's Marcia Lane in Chicago." Then he stopped. Marcia Lane was alive. He hadn't hurt her. What he'd done to her was entirely legitimate . . . so far. But Laval hesitated to tell Slesar the name of the other woman, Alice, in Boston. That could eventually prove awkward. "I don't recall the name of the other," he said. "Maybe I could look it up."

"That would help," Slesar said.

"I don't have the file here. I'll have to get it, Gordy."

"André," Slesar went on, "I'm on your side. This woman is a reporter. She exaggerates. I don't know what to think of your experiment, but I know you'd never do anything to harm these women."

"No, of course not," Laval said. "Gordy, I appreciate your loyalty. This is difficult. Things get misunderstood, and my career could be destroyed."

"Never," Slesar said.

The conversation ended. Both men hung up.

Slesar simply sat and stared at the phone, wondering what the truth actually was, worried about his own future. Could Laval do something to *him?* What if it ever came out that he was revealing Carly's confidences to Laval? If Laval were doing something wrong, and was exposed, he could stand trial. He might spill everything, no matter whom it hurt. Slesar didn't sleep. He had too much to contemplate, too much to worry about. Carly's new revelation about Washington was a bombshell. Maybe, he

thought, he'd shown too much loyalty to the wrong man.
He had a right to protect himself. *That* would put him at
ease. *Protecting* himself.

It was just good mental health.

Laval didn't sleep either. He felt a ring tightening around
him. Of course, Carly Randall still had no proof that he'd
been involved in any crimes, and he'd been so careful
about the murders he'd already committed. But any public
disclosure of what Carly knew would unleash a wave of
suspicion and possibly wreck everything he'd built up.
And there would certainly be public disclosure.

"I should have killed her already," he mumbled to
himself, pacing up and down on his plush blue carpeting.
"Why didn't I?"

But he knew why. He hadn't had a way of killing Carly
without bringing immediate suspicion on himself. He still
needed to perfect an airtight plan.

He'd thought it was all so brilliant when he began his
"experiment." He would become an immortal plastic surgeon by creating the immortal face, a kind of modern
Mona Lisa, admired throughout the world. Maybe it wasn't
so brilliant after all. Arnie Lemke always had a propensity
for screwing up, even in the days of his youth. He still
seemed to have that talent, he mused.

He stayed up until dawn, occasionally sitting in an
antique armchair—a gift from an admiring patient in Monaco. Periodically, he paced the room, mulling the perfect
plan he still needed. He worked on it, discarding possibilities, weighing the kind of people he might require.

And it came together.

Then, at eight A.M. sharp, he picked up his phone and
dialed his office at Burgess Hospital. One of his three
secretaries answered.

"Dr. Laval's office."

"Oh Giselle, this is Doctor," Laval said, trying to
sound nonchalant using his title as he always did, without
the "the."

"Yes, Doctor."

"Giselle, I've decided to schedule Carly Randall for some further work. Set up an appointment as soon as possible, would you?"

"Of course, Doctor."

"Next day or so would be fine."

"Doctor, I think you're booked solid for the next three days."

Laval hesitated. Show any sign of rushing or panic, and he'd give it away. He had to sound professional, medical, concerned. "My feeling is, the sooner we do this, the better," he said. "I've concluded that there's some risk of deterioration. Anyone we can move?"

Giselle went down the list. "Most of them are in the hospital already," she said. "But . . . Rusty Sims, the actress. That's minor. You said she shouldn't even have the work, but I think she wants it because she needed a topic for the talk shows."

"Yes, she told me that. How did her last picture do?"

"Grossed sixteen million."

"Move her."

"Yes, Doctor."

"And Giselle, order the same nursing crew that I had for Princess Isabel. I thought they were superb."

"I'll put it together," Giselle said.

They hung up. Nurse Becker, Laval recalled. Yes, Nurse Becker. Experienced, but shy and not too impressive. Not likely to be seen as the perfect nurse. She'd made some minor mistakes and been corrected by senior nurses.

Nurse Becker, not a fighter. The kind who was easily pushed around. Nurse Becker. Just an ordinary nurse who could easily make a mistake, and would probably accept blame quietly rather than going through the hell of an investigation and trial.

Nurse Becker. She'd have a new role now. Murderer of Carly Randall.

17

Strange.

It was a plain white envelope stuffed in Carly's mailbox, apparently by someone who had gained access to the building by waiting for a resident to unlock the lobby door.

Strange.

There was no return address, and the only writing on the outside was: CARLY RANDALL—URGENT.

Carly quickly ripped it open. Inside was an ordinary piece of white paper. Written on it: MARCIA LANE, CHICAGO—PATIENT, LAVAL THE FACEMAKER.

Someone knew.

Someone knew that Carly was tracking down women with her face. And that person apparently knew their names.

How?

How would one person know those things? Who *was* that person? And why did he, or she, stuff that envelope into Carly's mailbox?

Yes, Slesar knew she was searching. But Slesar surely didn't have the names. Laval had the names, but it was absurd to think that he was behind this. Mike Moran? Mike had no inside information.

Carly felt uncomfortable with the tip because it tended to confirm a theory of Slesar's: that whoever killed those women might be someone who worked with Laval, someone envious or jealous. But how would that someone know that Carly was investigating the plastic surgeon?

Wait a second, Carly thought.

Maybe that someone *didn't* know.

By simply sending the name to a woman who'd been given one of the identical faces, a woman who was also a reporter, a lot of wreckage could result.

Laval duplicated the faces. No doubt about that. But was someone else behind the murders in an attempt to discredit him? It was possible.

But it didn't make Carly feel any safer.

Mike Moran studied the name on the paper carefully, assuming his usual pose in his office, feet on desk, desk covered with the rubble of publishing, his suit probably unacceptable for donation to a respectable charity. "This is becoming a good movie, Carlykins," he said. "Now I think it's time for the detective to come in."

"I'm going to Chicago," Carly answered, not even acknowledging Moran's pressure to go to the police.

"Fine. Track down Marcia Lane. I've got no problem with that. But we're going to the constables."

"All right. When I get back."

"No, Carlykins, now. Pronto."

"Mike, I've got to have an edge on this. Look, I'm responsible for myself. Someone knows about me. Maybe someone's watching me. In a situation like this I trust me, not the cops."

"Have both. Look, Carly, this note . . . I mean, this isn't a board game for a rainy day. There's some kind of conspiracy here."

"I know. As soon as I get back, I'll do exactly as you say."

"*If* you get back."

"No melodrama, Mike. Please. What could the police really do to protect me? Put me in jail?"

"You get some good stories there," Mike replied. Then he threw up his hands. "Kidding. Peace. Only kidding.

Look, think about it. Delay your trip a day. Please, Carly. I'm spooked, and I don't mind saying so.''

"Bye, Mike.'' Carly moved to leave the office. Mike Moran knew her well enough to understand that she was trying to put the danger out of her mind, to suppress it—before it drove her mad.

"Okay, you win,'' he said. "I can't force you. Well, I *won't* force you. Go to Chicago. Find Lane. Dig up Mayor Daley if you can. But *I'm* going to the cops while you're gone. I can't be an accessory to a crime. Carly, I'm a citizen first.''

"Mike,'' Carly replied, "you should've stayed in politics. Or written a new national anthem.''

Now Mike Moran smiled at her, utterly amazed at Carly's spunk in the face of danger. He did worry about her, more than Carly could ever realize. He just couldn't come out with the words for it, but he hoped, in that muddled manner of his, that she would someday understand. "Be careful,'' he told her.

"Sure.''

And Carly knew Mike would do exactly as he said— he'd go to the police in her absence, and inwardly she was glad. It *was* the right thing to do. But at least *she'd* get a jump on Marcia Lane, in Chicago.

"Call me,'' Moran told her. "Maybe, when you come back, we should go over the whole thing. Y'know, order in half a pizza, maybe in my office at home.''

Carly loved it. It was the closest he'd ever come to passion.

As she was at her desk making reservations for Chicago, Carly's phone rang. She picked up.

"Ms. Randall?''

"Yes, Carly Randall.''

"This is Giselle in Dr. Laval's suite. The doctor has examined your records and wishes you to come in for that extra bit of surgery.''

Carly had almost forgotten about it. It was utterly bizarre, considering the circumstances. Here was a man she was investigating, who may have already killed, asking to put her under the knife. But she couldn't even hint at what she knew. "Oh," she said, "is it urgent?"

"There's no danger, Ms. Randall. But the doctor feels it should be done as soon as possible to avoid complications. Would you like to discuss it with him?"

"Uh . . . no," Carly replied, glancing at her watch. "I've got so much to do. Look, okay, I guess we'll have to do it. When?"

"Tomorrow, October fourteenth?"

"Impossible," Carly said. "I'm on assignment."

"Next day, then?"

"No," Carly said, "I'd better leave myself some time. Look, how about . . ."—she flipped through her calendar, looking for a relatively clear day not long off—"what about October twentieth?"

Laval stood over Giselle, listening, with Giselle gesturing to indicate what Carly was saying. Laval was not happy. He wanted this over fast, but understood that any pressure on Carly would look suspicious. He simply urged Giselle on with a hand gesture.

"I think the doctor wanted it sooner," Giselle said.

"Can't make it sooner. Let's do it on the twentieth. Okay?"

Now Giselle checked her own calendar, pointing out the date to Laval. Laval winced, knowing that the whole thing could blow apart before the twentieth, that Carly could come up with some devastating evidence against him. But he had no choice. She was resisting. Maybe he could apply some subtle psychology and get her to come in sooner, but, for now, he gestured his okay to Giselle.

"He does have a cancellation that day," Giselle told Carly. "Okay, we'll set it for the twentieth at nine A.M. We'll send you instructions."

"Right," Carly said. "I think I know those instructions by heart." She automatically went over them in her mind. They were standard for the hospital: Don't take any drugs before entering unless absolutely necessary; note all medications to the hospital staff; don't bring food; don't bring jewelry or valuables; have your insurance ID ready. Carly had read that list so many times.

They ended the conversation, and Carly hardly gave the subject more thought. Despite the bizarre circumstances, she really felt no fear about going under Laval's knife. If he was in fact a murderer, he was certainly too shrewd to try anything with other doctors and nurses around. She preferred to concentrate on her trip to Chicago.

At that very moment, André Laval was leaving Giselle's side to take a stroll through some of the supply rooms and laboratories of Burgess Hospital, planning his strategy for the day of the operation, planning Carly's untimely death— even the eulogy he hoped to give at her funeral.

But he was a troubled, deeply frustrated man. He could hear the bomb ticking, more loudly every moment. Anyone else in his position would destroy Carly immediately, he realized. But where? On the streets of New York? From a sniper's nest above Carly's building? The fact was, he wasn't a professional murderer, simply a great surgeon who had done what was necessary and had gotten away with it. Laval hated to lose control, but he was losing it. He feared being caught. He even feared the suspicions of Gordon Slesar. Yes, they were all after him again, just as they had been in the art school of his youth. Yes, they wanted Arnie Lemke out.

But Arnie would win. Arnie always won.

Carly took a cab in a pouring rainstorm to the main branch of the New York Public Library at Fifth Avenue and 42nd Street. She knew the library had a copy of the phone book for every major American city. *Allure* also had those books, but Carly didn't want to be conspicuous about her sudden interest in Chicago.

She raced up the library steps, past the two stone lions that were symbols of the building, and then took the elevator to the cavernous main reading room on the third floor. She quickly found the dog-eared phone book for Chicago.

There were four Marcia Lanes listed. Carly took down their names and addresses. As she did, she once again thought back to the mysterious note that had propelled this phase of her search. She accepted the working theory that someone close to Laval was disloyal to him. That someone might be willing to talk—to reveal the details that would expose Laval once and for all. But again, who was it? And how could Carly find out? One way, of course, might be through Marcia Lane in Chicago. Was she still alive? Would she have insight into what was going on?

But as she pondered the questions, Carly's heart began to sink. Why *should* Marcia still be alive? Laval was so thorough. So far, if Carly was right about him, he'd gotten rid of a good bit of human evidence. Carly realized her chances of finding Marcia Lane alive were probably not great.

But she would try. There was nothing else she could do.

Carly left the library and went to her apartment, where she got ready to call every Marcia Lane in the Chicago book. Now she thought of every conceivable obstacle. Maybe *the* Marcia Lane didn't live in Chicago proper, maybe she was indeed dead, maybe she'd used an alias, as some women do when going into plastic surgery. Maybe she'd moved, maybe she would lie or refuse to cooperate. Maybe she was involved in some way with Laval, maybe she'd been hypnotized.

The sharp ring of the phone interrupted, startling her. Leaning back, dreading a long conversation with a friend, she let the answering machine do the job.

"Okay, Carlot," Moran said, his voice thinned by the machine's tiny speaker, "I made a date with the police."

Smiling, Carly listened as Mike invited her to join him in his trip down to headquarters. She knew he probably cared for her more than anyone else ever did, or would. But her mind was absolutely focused on what she was doing. Mike could handle the cops alone.

And so she dialed the 312 area code for Chicago, then the number for the first Marcia Lane on her list. Carly very rarely rehearsed her interviews, but had a pretty good idea what she wanted to say, assuming someone answered.

The phone at the other end rang, and rang, and rang. Carly counted seven rings in all, waiting, her heart pumping, for someone to answer. She glanced down at the number again to make sure she'd gotten it right, and also scanned the woman's address—a building along Lake Shore Drive, Chicago's gold coast. Yes, that would be the kind of woman who'd probably have plastic surgery.

Finally, she heard a click as someone picked up.

"Hello?" The voice was firm, but seemed to crack a bit. Carly had trouble telling the age.

"Hello, is this Marcia Lane?" Carly asked.

"Marcia Lane, yes," the voice responded. "Always been Marcia Lane, even when I was married."

"I see." The voice now sounded older than Marcia Lane should be. "Uh, Ms. Lane, I'm a reporter doing a piece on plastic surgery—"

"You from the television?"

"No, I—"

"You know Dan Rather?"

"Well no. I work for a magazine."

"I'm angry at Dan," the voice said. "He did something on teeth and I was out of the room. I called for them to put it back on, but they said no. Angry at him. Not a nice man."

"Ms. Lane," Carly asked, "I wonder if you've had plastic surgery in the last—"

"Never touched it," the voice said. "Graven image, like the Bible says. I like the Bible. If Dan Rather read the Bible—"

"Uh, thank you Ms. Lane," Carly concluded. "I hope you have a good day."

"I'm going to the dentist."

They both hung up.

Carly glanced down at the next number on the list, and prepared to dial. But then she hesitated. This was foolish, almost amateurish. Even if Marcia Lane were home, and available, why should she want to talk? Why shouldn't she

be wary of any questions involving her surgery? No, a
phone call wasn't a very good idea at all, and Carly
wondered why she hadn't thought this out more clearly.
Simply calling on the phone was maximizing the chances
for failure, which were high enough already. She wouldn't
call Marcia Lane in advance of her trip to Chicago. She'd
simply go, cold, and hunt down the woman. Maybe she'd
even linger outside the houses of the several Marcias until
she hit the right one. Yes, Marcia would have to be
confronted in person.

There'd be no problem about recognizing her, Carly
knew. Carly would, in effect, be looking in a mirror.

Mike Moran arranged to meet Victor Hoover at a small
downtown Italian restaurant near New York's main police
headquarters. Hoover was a detective and thought it was
very bad form to receive members of the press in his tiny
office. Someone might think he was hunting for publicity,
or spilling the beans about some scandal inside the department. He preferred to do these things in the Italian restaurant.

Hoover was in his late forties, and always dressed in a
drab, dark gray suit that matched his smile-free face. He
was a superb detective, but a tormented man. People either
thought he was related to a vacuum cleaner or to one of
America's least popular presidents. He hated the name,
and kept it only because his father had threatened never to
speak to him again if he changed it. He was single, a
loner, a man married to the force and to his cases. Mr.
Excitement he was not.

Angelo's was his favorite restaurant, and he always
ordered the same two slices of mushroom pizza with a root
beer on the side. He was already eating when Moran
walked in. The two had met while Moran was covering the
trial of a socialite for the murder of her husband.

Hoover hardly looked up when he saw Moran, but
gestured with a mock salute, which Moran took as a high
compliment. Victor Hoover greeted only gangsters with a
smile, and shook no one's hand. Rumor was that he was
afraid of germs.

"So," he said to Moran, "sit down and tell me what I can do, Michael."

"Don't you even ask how I am?" Moran inquired.

"You're walking," Hoover answered. "That's all I have to know. If something was wrong, I'd donate you my blood. Now tell me why you won't let me eat alone."

"Vic," Moran began, as a three-hundred-pound waiter shoved a tomato-stained menu in his face, "one of my people has a problem."

"I don't fix tickets," Hoover said.

"This isn't tickets. This is corpses."

Hoover didn't miss a bite, letting part of his pizza drip back on its plate. "Inform me," he said.

"I have a writer, Carly Randall—"

"You introduced me once," Hoover said.

"Yeah, right, I probably did. Look, Vic, she had plastic surgery. Bad accident. They had to rebuild. I don't want to hit you with a play-by-play, but she found out—I mean, you're not going to believe this—but this doctor gave her face to other women."

Again, no missing a bite for Hoover. He didn't even look up. "So?" he asked.

"Well, we think it's wrong."

"I got a morgue full of wrong," Hoover said. "You'll have to do better than this."

"All right," Moran went on, showing no exasperation with a man whose methods he knew thoroughly. "The face thing can be a simple malpractice. Civil suit. Not your business. I agree. But Carly wanted to get to the bottom of why this happened. She started checking out these other women."

"Yeah, I see."

"So far, she found one missing and one murdered, and she's going after a third."

Now Hoover stopped eating, placing a piece of half-gone pizza back on his plate. "Here?" he asked.

"No. One California. One DC. She's heading for Chicago next."

"Out of my territory."

"Yeah, but the doctor lives here, Victor. Carly thinks he might be behind the disappearance and the murder."

"Why?"

"I don't know."

"Not too swift, Michael. Motive is three-fifths of it."

"Look, Victor, I can't tell what's in the guy's mind. But the guy gives the same face to four women. Normal plastic surgeons don't do that."

"You an expert on that, Michael?"

"I know about it. I checked it out."

"So, he's an oddball. Not my line."

"Then one of these women suddenly disappears. Another one is murdered, and her skull is gone. You give me the odds on two women from the same doctor, with the same face, having that happen."

"Odds don't make a case, Michael. But I'll check it out. I'll call LA and DC. I know guys there." Now Hoover made a note on the side of a newspaper that was on the table next to the pizza. He wrote over one pizza stain and gracefully avoided another.

"Victor," Mike went on, "this Carly Randall, my writer. I kind of like her. She's had some bad luck and . . ."

"Yeah, I get the picture, Michael. You're a-scared for her."

"Yeah, that's right. If I'm right about this doctor—even about someone around him—something could happen to Carly."

Moran knew that what was on Hoover's tongue, or even in his eyes, was no reflection of what he was thinking. The fact was, the stoneface often wrote checks larger than he could afford for charities, and worked weekends at no pay to close cases he cared about. So Moran wasn't discouraged by Hoover's surface indifference.

"I'll keep an eye out," Hoover said. "But so far you haven't exactly been an encyclopedia. All right, the faces, they're kinda interesting, I guess. I don't know what these fellas do. You just let me know what's happening, and you tell this girl not to take chances."

As the conversation continued, amidst the clatter of the

restaurant and an argument between two indicted politicians at the next table, Moran turned glum. His story
sounded far weaker than he'd imagined. There was no
smoking gun, nothing actually linking Laval to the bizarre
fate of the women in Los Angeles and Washington. Laval
certainly hadn't acted odd, and he'd done nothing to Carly
except save her life. And the duplicate faces? Laval could
probably explain that away, and might get the chance.

Moran knew only that he could count on Hoover's help.
But he also knew that, in the absence of something more
solid, the police weren't going to charge in full force—
André Laval was as politically well connected as he was
medically esteemed.

But at least Mike had made his first official contact.
Now he waited for Carly to report from Chicago, and he
hoped she'd find a bombshell.

18

Six days from the death that Laval was planning for her, Carly flew to Chicago, landing at O'Hare Field in the midst of that Midwest phenomenon—the ridiculously early snowstorm. Carly's still sensitive face was slapped by an icy wind as she tried to get a cab from the airport, giving her a sense that the omens for this trip were less than great.

Ultimately, with all cabs taken and businessmen making it clear that chivalry was indeed dead, Carly had to settle for the airport bus. She took it to the Palmer House, one of Chicago's better hotels, and, as she had in Washington, she dropped her bags in her room and started off on her search.

Carly had been in Chicago only twice before, both times on assignment for *Allure,* but she was unfamiliar with the neighborhoods. She'd grabbed a map at O'Hare, but was still depending on cab drivers. In New York that would have been a laugh. In Chicago a fair number of cabbies knew the city, and some had traveled it before.

Her first stop was on the South Side, in Hyde Park, near the University of Chicago. Carly gave her driver the address and tried to enjoy the trip, although the snow blocked out the magnificent view of Lake Michigan that she recalled from her last trip, and the skidding of the cab's bald tires provided a level of excitement that she hardly relished.

*   *   *

As Carly rode toward Hyde Park, the world's greatest plastic surgeon was in his Burgess Hospital office, making his own reservations for a trip to Chicago the next week. He too wanted to see Marcia Lane, and they'd finally agreed on a date. In a way, his trip seemed superfluous. Eliminating Marcia had been necessary when Carly Randall was his clear choice to be launched as the face of the nineties. But Carly would soon be dead. Why destroy Marcia?

As always, Laval had his reasons. Better to eliminate all the evidence of what he'd done, he thought. The experiment would have to be revised.

When he got off the phone, Laval went immediately to the television studio next to his office. It was remarkable, he thought. He'd started this series of tapes to share with his medical posterity the greatness of his achievements, the creation of the near-perfect face of Carly Randall. Now, he would share with these doctors of the future his prognosis for Carly's murder. They would marvel at the quickness of his mind, his ability to take a crisis and deflect it. They would certainly admire him for that.

He set up his equipment, sealed the soundproof door shut, and stood before the Minolta camera. He cleared his throat and attempted a smile, as if to show that he was totally in control, totally relaxed about dealing with his situation. Then he started, as he had so many times before:

"This is the seventh in the series. As you physicians know, my work has been disrupted. My hopes for Carly Randall have been destroyed by her own strange behavior, her pursuit of me, which I truly believe borders on ungratefulness. On reflection, I must concede that I've made some mistakes in choosing patients. Marcia Lane was a mistake. And I should never have put any faith in a reporter. Reporters are a particularly foul breed, with no personal loyalties and a superficial view of propriety. To these people, the Carly Randalls of the world, only the story counts. A physician's humanity, his contribution to society—these things mean nothing.

"The lesson here is that we surgeons are constantly being victimized by our patients.

"Carly Randall's last day on earth will be October twentieth. I will perform some touch-up surgery on her that morning. The operation will be conducted in full view of a group of students. They will be able to see every action I take. They will see nothing but artistry.

"But Carly will be injected with a drug toward the end of the procedure. At first, all will appear normal. But later she'll go into a stupor, linger for some hours, and die.

"I will express shock and demand an immediate investigation. But it will quickly become apparent that a particular nurse, supervising medications, gave Carly the wrong drug. No criminal charges will be brought, but I'd imagine Carly's estate will sue the hospital for malpractice.

"I don't think I have to tell you who will arrange for the mix-up in drugs. I have access to those things. I have plans. There is no way I can be blamed. After this episode, I will attempt another experiment."

Carly reached a brownstone in Hyde Park just as the bells of Rockefeller Chapel at the University of Chicago tolled three P.M. At that moment, Laval was finishing his tape and showing the precise syringe he would use to kill her.

The brownstone was next door to the former home of Richard Loeb, half of the esteemed team of Leopold and Loeb, who energized the Chicago press in 1924 with their attempt, unsuccessful it turned out, to commit the perfect crime—murdering a young boy without leaving a single clue. Leopold and Loeb found how elusive perfection could be when they were caught and convicted for the murder.

Carly checked the name on the brownstone's mailbox.

LANE, M.

Her heart pounded and she felt a dryness in her throat as she extended her finger to press the doorbell. She hesitated. If the name was still on the mailbox, that probably meant that this Marcia Lane was alive. If she were the right Marcia Lane . . . there were all kinds of implications.

Carly pressed the button. She heard the chimes go off.

There were footsteps.

"Yes?" came the voice from inside. It was the right age, Carly thought, and it sounded cheerful—the way someone would sound if she'd just had successful plastic surgery.

"Marcia Lane?" Carly inquired.

There was a silence. "What can I do for you?" the voice asked.

"Are you Marcia Lane?"

Another silence. Typical behavior for a big city, Carly thought. People were afraid—they panicked at the sound of their own names. Carly tried to put herself in Marcia Lane's position. "Uh, Ms. Lane, I'm a writer for a magazine. I have credentials. There's no one else with me. You can go to a window and look out, if you wish. I'm doing a story on plastic surgery . . ."

On those last two words, the door slowly opened a crack. It had two chains on it. Carly couldn't see inside, but did see the light of a human eye. She said nothing more.

"I guess it's okay," Marcia Lane said. The door closed again so Marcia could remove the chains. Then it swung open.

Standing before Carly was an elegant black lady in a business suit. "I'm Marcia Lane," she said. "Professor Lane. Physics Department at the university. I don't know a thing about plastic surgery. You probably want Milton Lane from the medical school."

Carly was deathly embarrassed. She knew she might hit some wrong people in her quest, but hadn't expected such heavy artillery. "Uh, yes," she said. "I think I've made a mistake. Sorry to disturb you."

"It's okay. If you ever need a quote about particle-beam generators, look me up."

"Yes. Yes I will," Carly replied.

Carly walked back down the steps, her mortification

unabated. Yet, there was really no better way to proceed. She pulled out the list of the other Marcia Lanes—there were two more—and decided to hail another cab.

It took more than fifteen minutes before Carly could get a taxi. She hopped into one, her ungloved hands icy from the miserable weather. Instead of announcing her destination to the driver, a transplanted Kentuckian who insisted on wearing a straw hat as he drove, she simply handed him the paper with the next Marcia's address written on it.

The driver studied the address, then turned around to Carly and stared incredulously into her eyes. "You nuts, lady?" he asked.

Carly couldn't fathom it. "No, I'm not nuts. That's where I want to go."

"Thinkin' of gettin' out alive?"

"Why, is that a bad area?"

"Bad? You talkin' bad? Lady, that's the combat zone up here. That's a part of town nobody should go to."

"I have to go there," Carly said, feeling a sudden clutching in her throat.

"You *got* to go? You don't look like the type to go there."

"Is it a . . . racial thing?" Carly asked.

"No, it ain't only racial," the driver replied. "I mean, they got colored there and all. But they got all kindsa boozers and druggies."

"It's daylight. I'll be careful. Let's go."

The driver shrugged his shoulders and turned back to the wheel. He gunned the engine and started down Woodlawn Avenue. Then he stopped.

"What's wrong?" Carly asked.

"Sorry lady" he replied. "I'm just not goin' down there. I gotta ask you to get out."

The next two drivers behaved in exactly the same way, and now Carly began to question her own sanity in taking this ride. She also wondered if it was futile. Would Laval actually have a patient in such an area? It was unlikely, she thought.

But unlikely wasn't impossible. Carly Randall was a

risk taker. She would get to this Marcia Lane, even if no cab driver would take her.

After two more tries, she gave up on cabs, asked a cop for directions, and boarded a public bus.

The ride took more than forty minutes, winding through some of the seamier neighborhoods of central Chicago.

Finally, Carly got off.

Instantly, she felt the fear the cab drivers had expressed. Even in the cold weather the streetcorner drug deals were open and blatant. The desperate, the down-and-out, the druggies too far gone to understand, the mental patients released too soon, staggered along the streets in their usual daze. This was the kind of area Carly would never have entered in New York. Here, it was part of the job.

She could hear the occasional screams of the deranged and she could literally count the liquor bottles strewn along the sidewalks and alleys.

There were some relatively normal residents as well, and a few of them eyed Carly as if she were totally crazy. At one point a man sauntered over and tried to sell her some crack, but she slid out of his way.

The area was well patrolled, though, and a policeman, after cautioning her about the neighborhood, directed her to Marcia Lane's address. It was a tenement. Carly had been pretty much resigned to that. But, from a distance, it seemed in somewhat better shape than most.

Carly walked toward the building, planning to find Marcia on the mailbox list and ring her doorbell. She did feel a tinge of uncommon fear as she realized the kind of nut Marcia might be. Was she crazy? An addict? Dangerous? Even armed? It was odd—thinking of someone with her face as a degenerate, but the area's flavor forced the thought.

The red-brick building loomed larger and larger as Carly approached. The snowfall had become heavier, and things started to look hazy. The white coating was starting to give the seedy neighborhood an almost antiseptic, cleansed look, covering over some of the trash left in the street and some of the cartons used by the homeless at night.

Carly reached the building entrance. She was about to venture inside when she saw a woman approaching from the other direction, her head down, walking quickly, but a little unsteadily.

Carly got a glimpse of the woman's cheekbone structure. There was something about it . . .

The woman got closer.

She looked up—directly at Carly.

And she froze in her tracks.

"Oh Jesus!"

"No, it's okay," Carly assured her.

"Oh Jesus!" Marcia Lane repeated. "It's a ghost. It's a goddamned ghost!"

"No," Carly said, now rushing toward her. "I can explain."

Marcia turned, then spun around. "I'm drunk," she said. "I'm high. Oh my God. She's me. I'm dreamin'."

Carly reached her. "Please calm down!" she pleaded.

But Marcia suddenly swung her bag at Carly. "Go away!" she shrieked, loud enough for the world to hear. "You can't be me! *I'm* me! Y'hear?"

"You listen!" Carly shouted, trying to slash through Marcia's hysteria.

But Marcia was too scared to listen. "Hektor!" she shrieked. "Hektor, help me!"

Suddenly, Carly heard an ancient window grinding open on the second floor. A man with a thick mustache and flaming eyes, wearing an old-style undershirt, peered out.

"Hektor!" Marcia shouted. "Look at her! Help me!"

Hektor vanished from the window and Carly could hear him barreling down the stairs.

Now Marcia stumbled, falling to her knees in the snow. Carly could practically taste the alcohol coming off her breath. "They're freakin' me!" Marcia shouted. "I did my time, but they won't let go!"

"That's not true," Carly insisted. "Let me explain!"

But then she saw Hektor charging out of the building, toward her. He swung a rusted machete over his head.

"Oh my God!" Carly moaned, and tried to run, slipping in the snow. "Police!" she screamed.

But Hektor kept charging. And there was no cop in sight.

Desperate, Carly tried to get up, at the same time turning back toward Marcia. "Dr. Laval," she screamed. "André Laval!"

Hektor was overtaking her.

In an instant he was on top of Carly, who was barely on one knee. But suddenly Marcia lunged forward. "No, Hek!" she ordered. "Don't kill her!"

Hektor held his machete high, but, at Marcia's command, did not strike. Instead, he looked curiously, incredulously, at Carly, then turned to Marcia. "You her sister?" he asked.

Marcia ignored him. Suddenly, she was intrigued with Carly, intrigued by the name she'd mentioned. "You tell me about Laval," she insisted. "He made my face."

"And mine," Carly said.

"Jee-zus!" Marcia cried out. "Look what he did to us."

It was a bizarre sight, the two manufactured faces, freezing against the snow, staring at each other in one of the worst streets in Chicago, a former mental patient standing above them, his machete ready for an act of neighborly love.

"I'm here to help," Carly said. "I'm trying to find out what Laval did. He did the same thing to other women. I'm not here to hurt you."

Now Marcia stared into Carly's eyes once more, and sensed, as only someone with her tumultuous background could sense, that this woman was a friend. "You come into the house," she said, "if you can stand it."

"I can stand it," Carly replied.

Marcia turned toward Hektor. "Thanks," she said. "You go now, Hektor."

And without another word, Hektor dropped his machete to his side and walked back into the building, like some well-trained animal who'd been patted on the head.

"I want to know all the stuff," Marcia told Carly. "I don't get a break from no one."

The two women, now walking side by side, entered the building and went to Marcia's two-room apartment. It was as drab an affair as Carly had ever seen. On the couch was a man, out cold from too much alcohol, and it was instantly clear that Marcia intended to talk around him, with complete nonchalance. Carly got the feeling that men had died in this apartment, their remains thrown out like garbage, to avoid police questions.

And she wondered once more how this woman and André Laval could possibly have met.

"You want somethin'?" Marcia asked. "I mean, I got a couple beers."

"No, that's all right," Carly said, shaking some of the water out of her clothing.

Marcia looked her up and down. "You come from some fancy place, don't you?"

"If New York is fancy, I guess so," Carly replied.

"You ain't a cop?"

"No. Reporter." She saw Marcia grimace and back away. "No, hey, I'm not that kind of reporter," Carly explained. "I don't do police stuff. The only reason I'm here is because I got one of these Laval specials."

Marcia snapped a beer from a refrigerator that stood right at the edge of the living room, and gave Carly another once-over, with no particular affection. "How you find out about me?" she asked.

"I really don't know. I got an anonymous note. That means . . ."

"I know what it means," Marcia snapped. "Look, lady, I'm no dummy. I had some bad luck comin' down, that's all. I'll get back on my feet and you'll see me take this town."

"Oh, I'm sure," Carly said. "Look, I didn't mean to say anything bad. At any rate, I got an anonymous note. I knew from before that there were at least two women with this same face—one in Los Angeles, another in Washington. One of the women is missing, the second was murdered."

Marcia's jaw dropped open at the word *murdered*.

"Yeah," Carly said, "it's pretty grim. I'm trying to find out exactly what happened."

"This Laval, he a bad piece of work?" Marcia asked.

"I think so. At least I know he's in the face-copying business. Uh, how did you and Dr. Laval . . . ?"

Suddenly, Marcia laughed. "Yeah, right, you still can't get over that this class-A face doctor would take me, correct?"

"Well, he usually does work in other areas."

"'Other areas,' she says. Look, uh . . ."

"Carly."

"Yeah, right, Carly . . . look, I'll tell you where he found me. I was in jail."

It registered. Carly recalled Laval saying that he'd done some work in prisons. "Yeah," Marcia went on, "there's a women's pison in Chicago. I stole some stuff, a lot of stuff, and they sent me there. I got beat up and needed a face doctor. So this Laval picks me to work on. I heard he was a big deal, so I had no sweat with that. I also liked what he did."

"We both liked it," Carly said. "Did he ever say that you were part of an experiment?"

"Naw."

"Ever threaten you?"

"Nope. Perfect gent. Even calls now and then to see how I am."

"Have you seen him since your surgery?"

"Sure. Couple times. But I got out of prison since then, so I go to a hospital here. Want coffee?"

"No thanks."

"What I can't figure," Marcia continued, "is why there's two of us."

"No one can figure that," Carly replied. "Look, if you had to . . . testify about this, would you be willing?"

"Testify?" Marcia's face froze, and Carly could read the fear. "Look, I had enough headaches with the law."

"All right, would you talk to my editor? There's a big

story here, Marcia. And maybe more than a story.'' She paused. ''There could be a movie.''

''Yeah,'' Marcia answered. ''And I'm Marilyn Monroe.''

''Think about it,'' Carly requested. ''You don't have to give me answers now. But we could do a big story, and it could be valuable in stopping this man. My magazine is *Allure*. Maybe you've heard of it. We aren't going to publish anything until I get more facts. Just think about it.''

''Yeah, I'll think,'' Marcia said.

''I can bring my editor out to talk to you, if you like.''

''Sure. I'll meet him. Talk don't hurt.''

Despite her rage at André Laval, Carly felt a surge of excitement. Here she was, in the same room with her artificially created ''twin.'' Here she was, face to face with the living proof of what Laval had done. Carly vividly imagined a press conference with the two of them— she entering from one side of the room, Marcia from the other. Dynamite. Absolute dynamite. It would move mountains, and Laval would be exposed. The rest would be up to the law. ''I'll bring my editor, then,'' Carly said. ''Look, I know how crazy this must be for you. I mean, just a few minutes ago you didn't know I existed. Well, it's just as crazy for me. The help you're giving us will be invaluable. It will help other women to avoid this. I'm sure you know that.''

''I know it now,'' Marcia shrugged.

''But,'' Carly continued, ''I want you to be careful. *Very* careful. If Laval tries to contact you, maybe you'd better avoid him.''

''Right. Sure. I follow,'' Marcia said. But now her eyes appeared glazed over and she looked out a dirty, cracked window at the windswept street. Other ideas were entering her head, and personal safety wasn't one of them. Carly *needed* her, Marcia knew. Marcia had a face that suddenly had value. She had a prize, and a prize has a price. A movie? Maybe. But Marcia always dreamed big. A movie might only be part of the deal.

But if Carly needed Marcia, Laval needed her even

more. She could be a menace to him. She could even destroy his career. What if Marcia confronted him and announced that she, Marcia Lane, had found out what he'd been doing with faces?

How much would Laval pay for silence? How much would Laval pay to have Marcia take a walk and never be seen in Chicago again?

Marcia Lane knew all about things like this. She'd gotten a fine education as a guest in the women's prison.

She also knew the kind of house she wanted. And she had her sports car picked out. The checks would come from André Laval. He'd write them . . . without hesitation.

The thoughts swam in Marcia's head, blotting out any concerns over what had happened to those other two duplicates.

She saw a better life ahead. This was the break she'd always dreamed of.

19

"I can't believe you didn't take a picture," Victor Hoover said, trying to get his fork into some too-soft lasagne, finally succeeding, then splattering it back on the plate.

"I just couldn't," Carly answered, sitting next to Mike Moran, who was listening intently as his reporter told the story to a law-enforcement officer for the first time. "You could see she was suspicious. I had to go easy."

"You had your Polaroid with you. You shoulda tried," Hoover said. "I mean, if you showed me a picture, even a Polaroid picture with that lousy color, I could say, 'Here is a duplicate face.' If I had to convince the brass that this is more important than the next parade, I could show them a picture and then show them you."

"As I said," Carly explained, "it wasn't possible."

"I hate to lose evidence," Hoover replied.

"I understand that." Carly managed to put up with Hoover, who barely looked at her, because Moran had briefed her on Hoover's weirdness.

"So as I understand it from Michael here, you are suggesting that he and you go to Chicago and talk to her again," Hoover said.

"Yes. She agreed to it. Look, she's been in jail. I couldn't lay a lot of cops asking questions on her."

"This I understand," Hoover said. "You show perception and this I admire. But there's one thing I don't understand.''

"What's that?" Carly asked.

"She's alive."

"I beg your pardon."

"I mean, we said that the duplicate-face game might be out of my line. I checked medical people. They said it was more for the lawyers and the disciplinary boards, the people with the letters after their name and the starch in their collar. But if this doc is up to somethin' else, well, that's my business. But all you got is one girl dead who coulda been aced out by anyone, and another one who's missin'. She coulda flew because she wanted to. This one, this Marcia, is alive."

"Maybe there was no reason to kill her."

"Right. The motive angle. I told that to Mike over pizza. They got good pizza here. But what if those other two, they just met with misfortunes? With this Marcia alive, where's the case?"

"I don't know," Carly said, reminding herself she still had nothing thoroughly solid except the fact that Laval duplicated faces. "Look, there may be other women."

"Oh yeah?" Hoover asked. "You holdin' back on me?"

"No," Carly replied. "But Laval has medical practices in four cities outside New York—Los Angeles, Chicago, Washington, and Boston. We know he duplicated faces in the first three, probably to keep them geographically separated. So why not the fourth?"

"This is a good question," Hoover observed, now guzzling a Classic Coke from a can, without a straw.

"I think I should check her out . . . if I can find her," Carly suggested.

"You got any hints?" Hoover asked.

"No, nothing," Carly replied. "I have no idea who she is, or even if she exists. I wish I knew her name."

"Names," Hoover mused. "I don't like names. I hate my name. People didn't vote for Hoover, at least not the second time. I got one of their vacuum cleaners. My rug is still dirty. Names are funny. No one should have names from birth. They should have numbers. Then, when they're old enough to be in the army, they should give themselves a name, like the Pope does." Then Hoover paused, and shrugged. "So, this'll take me maybe a day or so."

"What?" Moran asked.

"That's all. Why should Miss Randall go up to Boston to snoop around? If there was foul play, then this is for the officers of the law. I got friends up there. They know the medical business. You tell me where this Laval works when he's up in Boston. I'll check things out."

"But that's privileged information," Carly objected.

"Privileged? Did the lady say privileged? Michael, did I hear a toilet word?"

"Yeah, I'm afraid so, Vic," Moran said. He touched Carly on the shoulder by way of explanation. "Victor has people willing to help," he said. "These people need . . . favors occasionally."

"I get the picture."

"You learn quick," Hoover said. "Now, I understand that this Laval person is still your doctor."

"That's right. He's doing some minor surgery on me in five days."

"You don't got sweat over it?"

"Oh no. With all those people around? He'd never do anything in a hospital. He's too smart. Besides, if I try to avoid him, he'll get suspicious."

"Another good thought from you," Hoover said. "But I want you should hire a private nurse for your room."

"Why?"

"Becase that's the one place you'll be alone."

"I won't be there long."

"You think it takes a week to kill someone, Miss Carly? Hire one."

Carly paused. Her instinct was always to resist protective measures, but now her resistance faded. Here, after all, was a top detective, and he was becoming interested in the case. "I'll hire one," she said. "Now I think Mike and I should get back to Chicago."

"Hey wait," Hoover objected. "Lemme check out Boston first. If I dig up somethin', it makes things clearer. You could use my stuff in Chicago.''

"Good idea," Moran replied. He turned to Carly. "It's a day or two."

Carly knew that things were heading in the right direction. Moran and Hoover were moving with her. It would all come to a head soon.

October 16

As far as Laval was concerned, Carly had four days to live. It was remarkable, he thought. Here she was, tracking him, investigating the duplicate faces . . . and yet she would voluntarily go under his knife. In a way, he admired her. She had the kind of courage that would have been promotable for the face of the nineties.

Laval did consider, for the last time, an abrupt change of plans. He could still confront Carly, say he'd been tipped by someone in Los Angeles or Washington, and try to explain away what he'd been doing.

He rejected it.

She was a reporter. Her instincts would be to go with the story, with the possible Pulitzer, with the glory.

Carly appeared at Laval's office at Burgess on the afternoon of the sixteenth for a presurgical check. This was nothing more than a quick visual examination of the area to be worked on, and a discussion of the procedure, and was conducted entirely within the lavish office itself. As Carly entered, Laval was just returning from his private TV studio, where he'd made a tape giving details of how he was going to kill her. In his hand was a small vial of reddish liquid, which he placed on his desk. It was a turn-on for him. He assumed that Carly would sit in her chair and occasionally stare at it. In a few days, it would kill her.

"Wann-der-ful," he said, as he entered, extending his hand to shake hers. "Ms. Randall, every time I see you I become prouder of my work. You've come out so well."

"Thank you," Carly replied, trying to appear as normal and natural as possible. "That's what all my friends say. I'm having a ball!"

"Well, do sit down and do tell. I want pictures of you for all my students. You won't mind, will you?"

"No. Why should I mind?"

"Wann-der-ful. Oh, I see you're looking at the red liquid on my desk."

"Yes. Is it medical?"

"It is. It's a chemical we use during some procedures to aid the skin in healing. We'll be using it in yours."

"I see." Carly thought nothing of it. Nor did she think anything of the locked case on the floor, no more than five feet from her.

"Now, you've been seeing Dr. Slesar."

"Yes."

"Well, he's reported to me that your mental outlook is just grand. Just absolutely grand. I wouldn't continue with those sessions for more than a few months. You're in good shape."

"Dr. Slesar has been very helpful," Carly said.

"Yes, I like Gordon. He's helpful to me, too," Laval replied. "I assume you're back in the social swing."

"Oh, definitely."

"Traveling?"

"I get around."

"Are there any questions you have for me, Ms. Randall?" Laval asked. In a way, he was hoping Carly would confront *him*. But she wouldn't. He really had no idea what was in her mind now, where she was in her probe, what she'd learned most recently.

"I can't really think of any," Carly answered. "I'm sure you'll explain everything to me."

"Of course."

Laval realized that the tape he'd just made was on his desk—the tape giving the details of Carly's impending doom. Casually, he slipped it into a drawer. Then he got up and walked over to Carly, examining her right ear. "What we'll do is patch that little scar there and pull the skin back a bit. There's too much sponginess, and that's going to wrinkle unless we get to it. I really don't see anything else that needs to be done. After this, you'll be perfect.''

But she *was* perfect, Laval mused. It was so sad she had such a curious mind, so sad she had to snoop around. She could have been famous and wealthy, the toast of New York's chic set. Now she'd just be dead.

''And I'll only have to stay one night?'' she asked.

''That's all. Or maybe two. Only as a precaution.'' Laval returned to his desk. pretending to look up a date he already knew. ''I see you're scheduled for the twentieth, four days from now. That's fine.''

But he knew it wasn't fine. Each passing day brought greater risk that Carly would trap him in some way. He was almost desperate to move the operation date forward. ''Uh, I did have a cancellation for tomorrow,'' he told Carly, knowing he could always bump some other patient off the schedule.''It's always wise to be early with these things . . .''

''No, I'll keep the twentieth,'' Carly said, anticipating her quick trip to Chicago with Moran.

''Very well.''

All right, he'd have to wait it out. For Carly, the result would be the same.

Carly returned to *Allure* to find a note on her desk: ''See me. Quick! Mike.''

It had to be about Laval, so she rushed into Mike's office, not even bothering to knock.

She was surprised to see Victor Hoover.

''Something wrong?'' Carly asked, realizing from their expressions that something was *very* wrong.

''Sit down,'' Moran said.

Carly sat. ''Something's wrong in Boston, isn't it?'' Carly asked.

''Things could be better up there,'' Hoover replied.

''Tell it to me,'' Carly insisted.

Hoover pulled a half-eaten marshmallow bar from his

pocket and proceeded to finish it before answering. He savored the delay. "My friends in Boston, they got to Laval's records. All the patient pictures are missing."

"Missing?" Carly asked. "How could they *all* be missing?"

"If this here Laval wants 'em missing, missing they are," Hoover replied. "The man destroys evidence. He apparently is very good at it. I give him an A." Hoover crumpled the candy wrapper and returned it to his pocket. "We have a setback here."

"What do we do?" Carly asked.

"We're zilcho as far as the hospital up there goes," Hoover replied. "I could show *your* picture to the doctors and nurses, but it's bad tactics. Someone may tip Laval. But there's another way. If somethin' happened to some patient of this guy, the police files would have it—with pictures. I started 'em looking."

"How long will that take?"

"Day or two. I gotta send 'em your picture and find out if any lady who's missing or dead has that face."

"Then maybe Mike and I should just go on to Chicago without waiting," Carly said.

"I don't know, Carlykins," Moran broke in. "We'd be much more solid if we had facts from Boston."

"Second the motion," Hoover said.

Carly recalled something Laval had told her. "Look," she said, "Laval's got a surgery opening tomorrow. If I take it, it'll give you time to track down anything in Boston. I'll be out in a few days and Mike and I will fly to see Marcia."

"Why not?" Moran asked. "That's the schedule. It makes everything efficient."

"I'll set it up," Carly said.

Now, by her own decision, Carly would be under Laval's knife in less than twenty-four hours.

Laval was jubilant.

It was a gift from heaven, from the god of medical artists.

He'd get to Carly three days early, and that was three days less to worry about.

He immediately called his surgical team together and made certain that the nurse he would frame for Carly's murder would be available on the seventeenth, the new day of the operation.

She would. God was taking care of Arnie again.

He left his Burgess suite to go to his private office on the East Side. But as he rushed from the hospital, he never noticed a man watching from a parked car across the street. Laval hailed a cab for the short trip. The man in the car followed. As they traveled, the man picked up a cellular telephone next to the driver's seat and pressed one digit.

"Subject now proceeding south in a yellow cab, destination unknown," reported Sergeant Kelly, a surveillance man assigned by Victor Hoover. Hoover was now hot on the case, his stoicism finally moved, his interest aroused. He had a total of four surveillance men assigned to Laval at different times of the day. And he also got a court order allowing him to tap Laval's phones.

20

Death day.

A godsend for André Laval, for whom every hour had become a kind of torture. At the end of this day, Laval knew, the greatest threat to his freedom, to his eminence, would be eliminated. He drew up the draft of a statement he would make to the press, savaging the negligence that had led to Carly Randall's untimely passing.

As Laval prepared, Victor Hoover and Mike Moran were at LaGuardia Airport, ready to board the shuttle for Boston. Hoover had decided to go up personally and help the Boston police try to find another in Laval's series of duplicate faces, if such a face existed. He knew enough about police work to realize that Boston might assign some rookie to do the looking, and that the kid might spend most of his time looking out the window.

Hoover knew it was a shot in the dark. The only "evidence" that Laval had duplicated a face in Boston was the fact that he periodically practiced there, enjoying staff rights at a major hospital.

Moran had asked to go as well. He wanted to get into this probe, to be a part of it. With the discovery of Marcia Lane in Chicago, the story was growing, the exposure of Laval more staggering. The man who'd dreamed of creat-

ing the face of the nineties was becoming the medical
scandal of the century.

Carly arrived at the hospital at ten A.M. to start the
presurgical procedures. As she entered Burgess, she walked
right past the surveillance man waiting for Laval to leave.
She had no idea who he was. Hoover was not giving her
the whole battle plan.

Carly was given Room 502 in the plastic surgery wing,
the same private room she'd had before. She learned as
she waited to be prepped that her surgery was now scheduled for 2:15, and would be conducted before a class of
residents, if that met with her approval. She told a nurse,
who gave her forms to sign, that she had no objection. The
more witnesses, the safer she'd be.

Laval poked his head into the room to greet her. He was
wearing a green surgical gown and matching cap, having
just come from another operation. Underneath the gown,
in his pocket, was a small vial of the fluid that would kill
Carly Randall and end his problems. A few minutes after
Laval's brief visit, Nurse Eileen Becker entered Carly's
room. Carly remembered her from one of her previous
operations. Becker was twenty-eight and smallish, a shy,
friendly type who was easily intimidated by senior nurses
and almost any doctor. By the end of the day, according to
Laval's battle plan, she would be charged with the malpractice death of Carly Randall, and would have no effective means of fighting back.

"You're stuck with me again," Carly told her as Becker
checked Carly's chart and left some sedatives.

"I'm afraid you're stuck with *me*," Becker said. "I'm
going on vacation tomorrow and I've got a tenth of my
packing done, if you know what I mean. Panic time."

Becker had mentioned the same thing to Laval, and
Laval had made a mental note of it. Nurse assigned to
medication was going on a trip. Preoccupied. Uninvolved.
Just the kind to be distracted and make a mistake. Becker
was a wise, inspired choice.

"I want you to take these pills," Becker said. "One an

hour. We'll be in to get you at about one forty-five and
take you down. You should be out threeish. It isn't much
of a procedure, but the doctor likes to lecture to the
students.''

"I understand," Carly said."Uh, did you get these pills
yourself?" she asked.

Becker looked quizzical."Why . . . sure. I check all the
medications. Why?"

"Just asking. Nervous, I guess."

"Nothing to be nervous about. We're an old team here."
It was 10:47.

Moran and Hoover arrived at the main police building in
Boston sometime after eleven. Elise Ryan, a policewoman
whom Hoover had known when she lived in New York,
was assigned to help them. Ryan was in her forties, wore
civilian clothes, and was taller than both men.

She took them to a small room with a single metal table
near the department's records section. There she laid out
mug shots of a number of crime victims. Although Hoover
had specifically asked Boston to alert him to any murder
victims found with a head missing, the request had been
shunted aside and lost in the bureaucracy. Elise Ryan
knew only that Hoover was looking for a victim who'd
been "abused."

Carly's picture—rushed to Boston by police messenger—
still lay on some lieutenant's desk. As Hoover had told
Carly, it just wasn't priority.

There'd been some sixty-seven murder victims in the
last two years who'd been cut up, altered, or abused. At
Hoover's request, he was given the files on all sixty-seven.

Most had pictures. Some did not. He quickly determined that none of those in photographs had the face of
Carly Randall.

"Maybe she *is* still alive," Moran theorized, as he and
Hoover looked through the folders.

"And if she is," Hoover said, "like I said in New
York, I don't see a hell of a case. One missing, one
murdered, one living in Chicago, and one living in Bos-

ton. The missing, like we said, is no big deal. That leaves
a murder—one out of four. Not enough to call out the
National Guard. We're back to a doctor who manufactures
faces."

"I know," Moran said. "And that's not your line."

"Michael, you learn as quick as your pal Carly," Hoover replied, searching through a dusty folder filled with
reports and photos of a woman who'd been hanged.

It was noon.

Laval passed the drug storage area in the surgery section
many times each day. It was not unusual for it to be
unattended. Cabinets were locked. No one was concerned
about thefts. He had a key, as did most doctors.

At 12:34, the world's greatest plastic surgeon slipped
into the storage area, opened a cabinet and quickly replaced a legitimate liquid with the poison he was carrying
in his pocket. The two looked identical. André Laval was
very good at duplicating things.

He left the storage area and walked nonchalantly down
the hall, just as Nurse Becker was passing by. Laval
smiled at her, then stopped her.

"You know, Eileen," he said, loud enough for another
doctor in the hallway to hear, "you look tired. You said
you were under some pressure. I'm awfully concerned."

"Oh, I'm okay, Doctor," Becker replied. "Just getting
everything together."

"Well, you're a trouper. Truly wann-der-ful. I'm glad
to have you aboard."

As they parted, Laval made a mental note of the doctor
who'd overheard them, so he could later have support
when he claimed Becker was under stress.

Eileen Becker now went confidently to the drug storage
area and withdrew the vial that Laval had planted there
only moments before. She placed it on a small medicine
tray she was carrying and walked toward the operating
theater assigned to Carly Randall. She remembered that
she had to pick up a dress at the cleaner's and reconfirm
her airline reservation. At times like this she wondered

whether she should have been a nurse at all. It was so demanding, and she found herself easily exhausted.

Maybe there was something else, something better. Maybe she shouldn't come back to the hospital after vacation. Think about it, she told herself.

It was 12:38. Carly would be under the knife in less than two hours.

"Looka right here," Hoover said, going through the folder of a murder victim. "Skull missing, murdered late at night."

"All right," Moran replied, far less excited than he should have been, "but we've found two other reports on women with a missing head. The photographs of them don't match Carly's face."

"There ain't pictures here," Hoover said.

Moran paused, exploring the implication of what this means. "Well, that might change things," he said. "Why do you think there are no pictures?"

"Oh, uh, well in cases like this there can be lotsa reasons why there's no photos. I mean, maybe they couldn't get family pictures because there's no family. As far as pictures of the deceased subject, maybe they didn't take 'em because . . . well, Michael, there's no head. So maybe there's no face."

Moran shuddered at the thought. "What do we do?"

"I like this folder I got here," Hoover said. "It feels right to me. Right age of victim. But there's nothin' here about family or friends. She was a loner."

"Anything at all on her?"

"Worked for the phone company. Night operator. You get a lot of loners in jobs like that, where they work at night because they got no one. She musta known people in the phone office, though."

Without missing a beat, both men got up, closed the police file, and rushed to call the security office of the local phone company. They wanted the names of anyone who knew the woman in the police file—the woman without pictures, the woman who'd been found murdered, with her head missing. They knew the odds that this was a Laval-related case were strongly against them. They also knew that the most sophisticated criminals were caught by just this kind of detailed police work.

Carly was wheeled into the operating theater precisely at 1:45 by Nurse Becker and an orderly. She was smiling, trying to fake it. She raised her head and saw Laval, and also saw about sixty plastic-surgery residents glaring down at her from their seats above the floor. She felt like a piece of public property.

She had no real fear. In fact, her mind was cluttered with thoughts of Moran and Hoover in Boston. She wondered what, if anything, they'd discover.

She heard Laval clear his throat.

"Ladies and gentlemen," he announced to his students, "may I present a grand lady, an utterly delightful subject. Carly Randall is one of my very favorite patients, and a distinguished editor for the magazine *Allure*. I know you all read it. She has a wann-der-ful future, and I am personally very proud to have made a little of that future possible. Won't you greet her."

There was a round of applause—something of a Laval trademark. He always had the doctors applaud the patient.

"How are you feeling, Ms. Randall?" Laval asked.

"Just fine," Carly replied. What else do you say in front of all those students—that the doctor is a lunatic?

"Is there anything you want to tell the students about your case—from the patient's perspective?"

Carly thought for a moment. She hadn't anticipated such a bizarre beginning—show business in the operating room—but she sensed what Laval was looking for. Praise, of course. "Only that I have full confidence in my doctor," she said.

"And I thank you," Laval replied. He almost chuckled, but managed to hold it in.

Carly wondered what Laval would do if he *really* knew what she was thinking.

Out of the corner of his eye Laval watched Nurse Becker

as she laid out some of his instruments, and then placed the medications in their proper places next to the operating table.

Yes, it was there.

The . . . problem would be over very shortly.

"You didn't know her?" Hoover asked, sitting in the tiny living room of Blanche Selle, a night operator for the phone company whose apartment was only a block from where she worked. Blanche was in her fifties, very heavy, and wore a flower-printed dress that clearly had been bought when she was twenty pounds lighter.

"No, I really didn't. I never saw her even. I came there a week before she . . . went away."

"The phone company confirmed the police listing of her name," Hoover said. "Alice Boone. Ring a bell?"

"No. I mean, I know she was murdered, but like I said, I didn't know her. When I'm on company time, I do company business. No little chitchats with me—"

"You wouldn't recognize a picture?"

"Who knows? Maybe I saw her in a hall."

"What about this?" Hoover pulled a picture of Carly from his pocket and snapped it before Blanche. Blanche reached for her bifocals and slipped them on. She studied the photo, turning it in her hand to see it from different angles. "No, I don't know her," she concluded. "Doesn't mean it isn't her. But I can't say I've seen her."

"Okey dokey," Hoover said.

He and Moran left, discouraged. There had only been six operators on duty the night Alice Boone vanished, according to the phone company, and both Hoover and Moran assumed any one of them would recognize Carly's face—if in fact Alice had been given that face. Maybe she hadn't. Maybe this was a false lead.

Hoover and Moran cabbed to another apartment six blocks away to track down the second operator on their list.

It was at 2:14 that they showed their picture to Kenneth Zimmermann, a college student who sometimes worked nights as an operator to earn tuition money. They weren't even inside Zimmermann's apartment. All three were standing in the hall outside, Zimmermann in his socks, a political-science textbook shoved under his arm.

"That's her," Zimmermann said. "That's Alice."

"No doubt in your mind?" Hoover asked.

"No doubt," Zimmermann replied. "I talked to her every now and then. A real loner. No family. No friends. She came from another city, but, hell, I don't don't remember where. She just kind of existed."

"Ever mention plastic surgery?" Moran asked.

"Oh sure. Everyone knew she had some rearranging. She'd been in some kind of accident. When it was cold, especially, she said her face hurt. She once told me she was seeing this ritzy doctor. I mean, top of the list."

"Laval?" Hoover inquired.

"The name I don't remember. I know the whole plastic business was on her mind." Then Zimmermann stared at the picture once more. "Too bad," he said. "She looks so happy there."

"Except the she isn't she," Hoover said.

"What?" Zimmermann asked.

"Forget it. Look, fella, thanks loads. You did good for us."

"Hey, any time."

Zimmermann went back into his apartment. Hoover turned to Moran. "Michael," he said, "that for me is a clincher. There's a case."

It was 2:16.

Laval, before an operating theater packed with students, residents, and visiting doctors, was at work on Carly's right ear. Nurse Becker had struck vacations from her mind and was concentrating intently on her responsibilities.

"A great deal of plastic surgery is not permanent," Laval told his students. "People change. Faces change. The good we do can be undone by nature. I try to maximize everything so the changes can be delayed. I'm always amused when people think plastic surgery refers to the materials we use. Of course it simply refers to our ability to reshape and remold. But nature can do the same—to the best of us.'' He kept looking over at Becker, studying her. Everything had to be orchestrated perfectly. "Uh, Nurse Becker,'' he said, "that suture.''

"This one?'' Becker asked, simply wanting to confirm.

Laval glared at her. "Of course. You *know* that.'' And then, so others around could easily hear: "Get your mind off the Bahamas, Eileen.''

And Eileen Becker, compliant to the last, didn't even try to defend herself. She simply lowered her eyes.

"Of course, the majority of you have seen procedures like this before. You know, of course, that the original material used to rebuild this patient's ear came from her rib cartilage. For those of you who may be new to this area, the cartilage was removed from the patient's rib cage some months ago, whereupon I actually carved it in the shape of an ear.

"The exact shape was determined by tracing the patient's other ear, undamaged in her accident, then matching it.

"If you choose to enter this specialty, I urge you to practice this carving technique on cadaver cartilage, as I did for many years.''

Carly, only under local anesthesia, listened intently to Laval. The man was amazing. He inspired total confidence and loyalty. She was sure that no one in that room could have believed, or accepted, what he really was.

Again, Laval gazed over to Becker, and mumbled something impossible to understand.

"What?'' Becker asked.

With visible disgust, Laval turned to another nurse and loudly ordered her, "Nurse O'Hara, the remaining suture please. Near Nurse Becker.'' Then he glared at Becker, who seemed momentarily flustered.

"We must be artists,'' Laval told the students. He then looked up at some of the female students. "You may know that Alma Morani, the first woman to be board-certified in plastic surgery in this country, came from a family of artists. In fact, her father was disappointed that she didn't become a sculptor. But she knew a great deal about art, about the dimensions of the human form, and applied it to her work.''

Almost finished, Laval thought to himself. He'd performed brilliantly, humiliating Becker at precisely the right moments.

"Each of you should be aware of everything that could ease the patient's psychological transition after surgery,'' Laval said. "Don't think that commercial products are beneath you. There is now a new line of cosmetics called *Esteem*, just for people who've gone through plastic surgery. Familiarize yourself with it. Recommend products that help. Consider it a medical question—helping the patient recover.''

Laval knew that the fatal injection was only seconds away. Again, he glanced over at Becker. At this moment she didn't look particularly efficient or inefficient. She didn't look anything. She was perfect. "Nurse,'' he said, "would you prepare the syringe.''

Hoover and Moran were rushing by cab to Boston's Logan Airport for the flight back to New York.

"I want to call Carly from the airport,'' Mike said, checking the time on his original, certified Mickey Mouse watch. "Maybe she's back in her room. She'll want to know what we found. Y'know, I doubted her at first. I wondered if she were imagining things or had a grudge against her doctor. I feel like a creep. I'll have to take her to a restaurant where they have tablecloths.''

"Y'gotta doubt, Michael,'' Hoover said, taking some M&Ms from a jacket pocket and flipping them into his mouth. "I mean, my first hunch on this case was it was wacko. Not worth the mushroom on my pizza. And look, we don't know for absolute sure who's doing this. But if you wanna put down a hundred bucks, I'll bet on it.''

Moran was startled. "Who?'' he asked.

"Exactly who your Carly thought—Laval. He murdered them. I got the hundred bucks ready on that.''

"How do you know?"

"I figure—these ladies, with the same face, they must've meant a lot to him. He had to stay in contact. If one of them disappeared, or got killed, it'd show up in something he did. Maybe he'd go public, or run to the cops in those other cities. But he wouldn't just sit around and read your crummy magazine."

"I never thought of that," Moran said.

"You're not paid to think," Hoover rebounded. "You're paid to take ads."

"Thanks," Moran said. "I'll remember that crack the next time we do a cop centerfold." Then, after a few moments, he turned deadly serious again. "Why?" he asked. "Why would Laval—or anyone—do this? What's his motive?"

"I don't know," Hoover replied. "But I'm thinkin' of askin' him."

Becker loaded the syringe.

Carly was moments away from death. In his mind, Laval rehearsed his own reaction—the demand for emergency personnel, the panic, the anguish, the fury at his nurse.

"Inject the patient," he said, his heart now pounding out of his chest, his forehead breaking out in a rare sweat. *Seconds away*, he knew.

He eyed that syringe with the red liquid, eyed Becker's fingers, sure and experienced, moving without an instant's hesitation. Becker leaned over Carly, who was still awake, but groggy. Carly smiled up at the nurse. Now Becker lowered the syringe to a spot just in front of Carly's right ear. She moved her thumb to the plunger and took up a firm grip.

Laval was mesmerized, then realized that his intense interest was showing. He picked up an instrument and inspected it, trying to avoid any undue attention to this routine injection.

Becker touched Carly's skin with the needle. "This won't hurt," she said.

Carly moved her face slightly, forcing Becker to withdraw for a moment. Then she positioned the syringe once again.

She squeezed the plunger.

The red liquid oozed down the tube quickly, at a constant speed. Laval insisted on gazing at it out of the corner of his eye. In five or six seconds, the syringe was empty. Becker withdrew the needle. "Injection completed," she said.

Now Laval attended his patient once more, pretending to inspect the spot where the injection had been given. "That will aid in healing," he announced, glancing up to his students to make sure they had heard. "Should more work be required, we can probably use laser surgery."

And he waited.

The convulsions would begin in about a minute. All those witnesses would watch as Carly Randall left this world, her loyal physician at her side, calling for help and trying desperately to save her. They all had seen who had given her the injection. And records would confirm that Nurse Becker had obtained, and signed for, the drug.

Thirty seconds passed. In a way, Laval hoped the end wouldn't be too painful. He still liked Carly. He still had fond memories of his dream for her, the dream of the face of the nineties.

The time came up on one minute. Laval thought he saw a first twitch.

His heart slowed. He felt serene . . . and safe.

He continued to wait. The slight twitch did not immediately turn into a convulsion. Some people take longer, he reasoned. "When the patient is back in her room," he announced to the students, "I'll take small groups of you to visit her. I want you to observe her psychological condition. If she permits, you can speak with Dr. Gordon Slesar, her psychiatrist, who can give you an overview of her mental progress."

Still nothing. What is she, Laval thought, the iron lady?

Two minutes.

Nothing.

Laval couldn't understand it. Certainly by now . . .

"Imagine if I hadn't," Laval heard Nurse Becker whispering to another nurse.

"Excuse me?" Laval said.

"You talking to me, Doctor?" Becker asked.

"Yes. What was that you just said?"

"Oh, I didn't want to upset you."

Suddenly, Laval felt a tightness in his chest, a wrenching tug at his throat. What was this about? "Repeat what you said," he demanded. "Don't be coy, Nurse Becker."

"That drug we just used. I went to get it in the supply room, and, well . . ."

"Come on!" Laval snapped.

Nurse Becker moved closer to Laval and whispered, so Carly wouldn't hear. "When I picked it up I noticed some small bubbles. That's not the way it should look. I think something happened to it, maybe at the factory. So I got a fresh supply. God, what if I had used it? Maybe it would have . . . hurt her."

Laval just stared at Becker, the full extent of his shock hidden by the green mask that muffled every breath. "Jesus," he said, "you are wann-der-ful. To have that presence of mind, to be so careful. Thank you, Nurse Becker. I was a little rough on you before, and I apologize. You may have saved Carly Randall's life."

"Oh, it's okay," Becker said.

Laval had to force himself to go through the remaining steps in Carly's surgery.

All that planning. All that calculation. All that certainty—all destroyed by this little eagle eye, this weak, self-denigrating Clara Barton who just *had* to be the heroine.

Carly would live. That was the worst thing possible! She could still do damage. She could still destroy Laval and his magical career.

Again, Laval felt an incipient panic inside. What do you do now? How do you get rid of her? "Why me?" he asked himself over and over, the victim of a hostile world.

But he had a more immediate concern. Now that Becker had obnoxiously announced that *she* had discovered the tainted drug, she was in the clear. But what would she do with the drug? Would she turn it over to hospital security? There could be an investigation. The hospital would want to know who was in that drug supply area besides Nurse Becker.

Maybe they'd find out. After all, Becker herself had seen Laval in the area. There was no such thing, Laval knew, as the perfect crime. "What happened to that contaminated drug, Nurse?" Laval asked.

"I've got it in my locker," Becker replied. "It's marked. I'm turning it over to the administration."

"Excellent idea. It should be analyzed. We may have a problem with the drug company. But look, after this surgery is completed, come upstairs. Give the drug to *me*. I've got a little clout around here and I can move an investigation faster than you can. I want this accident nailed down!"

"Yes, Doctor," Becker replied, subservient and unquestioning.

Laval was on his way to heading off one crisis. But a much more serious one still loomed.

21

Carly was wheeled back to her room about twenty minutes later, the local anesthesia already wearing off and her grogginess just starting to disappear. Nurse Becker came to visit her, to see that she was all right, but mentioned nothing of the "accident." Nurses were under strict instructions from the hospital never to discuss such things with patients. Patients had lawyers.

About five minutes after she was put in her room, Carly's phone rang. She glanced toward it. It was still something of a blur. She reached for it, touching around, knocking it off the hook, finally grasping the receiver and placing it slowly to her ear.

"Hello," she said, her voice slurred.

"Boozing again?" Moran asked, squeezed into a booth at Logan Airport.

"Funny," Carly replied. "Only you would ask a question like that, Michael. I just got out of surgery."

"How do you look? I hope they didn't change the face. That ruins our story."

"Would you listen to him. Frankly, I don't know how I look. They haven't given me a mirror." Even though her mind was still foggy, Carly realized that Moran had to be calling from Boston. Then she heard the jet engines in the background. "You at the airport?" she asked.

"Yeah. Logan."

"All right, give it to me."

Moran sighed. The kidding had to stop. He really didn't

want to deliver this message, but he had to. He couldn't hold anything back from someone so involved in the story as Carly. "Well, we tracked down another Carly face."

"And?"

"Murdered. Same style."

"I . . . kind of expected it," Carly whispered. "Is Hoover convinced?"

"Yeah, he's convinced. And he's convinced it's Laval. We're coming back now. I think we should do what we said—next stop, Chicago. Talk to Marcia Lane. She seems to be the only one left besides you. Which reminds me, is that private nurse there yet?"

"Due any minute. She'll be here when the regular nurses go off duty."

"Make sure she stays with you."

"I told you, Mike, he doesn't do it in the hospital."

"You just be careful."

The conversation ended as Moran and Hoover rushed to catch their plane. Carly rested, assured of her safety by the arrival of the private nurse.

It was a relief to Carly that Hoover was now on board, but there was still one great hitch: all the evidence against Laval was circumstantial. What *proof* was there that Laval had killed his patients? Two women dead, one missing, all with the same face. Laval may have been a medical lunatic, but where was the smoking gun linking him to the killings?

Her worst nightmare was that Laval would get out of this untouched.

Later in the day, with her private nurse down the hall on a break, Carly telephoned Gordon Slesar. All right, she was a bit put off by his overgenerous personality and the constant cheeriness, but he'd been a good ear, and at this moment she needed that ear.

Slesar was seeing a patient when she called, but, when his nurse buzzed him and told him who was on the line, he ended his session, told the patient he wouldn't be charged, and went right for the phone.

"Carly," he said, slipping behind his modest desk, "great hearing from you. That surgery all finished?"

"Yes," Carly replied.

"Hey, thumbs up and up and up. So it's over. You'll be great." But Slesar was gripping the phone so hard his knuckles were turning white. He knew Carly wasn't calling just for a social chat. "What can I do for you?" he asked, with that exaggerated goodwill.

"I've got word on more duplicates," Carly replied. "One in Chicago, another in Boston. The one in Boston is dead. Murdered."

"Dear God," Slesar answered. "Carly, this is very serious. Ignore all my previous advice. Go to the authorities. Tell them *I* told you to go. Do you need my help on this?"

"Oh no," Carly replied. "It's already being handled. I just wanted you to know, and to know what you think."

"I think you're a very perceptive woman who was ahead of all of us."

"I appreciate that," Carly said.

"Look, you can count on me. I've never seen this before. I'm . . . shocked. I really can't believe André Laval would be involved in something like this."

"Neither can I."

"I want to spend some time thinking about it now," Slesar said. "Maybe I'll have a further suggestion. But please keep me informed."

"I certainly will."

They said their brief good-byes as Carly saw her nurse enter the room.

Now Gordon Slesar sank into a large easy chair, flipping his legs over the chair arm. This was terrible. Laval might be a murderer, undoubtedly *was* a murderer, and *he* had collaborated with him. It would come out eventually. It had to. And then would come the humiliation and ruin.

It struck him that Carly had mentioned a duplicate in Chicago. The anonymous letter had worked. The woman had to be Marcia Lane, and Carly had tracked her down.

Carly hadn't said much about Marcia, and Slesar wasn't about to ask, lest he place the suggestion in her mind that *he* had been the source of the letter. He couldn't admit to that now. It would raise too many questions about his complicity.

Yes, he could eventually prove by paper and ink samples that he'd written that letter, prove that he'd tried to help Carly, but what did that *really* prove? In fact, it proved only that he'd been working both sides of the street. Only now did he realize how that could blow up in his face.

Laval could even blackmail him: "Support me on the witness stand, Gordy, or I'll reveal that you passed on to me everything Carly Randall said. Support me, or I'll show how you disgraced your profession by not going to the police sooner."

Slesar felt utterly trapped. He had to do something. Of course, he could no longer pass information about Carly to Laval. He'd pretty much decided against that anyway, but now the decision was final. It was far too dangerous to collaborate with the revered plastic surgeon. Slesar had gotten too much information from Carly ever to claim that he hadn't been warned. He'd simply have to invent things if Laval probed.

He decided to go to a lawyer. Yes, that was the first step. Go to a first-class lawyer. Find out if his breaking of Carly's medical confidence would be considered legal if he argued that it had been done for the good of the patient.

Nurse Becker appeared at Laval's office suite, as ordered, with the little vial of contaminated fluid. She sat in the reception area, expecting to wait at least half an hour before being received in the royal chamber.

They were all out there, patients eager to see Laval, some of them in line for nose jobs at $3,500 a shot, some others carrying their copies of *Playboy* so they could show the doctor precisely what they wanted. Becker was used to this crowd, most of them hidden behind dark glasses. She was immune to them, and to their petty vanities.

"I want new eyes for Thanksgiving," Becker heard one woman say. It was the latest medical fad—plastic surgery for holidays. Face-lifts for Christmas were fun, and Mother's Day raised all kinds of possibilities. Becker had heard that one plastic-surgery mill in Florida was actually planning to sell gift certificates.

It took only a minute for Laval to come out. This was one of the "help" he wouldn't keep waiting. "Won't you come in, Nurse," he said, smiling mechanically at the other patients.

Becker entered the regal office, where her impeccable white shoes had never traversed before, and stood in respectful silence as Laval eased back into his desk chair. "You have it?" he asked.

"Sure, right here," Becker said, reaching into a pocket.

"Again, I want to compliment you, Nurse," Laval told her. "With all the sloppiness in medicine, the attitudes you see around here. You're a gem. Truly grand."

"Oh, thanks," Becker said, grasping the vial and placing it on Laval's desk.

Laval stared at it. Why did things go wrong? Why were things always against him? With a studied theatricality, he extended his right hand to pick up the vial. He grabbed it, pulling it toward him, his eye never off it. "I'll take care of this," he told Becker, "in the appropriate manner."

"I know you will, Doctor," Becker said.

"And thank you again, Nurse. You'll receive a written commendation for this."

Nurse Becker smiled, turned, and left.

Laval placed the contaminated fluid in a desk safe, never to see the light of day again. He'd simply tell Becker that the hospital's investigation was being handled "quietly."

The episode was over. Laval had failed in his first attempt to murder Carly Randall—the only botched murder in his career.

He would try again. Soon.

But he also had to deal with Marcia Lane in Chicago, another potential source of trouble.

22

Carly also had plans. Within hours after leaving Burgess Hospital after a two-night stay, she was at Kennedy Airport, boarding a United jetliner for Chicago with Mike Moran and Victor Hoover. Their objective: to interview Marcia Lane, to build the case against Laval.

Allure paid for Moran's and Carly's tickets, economy class of course. The New York Police Department paid for Hoover. He justified the trip by convincing superiors that Laval might be engaged in criminal acts in New York.

Upon returning, Hoover would consult with the district attorney for Manhattan, and possibly confront Laval directly.

"How do we trap him?" Carly asked on the plane, while over Pennsylvania. It remained the insistent dilemma that they faced.

Victor Hoover, still working on the pasta that United had served for lunch, and savoring each lumpy chunk, put down his miniature fork for a moment to answer Carly's question. "I dunno," he said. "It's drivin' me nuts. All I do is put on calories when there's somethin' like this goin' on. But listen, the first thing is to show Laval wasn't in New York during the time of the murders we know about. That's done, from the hospital records here. The second thing is to prove he was in those other cities on the exact day of the murders. That means Washington and Boston. That's a no-go. We can't do it."

"Why?"

"He wasn't goin' to advertise his whereabouts. You can

get in and out of Washington or Boston fast. You can take cabs instead of rentin' a car and leaving a credit-card number. You can wear dark glasses. You can never go near places where you're known. My theory is that Laval went to those cities to kill those women. He probably didn't even tell his office where he was. Maybe he said he was going to be with a friend, or another doctor. Maybe he said he was just takin' some time off. No one had to know where he was.''

"What does that leave?" Carly asked.

"It leaves us. Maybe this girl in Chicago can help. And luck. And good police work. He must've made a mistake somewhere.''

"Just great," Carly muttered. "The guy duplicates four other faces. We know some of those four women had something terrible happen to them. And we can't prove—''

"Carlykins," Moran interrupted, waving his black Cross pencil, "remember . . . it still could be someone who works *with* Laval.''

"But Laval was out of town when those women—''

"Circumstantial," Hoover broke in. "Like I said, if we can't prove he was in those other cities, there's no case. Look, I think it's Laval. But we need criminal-court proof.''

"All right, we talk to Marcia," Carly said. "But what if she comes up with nothing?''

"Then we have to blow it open," Hoover answered. "Full investigation. Bring in Laval. Bring in everyone who works with him. He'd be on guard then, obviously. But we may have to do it. Trouble is, it'll mess up his reputation.''

"Big deal," Carly said.

"Could be a big deal," Moran broke in.

"How so, Mike?" Carly asked. "You concerned about hurting his feelings?''

"No, I'm concerned about his lawyers. If his reputation is damaged and he's innocent, he'll come after us.''

Carly pondered it. A slow, burning rage began to well up inside her, the rage of the victim who sees her assailant slipping through one legal loophole after another. "So,'' she said, "not only could he get off scot-free, he could even win a lawsuit and come out with millions."

"That's unfortunately correct," Moran said.

Now Carly could just see him—hiring a million-dollar lawyer and presenting to a jury all the women whose lives he'd made whole again. Humanitarian. Teacher. Inspirer. Savior. She'd been to too many trials, heard too many facts twisted out of shape, to trust to the luck of the judicial system.

She thought back to Margaret Shirmer and her daughter, Kathleen. She thought of Laval's dead patients, realizing there might be many more than she knew about. She thought of her own face, how Laval had made her part of his bizarre scheme. And she thought of the man himself, and the veneer that covered a sick, driven mind. "I'll get him," she said quietly, but making sure the two men heard.

They did, and both seemed startled by the use of *I*. "I'll never rest until I get him," she concluded, and then fell silent.

Carly, Moran, and Hoover landed in a balmy Chicago this time, treated to a burst of warm air and gentle breezes. The skyline of the city stood out in sharp relief against a pure blue sky. Only a local corruption scandal, highlighted by the murder of a crooked judge, seemed to sully the atmosphere, but Chicagoans took the news in stride. It was one less judge to pay, and worry about. The bribes he was scheduled to receive would simply be given to another public servant to advance the cause of good government and equal justice under law.

Carly, Hoover, and Moran didn't even check into a hotel. Instead, they went immediately to Marcia's apartment building in her run-down neighborhood. As they entered the district, which seemed to begin abruptly as if it were another country, Moran looked around skeptically. "Laval took a patient from *here?*" he asked.

"Amazed me, too," Carly answered, "but remember, she was a prisoner. He must have had a reason. Maybe he thought her bone structure was unique."

"It's all a bunch of theories," Hoover said. "We still don't know why he's into all this. I think, if I was him, it would have something to do with bein' an artist. Maybe he's tryin' to prove somethin' with these faces. Why he kills them? Well, I've seen lotsa crazy people."

They entered Marcia's building and walked up to her apartment. The doorbell wasn't working, so Carly rapped on her door. There was no answer.

She rapped again, insistently.

"Sure she knew we were coming?" Moran asked.

"Of course I'm sure," Carly replied. "I called to make the appointment, then confirmed it." But as she rapped again, she wondered. Marcia was hardly the picture of responsibility, and maybe she'd just be late getting back. Or maybe she wouldn't show at all. Or maybe she was drunk on the floor. Or maybe she was sitting in there and had just decided not to answer.

They waited almost five minutes, but all they got from inside Marcia's apartment was silence.

"Can we knock it down?" Moran asked.

"Negative," Hoover said. "I got no authority. No warrant. Besides, I'm a visiting officer. The Chicago boys would have to do that."

Carly went to the next apartment, from which she'd heard a crying baby, and rapped on that door. After more than a minute an obese young woman who looked as if she were in a perpetual daze answered, opening the door slightly, peeking through, but not unfastening the chain that provided her some security. "Yeah?"

"I'm trying to find Marcia Lane," Carly replied. "Do you know where she is?"

"Marcia?"

"Yes. Marcia Lane. Next door."

"Last I saw her was two days back," the woman said. "I don't know where she is."

"Does she go anywhere in particular?" Carly asked.

"Look, lady," the woman replied, "I'm not her momma, y'know? She goes. She comes. She ain't here now. Big deal." The door closed.

Carly tried two more apartments on the floor, but no one answered.

"Carlykins," Moran said, "this is more than disappointing. I expected some stimulating conversation, a tour of the duplex—"

"Michael, stop that," Carly snapped, in no mood for levity. She sensed something was more than wrong. "Can you get the police?" she asked Hoover.

"Yeah, I can," Hoover answered. "And I will. I got friends here."

Carly and Moran waited while Hoover went to make his call. It took only eight minutes for a Chicago police car to arrive. Two patrolmen, one bearing an ax, rushed upstairs with Hoover to Marcia's apartment.

They didn't need a search warrant. There was reasonable cause to believe the occupant in the apartment was either unconscious or had met with foul play, so breaking down the door was legally justified. One of the patrolmen, small but muscular, started swinging away at the wood door, and splinters began to fly.

The door, already rotting, came down with only four swings. The patrolmen, followed by Hoover, Moran, and Carly, rushed in. Instinctively, they started sniffing loudly, anticipating the aroma of death. But there was none.

They looked around, snooping through closets and drawers. This part wasn't precisely legal, but the Chicago cops ignored the infraction. They wanted to help Victor Hoover, and they saw the chance for some glory should this cop from New York discover something major.

"Palmer House," Carly suddenly said.

"What?" Hoover answered from across the ramshackle living room. How could an elegant hotel be mentioned in these surroundings?

"There's a phone book here, turned to the page with the Palmer House."

"Lots of other things on that page too," Hoover observed, moving over to Carly and looking over her shoulder.

"But that has a little pencil mark next to it," Carly said, "Could she be there?"

"Are you kidding?" Moran asked. "She couldn't afford ten minutes at the Palmer House."

"How do we know?" Carly wondered. "How do we know what she had stashed away? How do we know what kind of friends she had? How do we know what business she was in?"

"But why would she go there?" Moran insisted.

Hoover grabbed the phone and dialed the Palmer House number. No, no Marcia Lane registered there. But she could be registered under an assumed name. He had one device to find out quickly if she were at the hotel—Carly's face. "Let's go down there," he said.

With Moran still shrugging his doubts, the three left Marcia's building and accepted the cops' offer of a ride to the Palmer House. It was true that it just wasn't the kind of place Marcia would go, unless she had a very good reason. On the ride over, Victor Hoover wondered what that reason could be. What could be important enough for Marcia to break, without notice, her carefully arranged meeting with Carly Randall?

They arrived at the hotel, zipped past the doorman, and went immediately to the front desk. Hoover flashed his badge and started making the rounds of lobby personnel, lugging Carly with him. His question was always the same. "Did you see a woman here who looked like this?" The hotel people assumed that Carly was the missing woman's twin sister.

All Hoover got was shrugs. The hotel manager suddenly appeared. He was only about thirty-five, slim, perfectly groomed, and management-school efficient. But he was clearly troubled by the presence of a detective at the hotel. He whisked Hoover into a corner for a quick conference. "What's wrong?" he asked. "Did anything happen here?"

"We don't know," Hoover replied, the side of his mouth slightly painted with the remnant of a Milky Way. "We're lookin' for a missing person and have reason to believe she might be here."

"I'll give you my security people," the manager said, balancing between cooperation and concern for image.

"We'll call 'em if we need 'em," Hoover replied. "Are most of these people on shifts?"

"Yes, of course. We operate twenty-four hours."

"I may have to ask for lists of employees and start checkin' 'em out."

"Yes, anything. Just, uh . . ."

"Don't worry. There'll be no press conference."

Reassured, the manager worked out a plan with Hoover. He would call a small group of employees down to his office, where Hoover would interview them. If nothing turned up on the shift, Hoover would return later.

Groups of four started descending on the manager's office—clerks, maids, maintenance men, waiters, bellhops, even security guards. Each was asked to study Carly, as if she were in a police lineup. Not one recognized her.

The next shift came on three hours later. As Moran made reservations to stay at a hotel—a less expensive one than the Palmer House—Hoover and Carly started quizzing a new batch of people.

"Did you see a woman like this?" Hoover asked a night reservations clerk barely out of high school.

"I think so," he said, the first positive response Hoover had gotten.

"When?"

"I don't know. Wait a second, maybe I didn't see someone like her. Hard to say. I'm usually looking at papers, y'know? I'm not so sure."

"Don't want to get involved?" Hoover asked.

"I don't know. My eyes aren't that good."

"The woman who *might* look like this, the one you *might* have seen," Hoover went on, "what can you tell me about her?"

"Nothing. I get so many people. I mean, early evening. That's big around here. Y'see, the airline flights come in—"

"Yeah, yeah, I know," Hoover said. He took the man's name and moved on.

Forty-four people passed through the manager's office. It was 6:35 P.M. and Hoover's stomach was reminding him of fine Italian cooking. But there were times when even eating took second place, and this was one of them. Why had Marcia Lane's phone book been turned to the Palmer House?

A group of four maids was ushered in. Hoover was about to start questioning them when one, a plump older woman with frizzy, grayish hair, stared at Carly, then pointed to her with a smile.

"You know someone who looks like her?" Hoover asked.

The maid just shrugged.

"I ask again, you know someone like her?"

"She only talks from Poland," another maid said.

"Polish?" Hoover asked. He could get by in three or four languages, but not Polish. "Who speaks Polish here?"

No one did.

"I need someone who speaks Polish," Hoover announced, watching the maid as she gestured again toward Carly.

Hoover rushed out to the front desk. "You got all kinds of services here," he told the clerk. "I need a Polish talker."

"You want a talk given in Polish?" the desk clerk asked.

"No. Someone who talks Polish. I'm interviewing a Polish maid."

The desk clerk shrugged. "I don't know anyone who speaks Polish. Maybe in the morning—"

"You got a personnel roster for this shift?" Hoover asked.

"Sure. We keep one right at the desk, in case one of our people gets a phone call or—"

"Yeah, right. Lemme see it."

Hoover looked over the roster and instantly found two Polish-sounding names. He had the people paged.

In a few minutes Hoover had his Polish translator—the headwaiter of one of the hotel's restaurants. In full tuxedo, complete with towel, sporting a Vandyke beard, the man slipped into the manager's office to perform the only service of the evening for which he would not be tipped. And he was not pleased. As soon as he arrived he stared glancing at his contraband Rolex watch, eager to get back to the money machine. He had only condescended to do this because one of the hotel's assistant managers had convinced him that the establishment's image was on the line.

Hoover didn't even bother to introduce myself. As the headwaiter entered, Hoover simply gestured to the Polish-speaking maid. "Ask her if she knows someone who looks like this lady."

With obvious disgust at even having to address a maid, the headwaiter asked the question in elegant Polish.

The maid gave a bubbly answer, accompanied by large hand movements.

"She says yes, she saw this woman come in yesterday. She wonders what she's doing here."

"We'll get to that later," Hoover said. "Was she with anyone?"

The headwaiter passed on the question, trying not to look the maid directly in the eye. The maid replied that the woman was with a man.

"Describe him."

The maid went through a description in Polish, complete with a drawing in the air. "She says," repeated the head-waiter, "that he was tall but wore large sunglasses and a hat. She wondered why a man would wear sunglasses in dark weather. Maybe there was something with his eyes . . ."

"Maybe," Hoover said. Could she identify the man?

The question was asked, and the maid replied, her answer accompanied by shrugs. "Probably not," repeated the waiter. "She saw him come into the room with the woman, but not after that. And with those glasses, and a big coat and—"

"She see the woman again?"

"No. She expects to. She's in her room."

"In her room?" Hoover asked, suddenly becoming animated. "How does she know?"

"How do you know?" the headwaiter asked the maid in Polish, listening to the answer and repeating it for Hoover. "Because there's a Do Not Disturb sign on the door. It was there when she went off duty last night. And it's there again now. This lady must rest a great deal."

"What room?"

"Room 360."

Taking Carly, the maid, Moran, and the headwaiter, Hoover dashed out of the manager's office, commandeering an elevator. As they rode up, Carly was charged with excitement. She would see Marcia again—the one living link left to Laval's crimes.

They got out on the third floor and went to Room 360. Hoover rapped hard on the door.

As at Marcia's apartment, there was no answer. Hoover rapped again and again. Still no answer.

Hoover took the maid's master key and inserted it in the lock. "I go in first," he said.

He snapped open the lock, then pushed the door open. The room was dark. Maybe Marcia had simply left the sign on the door and was out of the hotel.

Hoover entered.

He flipped on the light.

"Oh Je-zus," he moaned.

He turned back to the others. "Stay out," he ordered. "It isn't very nice."

But Carly pushed ahead. She felt an affinity with Marcia and rushed into the room, taking one look and instantly spinning away. Marcia was on the bed, soaked in her own blood.

"Oh my God!" Carly sighed. "Poor Marcia. She never had a break in this world." And then she turned to Hoover. "That's all four," she said. "All the faces, except mine. Three murdered, Kathleen Shirmer missing. I'm guessing Kathleen is dead also."

"Too bad about this one," Hoover said. "She could've helped. We're nowhere."

"What do you mean, nowhere?" Carly asked incredulously. "This clinches it. Laval murdered these women."

"No he didn't."

Carly and Moran were stunned.

"Vic, what are you talking about?" Moran demanded. His voice was laced with frustration, and a touch of anger.

"It can't be Laval," Hoover explained. "I've had him under surveillance. He never left New York. He's probably an innocent victim of someone tryin' to frame him. Just like we always said. Maybe someone jealous, or someone he didn't treat right."

"Wait a second," Carly demanded, not quite believing it. "You said you were *sure* it was Laval because he undoubtedly kept up with his patients, and would have done something—worked with the police or put up a reward—if he'd found out these women had been killed. . . unless *he* was the killer."

"And I messed up," Hoover said. "Fact is that surveillance reports up until two hours ago—when I called New York—showed Laval doin' his local thing. This woman was alive last night, remember. And she didn't go to New York to be murdered and fly back here herself."

"I guess not," Moran conceded, a look of dejection on his face.

"I still can't believe it," Carly said. "I just can't believe it. It *has* to be Laval. These are all his patients."

"The people around Laval knew who they were," Hoover countered.

"Maybe Laval *hired* someone," Carly suggested.

"That's always a possibility. But I doubt he'd want anyone else involved. Very dangerous. *Extremely* dangerous."

"All right," Moran said, "let's hit the bottom line. What do we do next?"

"We start over," Hoover told him. "Funny, I'll probably need Laval's help on this. Maybe he'll be a good guy."

"Oh, come on!" Carly snapped, not quite ready to make Laval out for an angel. "Don't forget that he duplicated faces."

"You don't forget it," Hoover answered. "You want to sue him, I got lawyers. That's all I can do."

Stupefied, they all just stared at each other. All the underpinnings of their case, their story, had been yanked from under them.

The work had all been for nothing.

André Laval was getting a clean bill of health.

23

Laval stood before the television camera in his East Side office preparing to make his latest tape. He was remarkably upbeat. Things had turned his way. One potential witness in Chicago had been erased, and he felt sure he could remove Carly on the next try. His plan was in place, and it did not depend on the nurses at Burgess Hospital.

He waited for the rattling of jackhammers at a nearby construction site to stop. And he wondered what doctors studying this tape years later would think. Would they understand what he'd attempted to do? Would they recognize that in trying to create the face of the nineties he was advancing medicine? Would they respect the importance of art, and of him as the artist? Or would they be mere technicians, unable to comprehend how one physician could move his profession forward?

Laval worried over that. It was hard, after all, for the world to appreciate genius.

He cleared his throat, and began.

"I may have mentioned one Marcia Lane of Chicago. Marcia was a prisoner when I met her. She was in for some middle-level offense, I don't remember which. She had the right bone structure for my experiment, so she immediately attracted my interest. Marcia was not an elegant person, but she possessed an earthiness that I thought could be turned into charm.

"I was wrong, one of my few character misjudgments. The girl just had no class whatever. She was vulgar, truly

211

was. And I just hadn't the time to play Henry Higgins with her.

"When this recent series of misfortunes occurred, I decided Marcia had to be withdrawn. I went out to Chicago yesterday for that purpose.

"But the woman had other designs. She claimed she knew all about me, and had some facts to back it up. And it was true, she did. She refused to say where she got the information. I am guessing it came from Carly Randall.

"Marcia wanted me to pay for her silence. Her first demand was a room, permanently, at the Palmer House. Amusing, isn't that? But I realized this was an opportunity, not a setback, for a hotel was a wonderful place to terminate her. The police would think she'd made some money at something illegal, celebrated at the hotel, and was killed by one of her pals, possibly for the money.

"I wasn't recognized when I took her to the Palmer House. We even ordered a dinner from room service—another of her demands. And she presented me with a list, including a red BMW.

"I killed her during dinner. But she did get that last bite of steak."

"That leaves Carly Randall, the sole survivor of my New Faces group. One attempt to kill her has not succeeded, but has not led to an investigation either. It was very close, a superb plot that would have resulted in a nurse being blamed.

"I'll try again. She's investigating, and I don't know how much damage she's done. But I know that, no matter what they have, they haven't got enough to convict me of anything. I leave no tracks.

"Carly must die. Once she's shut up, I'll be safe. And then maybe I'll make another face just like hers."

Abruptly, Laval stopped the tape. He sat down and leaned back in his chair. Ingratitude, he thought. All his problems stemmed from ingratitude. Carly was typical of them all—take everything, give back nothing. He'd labored hours on her, and what did he get? An investigation into his past.

"There's no decency," he mumbled, then closed his eyes to rest.

Gordon Slesar paced his small bedroom near Columbia University, his palms coated with sweat.

He was afraid. Carly's bombshells had hit home. Now he decided, once and for all, to confess to her that he'd kept Laval informed. Sure, she'd be shocked, but she'd also be understanding. He'd been doing it for *her*, after all. He was simply consulting with Laval, passing on information showing Carly was mentally distressed. Oh, of course it was wrong to break a patient's confidence, but it was an innocent mistake. Who knew what Laval really was?

Slesar would tell Carly that he'd stopped the consultations as soon as he began suspecting Laval. She'd see this as proof of his goodwill. No doubt about it. Slesar would be off the hook. He'd come out a hero yet.

But thoughts of malpractice danced darkly through his mind. What if Carly were not so understanding? And Laval could easily drag him in if Laval went to trial. Thoughts of having his license lifted, of testifying before juries, of being humiliated within his profession, kept hounding him. He always thought of himself as a "healing guy." Healing guys went into psychiatry. But he was also an ambitious guy, and now he realized just what his ambition had cost him.

He sat down at an ancient rolltop desk that he kept at one corner of his bedroom, and started writing:

Dear Carly,

I know this is an unusual way for a physician to communicate with his patient. But the situation is unusual, and I ask your understanding.

While treating you I became concerned about some of the statements you presented, especially those involving Dr. André Laval, whom I recognized as a superior plastic surgeon. I felt your revelations might have been based on hallucinations, or some deep-seated resentment that even you could not articulate. I felt I needed further information to fully understand what you were telling me.

It was my *medical* judgment that Dr. Laval should be consulted on your case. I knew that we were both interested in your welfare, and saw nothing improper about revealing to him all that you had said to me. I was certain that he would be sympathetic.

I did this on several occasions.

I now realize that I've made a terrible mistake. I am trying to correct that mistake by writing to you, so that you are alerted to everything Laval knows. You have my pledge of full cooperation if you are contemplating legal action against Dr. Laval. I realize that you may also contemplate legal action against me, but I urge you to discuss that with me first.

Of course, I stopped passing information to Laval as soon as I became convinced that your suspicions had merit. He does not know about your latest findings, in Chicago. He has not asked me about you in some time.

I regret any distress this may cause you. Sometimes, even physicians make misjudgments in pursuit of the best care for their patients.

Of course, there will be no charge for my services.

Sincerely,
G. Slesar, MD

Slesar leaned back and studied the letter. He was impressed by his own ability to project sincerity. Should it be sent? Hand-delivered? Home or office? Should it be shown to a lawyer first? He'd never had to do anything like this before, and this time he couldn't ask his mother's advice.

He couldn't decide. In fact, for the moment he couldn't decide anything, not even whether to use the note. He wanted to alert Carly, to get on the right side of this case, but wasn't the note a little wimpy? Maybe he should go to her office, or ask her to come to his. Maybe he could simply call her. That would be personal, but would avoid the ugliness of a direct confrontation.

He shoved the letter back in his drawer. Decisions were really hell.

The day after returning to New York, Carly, Mike Moran, and Victor Hoover met in the rear of a crumbling, little-used church on Manhattan's Lower East Side. Hoover felt close to God here, but not bothered by a pushing, shoving congregation. It was like a personal church, a divine resort in the midst of a New York slum. And it was very private.

As they spoke in hushed tones, only a lone parishioner knelt toward the front of the church. A janitor pushed a large broom in a hallway outside, softly chanting as he worked. Other than that, the church was silent.

"I got something," Hoover said, leaning his arm back on the top of a cracked pew and pulling a paper from his jacket with his other hand. "I been snooping around Burgess Hospital. I get tips from friends there. Miss Carly, you aware of what happened during that last operation?"

"No. It was normal."

"Yeah, normal," Hoover said. "So normal you almost got a one-way ticket to the coroner's office."

"What do you mean?"

"I mean there was a mix-up in some drug. A nurse noticed it at the last minute. If you had gotten it, you wouldn't have been on that super-saver flight to Chicago. . . ever."

"I never knew," Carly whispered. "No one mentioned it. But I'd love to thank that nurse."

"You forget the gratuities right now," Hoover told her. "You put your arithmetic hat on. Know what the odds are of that happenin'?"

"Not very good, I guess."

"Not very good is right. I got bookies. Any of 'em would give you money that it wouldn't happen. Not in a class hospital like that. Unless someone wanted *you* very dead . . . and wanted to blame someone else."

"Laval would know about drugs," Moran said.

"Michael, stop bein' so Sherlocky. You don't know this trade. Laval wasn't in Chicago, remember? He didn't kill this Marcia Lane out there. It's not Laval. It's someone else. We always said it might be someone close to Laval, for a reason we don't know. Maybe a nurse, or even one of his students."

"Unless it's Laval *and* someone else," Carly suggested, her voice touching off a slight echo through the church.

"No way," Hoover insisted, now hoisting his leg up on one of the pews. "Laval's no team player. I can't believe he'd get involved with someone else."

"Are the police investigating?" Carly asked.

"Again you're watching TV mysteries," Hoover retorted. "Number one, our guys got too much to do. Drug mix-ups aren't priority. Number two, the hospital hushed things up. They got clout with the mayor. No cops, if you catch my words. Number three, I personally don't want *any* official stuff on this. It'll tip our little killer. I'm on the case. That's all you need."

"I follow," Carly said.

"Now, we got to take some action," Hoover continued. "First," he said to Moran, "we put a watch on Carly."

"A bodyguard?" Carly asked.

"More of a guy followin' you around. You got to. You're a target."

Carly was sufficiently frightened by now not to resist.

"Next," Hoover went on, "I'm going to Laval."

Neither Carly nor Moran responded immediately. Although Hoover had mentioned confronting Laval before, this was the first time he absolutely declared he was going to do it.

"What do you ask him?" Moran inquired.

"I tell him the truth," Hoover said. "We got nothin' to hide." He took a Rolaid from his pocket and flipped it into his mouth. "Damn anchovy pizza. My mother always said I shouldn't have it."

"You'll tell him about me?" Carly asked.

"Oh no. Just that we learned some of his patients were

winnin' look-alike contests and were goin' from living to dead in a hurry. Why not? I'm a cop. I get stuff from cops in other cities all the time.''

André Laval would now get the opportunity of his dreams—the chance to point the accusing finger at someone else on his staff, and to put on the performance of a lifetime.

24

Hoover wasn't at all nervous as he waited outside Laval's Burgess Hospital office. Power, influence, and prestige never daunted him. He knew that cops enjoyed a special kind of status—a glamour, an aura of adventure, and the authority to arrest—that gave them a certain importance not reflected in their paychecks or brand of car. Ears always perked whenever he was introduced as "Detective Hoover." So, he convinced himself, he was as important as this plastic surgeon, who, after all, had never shot it out with a killer on a city street.

The only bow that Hoover made to Laval's prestige was a neatly pressed suit without candy wrappers dangling from the pockets. The shoes were unshined, but he'd kicked the mud off.

Hoover had made an appointment, but Laval made him wait. Hoover knew Laval was in his office, and knew there was no patient in there. "He's dictating notes," the receptionist said.

So Hoover waited.

Inside his office, Laval wasn't dictating anything. He just didn't want to appear overanxious—a sure giveaway of guilt. He fought to keep his hands steady, to prevent the sweat from popping out all over.

He couldn't figure what Hoover wanted. When he'd called for the appointment, Hoover had simply said it was about "police business." Had there been some breakthrough in the deaths of the duplicates? Did something go wrong that would point to the world's greatest plastic surgeon? Or had word gotten out about Carly's brush with death in the operating theater? Was it about something entirely different? Maybe Hoover was simply checking on a patient, or another doctor. Laval, seated behind his desk in an elegant dark gray suit, resisted paranoia, but not very successfully. He'd put his videotapes in a personal vault in case Hoover had a search warrant. He was living his nightmares, but fought to stay serene, the picture of confidence.

Finally, he picked up the microphone of his dictation machine, assumed a professorial pose behind the desk, and buzzed the receptionist to send Hoover in. Then he started dictating: Mrs. Pearl is a very well spoken lady who presents a fascinating example of the relationship between CAT scanning and cranial facial surgery. The fact that we can now study the structure of underlying bone and tissue before the operation, then apply that knowledge during surgery, represents a remarkable advance, one made possible only in the 1970s. When you consider that our science of plastic surgery began in India around 700 B.C., you realize . . .''

The door opened. Laval looked up. "Detective Hoover," he said, "grand to meet you. Please come in."

Hoover strode in, maintaining a studied indifference to the opulence of the office, giving the bust of Laval only a passing glance. "If you're working, Doctor, I'll wait," he said.

"Oh no, I can continue this later. Just making notes on an absolutely delightful patient." He placed his microphone down on the desk. "Uh, please, please sit down, Officer. I hope this isn't too serious."

Hoover did not sit, always preferring to remain above his subject. "Pretty serious, Doctor, It's about life and death."

Laval frowned, then let the frown mellow into an expression of concern. "Oh, well, that *is* serious. I assume, then, that it deals with a problem here at Burgess."

"Yeah. Partly. We'll talk about that."

"I'll be glad to cooperate with you in any way."

"Good. Can we start with a few questions, then?" Hoover asked.

"Of course," Laval assured him. "Anything you like, Officer. You're sure you don't want to sit?"

"I'm sure." Hoover felt his stomach suddenly churn and knew he could kill for some ravioli, but he fought the feeling. "Uh, Doc, you know that we police have contacts in many cities."

"I'd imagine so," Laval said. His heart began to pound with the mention of other cities. This could be the worst.

"And, uh, we got some reports that might disturb you."

"About the girl in Los Angeles?" Laval asked urgently. "The one who disappeared?"

"Among others."

"Who?"

"Doctor, three of your patients have been murdered."

Laval did not respond immediately. Instead, he just stared at Hoover. "You are joking, Detective."

"I don't get humorous about women with their heads missing," Hoover replied.

Laval let his mouth drop, ruining the sophisticated line of his face. "Why haven't I heard of this?"

"I assumed you had," Hoover replied. "Maybe I'm wrong—I guess I am—but don't doctors keep up with their patients?"

"It depends on the case," Laval answered. "Look, Detective," he said, now rising and starting to pace the room, "this is a terrible, terrible shock, and you haven't even told me who these women are. And why have they been killed? *My* patients?" He revved up his act, his face turning red, his lips quivering. "*My* patients?"

"These women," Hoover went on, "looked a lot alike."

"Alike?" Then Laval struck a curious pose, as if pondering the whole thing. "Oh my dear Lord," he finally said, "the experiment. I know who you're . . . oh Lord. All three of them? Of course I know who they are. Why didn't someone tell me? I have friends in those hospitals. They should have—''

"Now Doctor," Hoover said, "I want you to know right off that you're not a suspect."

"Officer," Laval shot back, approaching Hoover as if to challenge him, "that is not a concern of mine. My *patients* are my concern."

"Of course," Hoover said. "And y'know, it's funny. I was wonderin' why you didn't know about those murders. I mean, you mentioned this was some kind of experiment. You didn't keep up?"

"For a time, yes. But . . . look, I can't go into a whole lesson on medical procedures. This was an experiment in precise molding of facial parts." He walked back behind his desk and sat down. "I'm just . . . Mr. Hoover, these were grand women, really wann-der-ful. They had this thing in common, this similarity of facial structure, that I gave them. Yes, it was an experiment. But if they've been killed, then it's no coincidence. Do you agree?"

"Oh yeah."

"Then who's doing this? Why isn't there an investigation? I insist on one."

"I'm it," Hoover said.

"Oh, I see. Look, it's interstate. Can't we bring in the FBI? No offense, but they've got all these resources."

"We'll get them," Hoover replied. "But there's a bigger thing. You asked it. Who would want to kill these ladies? Who would go from state to state?"

Laval leaned back in his chair, trying to strike a pose that crossed a philosopher with an angry surgeon. He waited for more than thirty seconds before answering. "Mr. Hoover," he asked, "do you know who I am?"

"You're André—"

"No. I mean, do you know where I rank in the world of plastic surgery?"

"Right up in Topsville, I hear."

"Yes, indeed. Right up there. At the *very* top, actually. And when you're at the top, people get jealous. There are doctors who would like me dead. There may be some nurses too. I'm demanding, Detective. You don't get to my level without being demanding.''

"Yes, sir.''

"It sounds like someone is trying to hurt me through my patients. Does that sound logical?''

"Yeah,'' Hoover replied. "Any names?''

Laval leaned back again.''Let me think,'' he said.

So Hoover watched him think. Still, something was curious. Laval had readily admitted that these other women had the same face, and now he knew they were dead. Yet, he never mentioned Carly. Why not? Carly was alive. Why wouldn't he want to protect her?

''I can think of no one,'' Laval finally said. "Yes, certainly, there are frictions, and the jealousies I mentioned. But I can't imagine anyone associated with me actually doing these terrible things. It might be someone in another hospital, a rival, maybe even someone who thinks I didn't treat him right.''

"I follow that,'' Hoover said. "Oh, by the way, anyone else with that same kind of face?''

"Yes,'' Laval replied. He'd have to be accurate now, or arouse Hoover's suspicion. "Her name is Carly Randall, and she lives right here in New York. You've *got* to protect her!''

"We'll take care of it.''

"God, please. God, please. She's a wann-der-ful woman. It would be horrible if something . . .''

Laval had almost choked on his words. The last thing he wanted was for Carly to receive protection. But the act had to be played out. And now *he* had a question festering in his mind: Why *didn't* Hoover suspect him? Or was saying he wasn't a suspect merely a device of some kind?

"You give us all the data on this Randall girl,'' Hoover said. "We'll watch her.''

"You'll have everything I've got. Detective, we have a monster on our hands. You said he took their heads?''

"Yes, sir, he did.''

"Look, I'll give you a list of people who've worked

with me in all these cities. I'll explore every possibility, even ones I think are ridiculous."

"Thank you, sir."

Then Laval's eyes widened. He seemed to hit on something. He got up, as if ready to make an announcement. "Eileen Becker," he said.

"Who?"

"Eileen Becker. She's a senior nurse here."

"Why do you bring her up?"

Laval sat down again, becoming pensive. "I'm not quite sure, Detective. I've always felt Nurse Becker had a resentment toward me. She's the quiet type—the kind you always wonder about. And I've had to discipline her a few times when her mind seemed to drift during surgical operations. I just wonder if . . . well, consider this, Detective Hoover: I don't know if you're aware of it, but there was an incident during Carly Randall's last surgery. A potentially lethal drug was found on the drug tray just before it was to be administered to Ms. Randall."

"I've heard reports of an incident," Hoover said. "Who discovered it?"

"Well, that's just the point," Laval replied. "Nurse Becker *said* she detected it. We assumed it was a mix-up. These things do happen occasionally. But what if it wasn't? What if she'd planted it? What if she'd planned to kill Carly Randall to discredit me, but just couldn't go through with it, or thought she'd get caught?" Laval started tapping a pencil against his desk. "You know, there might be something here. She *did* have that stuff in her hands. Maybe you should . . . do some checking."

"I'll make a report to my division head," Hoover replied, intentionally evasive, still fearing that a police presence might put the killer on guard. He whipped out a pad and started making notes. "Anything else about this nurse?"

Laval played at pondering it. "She goes on trips," he replied. "Lots of vacations. She takes unpaid time. I've had to approve some of her little excursions. She could easily get to those other cities."

"Yeah," Hoover said, "but we can check her service

record to see if she was here when those other women were killed."

"Irrelevant," Laval broke in, now waving his finger at Hoover. "Those records are faked all the time. Nurses cover for each other. A nurse could be absent for two, three days, but some friend signs her in and out."

"Interesting," Hoover said. He was, however, skeptical. Laval had produced nothing convincing against Becker. "But I'm not satisfied," he went on. "We're lookin' at everything. You got a computer?"

"Yes."

"Your files on it?"

"Of course."

"Then someone could break into that computer."

"Yes. Yes, that's true." Laval was thrilled that this whole discussion was about *other* suspects. "You know, Detective, it's remarkable. We had a seminar here last year on the security of records. All of us have been worried about these hackers, these people who can break into computers. Maybe one of them . . ."

"Maybe."

"I'll review my records," Laval said. He felt he had Hoover where he wanted him—going off in all directions. And he knew how to ingratiate himself even further. He suddenly began staring at Hoover, tilting his head as if studying a fine picture rather than a New York City detective.

"What are you starin' at?" Hoover asked.

"You, Detective," Laval replied. "Excuse me, but it's a habit of plastic surgeons. I hate to digress from our important concerns, but a face to us is life itself."

"Not much of a face here," Hoover observed.

"Ah, don't say that. I think it's a wann-der-ful face. A bit sad. Somewhat dour. Like Lincoln's."

"A Hoover has a kisser like a Lincoln?"

"Yes. It has character, the character of experience. There are some . . . problems, though."

"Oh yeah?"

"No offense, but those little bags under the eyes, and

he way the mouth turns slightly down. I'm sure that's
bothered you.''

"Well . . . uh, I don't exactly like lookin' in the mirror,'' Hoover said.

"I can fix that.''

"No kiddin'.''

"And you *should* have it done. I'll take care of it.
You'll be a new man . . . and don't worry about the
cost.''

Hoover managed a faint smile."Well . . . maybe,'' he
said. "I appreciate that. But I better crack this case
first.''

"Yes,'' Laval said. "I agree fully. This is awful.''

And then a new thought struck Hoover, one that seemed
so obvious, yet one that he'd completely overlooked. "Uh,
Doc, a question,'' he said. "You been around the country
recently?''

"Of course,'' Laval replied. "Detective, a man in my
position is called to teach and lecture in other cities. I'm in
most major cities every year.''

"Really?''

"Really.''

But if that were true, Hoover reasoned to himself, how
could Laval *not* have heard of those murders? Surely *one*
of his medical colleagues in the murder cities would have
brought up the violent death of a Laval patient. Something
wasn't right.

But Laval hadn't been in Chicago for Marcia Lane's
killing, Hoover reminded himself. His own department's
surveillance report placed him in New York. Maybe he
was making too much of minor contradictions. It was
common in police work. It was the detective's curse.

Laval again pledged his full cooperation and Hoover
left, taking some of Laval's photocopied files with him.

With Hoover gone, Laval slumped behind his desk,
grateful that the meeting had gone so well. He'd never
been a religious man, although Arnie Lemke had been
brought up in a religious home. But now he prayed, and
expressed thanks for his deliverance.

But deliverance would never be complete without eliminating Carly and making sure he wasn't blamed for her death.

How could Carly be safely killed? Laval had no ready answer.

But he knew he'd come up with one.

He rarely failed. Rarely.

25

Carly flew back to Chicago to attend Marcia's funeral. The service was delayed by the need for an autopsy and the procedures of the Chicago Police and the Cook County Coroner's Office. It was held in a local church and attended by only four of Marcia's friends, all from her building, three of them single mothers who came with crying children. Through Carly's generosity, Marcia was buried in a decent plot in a well-kept cemetery. In a way, Carly felt as if she were burying part of herself.

She returned to New York, to *Allure*. There was little more she could do in probing the duplicate faces. The investigation was now in Hoover's hands. At Moran's insistence, Carly started to sketch out the story she would eventually do on her plastic surgery, and the nightmarish discoveries that followed it. She had to confront the reality that Laval wasn't guilty of the murders, but the bizarre nature of his "experiment"—duplicating faces—still horrified her. There *was* something wrong with that, no matter how much he might try to justify it.

Her life wasn't normal. Each time she left her apartment she saw Hoover's surveillance man outside, there to protect her. Another one was posted right outside the *Allure* office. Carly felt safe, if a bit smothered. She wished for the day when it would all be over, when the murderer of her look-alikes was finally caught.

Staff members were very protective. They tried to shield Carly from the constant stream of publicity-seekers who knocked at *Allure*'s door each day, seeking space in the magazine's pages for their latest dress design, rock album, or marriage manual.

Even the office boys helped. There was one clerk in the mail room who knew how much Carly hated those solicitations, especially from doctors who liked to parade their expertise in the public print as a means of recruiting patients.

One day a hand-delivered letter came into *Allure*, addressed to Carly, and bearing the return address of a Dr. Gordon Slesar. The envelope was marked URGENT.

Another phony, the clerk thought. One more MD with a new diet or a cure for baldness. It couldn't be very important.

So he filed it in a box of old press releases, to be delivered to Carly when she fully recovered. He was doing her a favor, he was sure. He had her best interests at heart.

Mike Moran invited Carly into his office to discuss her articles. She immediately noticed something different as she closed the door behind her. The office was neater than it had been. Papers were piled respectably on the desk. Mike actually had his jacket on, something Carly hadn't seen in years. And he seemed a little tense, not his usual California free-swinging self.

"How's it coming, Carlykins?" Moran asked, slapping his hands behind his head and flinging his legs up on the desk with a thud.

"Fine, Mike," Carly answered. "I'm just working out the details of my accident. I want the right hook—you know, I want the readers to understand *why* people need this kind of plastic surgery."

"Yeah. That sounds good. But don't make it a soap opera."

"Mike, I don't write soap operas."

"Right. I know. Uh, Carly . . ."

"Yes?"

"I was thinking about these articles. Maybe you need some perspective on things."

Carly frowned. "Define that, Mike."

"Well, I don't mean real help. I mean, another point of view . . . like my point of view. And not just an occasional visit to my office."

"Sure," Carly shrugged. "Mike, I have no problem with listening to your view on what I'm doing. You *are* the editor. I'll send you memos."

"Well, memos are fine," Mike answered, fidgeting with his hands, "but maybe this requires greater depth. These are important pieces, Carly. So I thought . . . why don't we do some *after* hours work? Now, I know it's unfair. You've got other things to do. But, look, I've got some theater tickets. Well, all right, movie tickets. We could go. You *need* some relaxation. Then we could have a *working* dinner. I know a quiet place. Very neat. Wonderful tablecloths."

She grinned. He was talking about . . . a date. This was as direct as it was going to get. "Sure," she said. "A working dinner. Why not?"

And Mike Moran beamed. Then he caught himself and turned it into a shrug. "I'll write it down," he said. "I'll try not to cancel."

They were interrupted a few moments later by Victor Hoover, who knocked at Moran's door, then opened it without being invited. "Can an old cop come in?" he asked.

"Sure Vic, sure," Moran replied.

Hoover swept in, carrying three hot slices of sausage pizza in a brown paper bag that was starting to leak. "I figured this was a better place to eat than Burgess Hospital," he said. "Too many germs in a hospital, Michael." He turned to Carly. "You know about that, Ms. Carly."

"Unfortunately, yes," Carly answered.

"I just got back from there," Hoover reported. "Spoke to most of Laval's nurses. I like 'em to gossip about each other, and about anyone else. I may have some leads. The man is admired, but not liked. That personality—he acts like a king, y'know."

"They giving you a hard time over there?" Moran asked.

"Naw. Very cooperative. And Laval, I gotta say, he's been handin' over records and makin' lists."

"You're still convinced he's not involved?" Carly asked.

"I'm pretty sure. We know he wasn't in Chicago. And I still don't think he's the type to work with anyone. Also, no one's found physical evidence to link him with any of those murders. Everything normal with you, Ms. Carly?"

"Normal?"

"With all my guys' eyes on you."

"Oh." Carly laughed. "I'm probably safer than anyone in New York with those eyes," Carly replied. "Your men are great. I've gotten to know some. And they do watch." Then she wagged a teasing finger at Hoover. "But not yesterday afternoon."

"Oh? What's that mean?" Hoover asked.

Carly fell silent. "It was nothing."

"It was *something!*" He was turning red.

Carly had never seen him angry before, but it was his way of getting her to talk. And she hated to, because some guy might get in trouble. But now, challenged, she felt she had to come out with it. "Well, one of your men was parked in his car when I arrived home," she said.

"Briggs," Hoover said. "That's when he was on."

"Out is a better word."

"Out?"

"Like a light. In his car."

Hoover shook his head in disgust. "Cooping, we call that," he said. "The department once had a scandal about it. I hate that. I just *hate* it. Briggs. He's not our best man. He's got some kind of disability—probably faked—so they assign him to this stuff." Hoover started unwrapping his pizza. "I'm glad you told me, I—"

And then Victor Hoover froze in place.

"What's wrong, Vic?" Moran asked.

Hoover dropped the pizza onto Moran's desk. One piece landed upside down and ruined a memo. Hoover ignored it and stared into space, a lemony sourness in his eyes. "Cooping," he mumbled.

"What?" Carly asked. Instinct told her that this was

either a breakthrough or a disaster—Hoover's face made it impossible to determine which.

But without a word, Hoover jumped up, left his pizza, and rushed from the office, leaving Carly and Moran dumbfounded.

Victor Hoover dashed from the *Allure* building and grabbed a cab. He flashed his badge and ordered the driver to speed to main police headquarters in lower Manhattan. And he cursed himself, hated himself for not having thought of one possibility before. To him, this was both disaster *and* breakthrough.

The yellow cab screeched to a skidding halt outside the red-brick building that serviced the New York Police Department. Hoover rushed to a small office on the third floor that handled the surveillance requests and sent out the officers to keep watch on Carly and Laval. An aging sergeant, Sam O'Rourke, whose five sons were also police officers, was seated at an ancient wooden desk, which he'd brought with him when the old police headquarters on Centre Street was closed down.

O'Rourke had never seen Hoover so agitated. "Victor," he said, looking up with intensely bloodshot eyes, "you sick?"

"Maybe," Hoover replied. "Look, O'Rourke, I got no time for family talk. Here, I wrote on a paper a date and time. Tell me now, who was assigned to watch this Dr. Laval in this period? Tell me now."

O'Rourke shrugged, baffled by Hoover's case of nerves. But he checked immediately through a raft of yellow sheets, squinting at some of the funny handwriting that was scrawled all over them.

"C'mon, O'Rourke," Hoover insisted. "Move quicker."

"Jesus," O'Rourke answered, "I'm tryin', Victor. My old eyes can't move that fast. My doctor says—"

"No medical stories, O'Rourke. Gimme the data."

O'Rourke found the entry. "Briggs," he said.

"Where is he?"

"Y'mean now?"

"What the hell else could I mean? Where is he? Puerto Rico? Italy?"

O'Rourke checked assignment sheets. "He's here," he replied. "Desk work today. Inner-ear problem or somethin'. A doctor once told me I had that. I—"

"What office?"

"Uh, check 602. If not, check any couch."

Hoover left O'Rourke without a thank you, and ran upstairs to Room 602, which was temporarily being used to process requests for pistol permits from New York's retail merchants. There were six policemen working in the office, and Hoover instantly spotted Briggs studying one application and stapling it to some official forms. "Briggs," Hoover shouted, startling the serenity of the office.

Briggs looked up. He was about thirty, with a pudgy, roundish face and a premature double chin that quivered like Jell-O whenever he moved. "Oh, hi Victor," he replied. "You want me?"

"I called you, didn't I? Out here."

Slowly, Briggs got up and ambled across the room. Hoover thrust his hand out, grabbed Briggs by the sleeve and yanked him through the door opening into the hall. "Hey!" Briggs snapped. "What's goin' on, Victor?"

"You were assigned to Laval?" Hoover asked.

"Yeah," Briggs replied. "Nice work."

"I bet. Briggs, I got a problem."

Suddenly Briggs gulped and stood back a step. "Uh, Victor, don't come down on me. All right, I did it. You got a report from Internal Affairs. It won't happen again. I mean, I got medical problems. Somethin' in my blood."

"You were cooping."

"Well . . . this medical problem."

"Last Sunday . . . when it rained?"

"It hit me that day, Victor."

"You jerk, Briggs. You file a false report?"

Briggs's head sank. "I won't do it again."

"You'll never get the chance!" Hoover turned and ran down the hall, first stopping at O'Rourke to order that protection of Carly Randall be doubled immediately.

Now he knew. Now he knew the truth: On the day that Laval had gone to Chicago to kíll Marcia, Briggs had been assigned to watch him . . . and Briggs had fallen asleep in his car outside Burgess Hospital. Trying to cover, Briggs had then filed a false report, stating that Laval had spent the entire day at the hospital. But Laval had gone to Chicago. Hoover was sure of it.

It was stupid. A blunder. An oversight that Victr Hoover could never forget, or forgive. And yet it might have led to one positive development: in his talk with Laval, Hoover had made it clear that Laval was *not* a suspect. Maybe Laval would relax, make a mistake, reveal himself.

Hoover shot out of the building.

He wanted to tell Carly and Mike Moran . . . in person. Carly had been the shrewdest detective of all of them.

Gordon Slesar canceled all his appointments for the day. He was too nervous to see patients, too obsessed with Carly Randall. He couldn't understand why she hadn't called. The messenger service had confirmed that the letter was delivered, and that the messenger had been told that Carly was in the office. What was Carly doing? Was she too angry to call? Was she notifying the police? Was she confronting Laval?

Slesar paced his office, clasping his hands together so tightly that his knuckles turned white. By four P.M. he could stand it no longer. His whole life might depend on how understanding Carly was, on whether she could accept his story that he'd only been acting in her interests when he'd broken her confidence. He was almost beginning to believe that lie himself.

His hands throbbing, he went for the phone, and called *Allure*. In a moment, he heard the nasal-voiced switchboard operator. "Good afternoon. *Allure*."

"Carly Randall please," Slesar replied.

"One moment. Is this an unsolicited submission?"

"Uh no, this is Ms. Randall's . . . doctor."

Slesar heard the usual clicks, then two rings of a phone.

Someone picked up. His heart almost stopped in anticipation. "Carly Randall," said the voice.

Slesar summoned all his strength. "Uh, Carly, this is . . . Dr. Slesar."

"Oh, hi," Carly answered. "I'm surprised to hear from you."

"I know," Slesar said, trying for a little laugh. "It's usually the patient who calls the shrink."

"Yeah, I guess."

"But, uh, this is a special situation."

"Oh?"

Slesar realized that Carly *hadn't* seen his letter. "Well, I was wondering about your discoveries, and what you were doing."

Carly was baffled. What was so special about that? "It's all being taken care of," she answered. She couldn't talk with people around her.

"Hey, that's good," Slesar said, trying to turn on the cheer. "You know . . . I was wondering, I sent you something by messenger—"

"You did?"

"I guess you didn't get it."

"No, I didn't get anything from you, Doctor. I'll check our mail room, unless you want to tell me now what it was."

"Oh, that's all right. Well . . . it isn't all right. No, it isn't all right at all. Actually, I wanted to discuss something with you, about your case." Slesar was inexplicably gaining courage now. If Carly didn't have his letter, he'd confront her directly, like the man he wasn't.

"Is it urgent?" Carly asked.

"I'd say so, but I'd prefer not to discuss it on the phone. Look, uh, could you come to my office tonight, say eight o'clock?"

It was a startling request. Psychiatrists usually didn't do this, Carly knew, unless a patient was in desperate straits. What did Slesar know? What was he holding back?

"I guess I could," Carly replied. "Let's make it eight sharp. I hope there's nothing . . . seriously wrong."

"I wouldn't worry too much about it," Slesar said.
"We'll talk. You'll be fine. Hey, I'll be seeing you soon."

He hung up, leaving Carly a little shaken. She left her
desk and rushed to the mail room, hoping to find the letter
he'd mentioned. But the mail had been dispensed and the
mail room closed for the night.

Carly told Mike Moran about the call a few minutes
later. She was just finishing when Victor Hoover rushed
in. He was out of breath, barely able to speak. He hustled
Carly and Moran into Moran's office, slamming the door
behind him. Finally, he caught his breath. He calmed
down. He forced the words out.

"All right, here's the mea culpa," Hoover said. "I'm
givin' it to you straight, no foolin'. We screwed up the
surveillance of Laval the day he would have gone to
Chicago. We missed everything. We've got to assume
Laval was out there. Confession completed."

Moran and Carly stared at Hoover incredulously. They
were completely off balance. In just seconds, everything
changed. Carly felt a surge of anger at Hoover, at his
almost flippant confession, yet she knew it wasn't his
fault. It was the usual screw-up, the botched operation, the
surveillance that went blind.

So it *was* Laval. It had been Laval all the time. They
were back at the beginning.

"Credit goes to Carly," Moran sighed, with unusual
softness, flipping a pencil onto his desk in frustration.

Silently, Hoover seconded the motion.

"Credit isn't what I'm after," Carly replied. "Laval is
what I'm after. All right, a mistake was made. We know
the truth now. What comes next?"

"First off," Hoover answered, "you are to go nowhere
near Laval. I don't care what his methods are. Stay away.
I've interviewed him. Sure, him and I talked about it bein'
someone else, but *he* knows the truth and maybe he thinks
we're closin' in. He could panic. He could do somethin'
crazy. You stay away, even if you need a new face by
Monday."

"How do we get him . . . how do *you* get him?" Moran asked. "There's still no evidence."

"Don't you think I know that, Michael?" Hoover answered. "That's the whole dilemma. I've got nothin' solid on the man. It's all circumstantial. We've got no witnesses."

"Someone must have seen him go in and out of the Palmer House," Carly said.

"They saw a man with Marcia, and he was wearing dark glasses. Even dark glasses are enough to throw the whole world off. Look, this may take time. They all leave clues somewhere. I gotta go back and trace everything."

Again, there was the sense of running in circles. They had enough about Laval's duplication of faces to ruin his reputation and destroy his practice forever, but not enough to convict him of murder. And Carly feared that this was as far as they might ever get.

26

Laval had only one goal—to destroy Carly Randall without getting caught. It had to be perfect, just as the others were perfect. He could leave no trail, especially this close to home. He needed a breakthrough, and he needed it fast. He also needed information on exactly how far Carly had gone, how much she knew. Laval had to assess the damage, to determine how he had to maneuver.

There was only one person who would be able—and willing—to help him. Sitting behind his desk at Burgess, Laval flipped through his black address book, and dialed the number of Gordon Slesar.

The phone rang in Slesar's office.

Jumpy, apprehensive about his impending visit from Carly, Slesar answered on the first ring. "Yes?"

"Gordy," Laval replied, "it's André, Gordy. Why so panicked?"

"Oh, André," Slesar answered, almost relieved that it was Laval, and not a suspicious Carly or an equally suspicious cop. "I'm not panicked. I was expecting a patient who's having his problems."

"Oh, I see. You have another line, don't you? I'd hate to tie up your phone."

"Sure. I've got two phones."

"Just grand. Y'know, Gordy, I called because I was reviewing Carly Randall's folder. Very strange situation, I think. And I was wondering whether she's said anything to you that could prove . . . helpful.''

"Uh, not really, André.''

"She hasn't had more of those suspicious ideas?''

"Well, I haven't heard any recently. Of course, I haven't seen her that much.''

"You seeing her again soon?''

Slesar balked at the question. Why was Laval asking? Did he know something, or suspect something? "Yes, I'm actually seeing her tonight,'' he replied. He really didn't want Laval to know he was seeing Carly, but he couldn't lie. What if Carly called Laval for some reason and mentioned it? What if Laval already knew and was just testing? Why provoke Laval?

"Tonight?''

"Yes, about eight o'clock.''

"Eight o'clock. I see.'' Now Laval had it. He had what he wanted. "Gordy,'' he asked, a contrived warmth in his voice, "I wonder if I could drop over about seven.''

"Drop over? Is there a problem, André?''

"No, but it's about this case. I'd rather discuss it with you in person.''

Slesar didn't want to antagonize Laval, didn't want to alert him to his own suspicions, "Sure,'' he said. "Come on over. You know where I am.''

They both hung up. A broad smile formed over Laval's face. This was a gift. The smile deepened into a grin, then into a heavy laugh as Arnie Lemke recalled his favorite fairy tale—"Little Red Riding Hood.'' He'd always liked that story as a child.

He liked it even more now.

27

Laval took a taxi to Slesar's office just before seven P.M. He was followed by two plainclothesmen in an unmarked Plymouth Horizon. After Laval arrived, the plainclothesmen waited down the block, talking and joking in their car, and filling out the log showing Laval's movements. It wasn't very interesting.

Slesar opened the door with a smile, trying to hide his anxiety at even seeing Laval. "André, come in," he oozed, then closed the door behind the surgeon.

"Thanks for letting me intrude, Gordy," Laval said. "I know your schedule is as heavy as mine. But this Randall case concerns me." He flipped off a light coat and tossed it onto a chair, a gesture that instantly struck Slesar as strange. The elegant Dr. Laval never flipped clothing around.

"Sit down, André," Slesar said, as he ushered Laval into a small living room.

"That's all right, Gordy. I've been sitting in that cab, and I'd rather stand."

But Slesar sat.

"You know, it's funny," Laval said. "I don't think I've been here more than twice. It's a lovely place, Gordy. Truly grand."

"Thank you, André. I like it myself." No, this wasn't typical of Laval, who never lavished praise on a lesser doctor. What was wrong with him?

"Of course, I've always enjoyed the Morningside Heights

area," Laval went on, slowly pacing up and down. "But, uh, how do you . . .? I mean, no offense, but the neighborhood—"

"Crime, André?"

"That's what I was trying to say. I mean, you must keep drugs here, Gordy. You have a cabinet, or a safe?"

"A locked cabinet, right in the next room. But it's inside a wooden console, so unless they knew, they'd need time to find it. And I keep the only key with me."

"Good idea." Perfect, Laval thought. Now he knew where the drugs were, and that Slesar carried the key with him.

"André, what about Carly Randall?" Slesar asked, eager to learn why Laval had taken the time to come over.

"Yes, let's get to that," Laval said, glancing at his watch. "I wouldn't want to be here when she arrived."

"Of course not."

Slowly, Laval pulled a brown business-size envelope from his jacket pocket and started opening it. "Gordy," he said, "I want to show you something. These are observations of Carly Randall made by a nurse during the patient's recent surgery at Burgess." Laval walked closer to Slesar, standing over him. "Here, Gordy, I think this will concern you. Take a look."

He handed Slesar the paper and Slesar started reading it carefully. As he did, Laval reached into a side pocket and clasped his hand around a tubular object. He withdrew it.

Slesar looked up. "André, you sure this is the right thing? This is . . ." Slesar's eyes flew toward Laval's hands. "André, what's—?"

Laval jammed the needle into Slesar's neck, and squeezed the plunger.

Slesar said nothing. He stared at Laval, his eyes wide and frozen. His throat gurgled, and he slumped over.

"I'm so sorry, Gordy," Laval said, "but I'm the better doctor. Nothing must happen to me."

Then, almost casually, Laval took a paperweight from

the desk and slammed it against Slesar's head. He wiped the fingerprints from the paperweight and returned it.

Laval searched through Slesar's pockets, finding a small key case. He took the keys into the adjoining room and opened the wooden console. The cabinet was right inside, protected by a heavy lock. One by one, working quickly, mindful of the time Carly was to arrive, Laval tried each key. Finally, he hit the right one, and opened the drug cabinet.

He reached in and intentionally spilled some bottles, breaking two of them. He took some others that contained narcotics and stuffed them into his pockets.

He debated with himself whether to move Slesar. The body was in a room that could easily be closed off. Carly certainly wouldn't be able to see it. But the murder scene looked suspicious. There was no sign of a struggle, no indication that Slesar had tried to defend himself or his supply of drugs.

Laval studied the body. The blood that trickled from Slesar's postmortem head wound stained only his shirt and hadn't splattered on the floor. That was good. Slesar could be moved without leaving a trail.

Using extreme care, Laval grabbed his colleague by his arms and dragged him to the drug cabinet. He dropped him there, then got the paperweight and planted it beside him. He left the room and closed the door.

"Attempted robbery," the police report would say. Slesar had resisted, and had been killed by a blow to the head. Yes, it was possible, Laval knew, that the coroner would discover the needle mark and the killer drug in Slesar's system. Laval had used the drug to eliminate any chance that Slesar could resist. But there were many people in New York with access to those drugs. Why would anyone suspect an eminent plastic surgeon?

Everything had worked.

Now Laval settled back in Slesar's desk chair and waited for Carly.

Carly was driven back to her apartment from *Allure* by a plainclothesman. It was 7:28 P.M., and she wanted to freshen up at home. She stayed in the apartment fifteen minutes, then prepared to leave for the ride uptown to Gordon Slesar's office.

But she had a final thought. It was an unusual hour for an appointment, and maybe it would be best to call to confirm. Why go all the way uptown and find that Slesar thought she was due another time?

She walked back to her phone and looked up Slesar's number in a small leather book. She picked up the receiver and dialed. All she got was a busy signal.

She called again. Same result. All right, at least he was there. She really couldn't stay until the line was clear to call again.

Carly left the apartment.

Another step in Laval's plan had fallen into place. He knew patients called to confirm. So he'd left both Slesar's phones off the hook. Carly would think Slesar was on one phone, holding someone on the other, conducting business as usual.

The ride up to Slesar's office took only eight minutes. Carly was driven by Patrolman Fred Larkin, a two-year veteran of the force, who found the work dull and was seriously thinking of becoming a deep-sea diver. Thin and wiry, Larkin had virtually nothing to say to Carly during the ride. Finally, they neared their destination, Slesar's brownstone just outside Columbia University.

"I'll drop you here and wait," Larkin told Carly in a monotone.

"Oh, don't bother," Carly said. "Why don't you grab something at the luncheonette? We can meet here at, say, nine. How's that?"

Larkin shrugged. If the lady didn't want him hanging around, why hang around? "Sure," he replied. "It's not regulation, but it's okay."

"There's nothing to worry about," Carly said, as Larkin stopped outside Slesar's office. It's my psychiatrist." She laughed as she got out, and waved Larkin on.

As the car pulled away, Carly climbed the steps leading

o Slesar's brownstone. She noticed one unusual thing—all he shades and blinds were closed. But so what? Maybe Slesar was seeing someone who wanted privacy.

She reached the top. She rang the buzzer.

28

Moran was about to leave his office when the phone rang. He assumed it was a California call since it was only five P.M. in Los Angeles, and the Coast often called about this time. California calls usually meant hot stories on celebrities, a staple for *Allure* readers. Moran picked up the receiver.

"Mike Moran."

"You sound so official, Michael," said Victor Hoover, at his gray metal headquarters desk.

"Hello, Victor," Moran answered. "I thought it was one of our West Coast people. I didn't know you worked this late."

"Twenty-four hours, Michael. Always on call. Always on watch." Hoover's words weren't completely clear since his mouth was half filled with spaghetti. "I phoned you just to say that a strand of hair found in Marcia's hotel room in Chicago seems to match Laval's hair color. I gotta say *seems*. We don't have a hair sample from Laval, so it's all by observation."

"I'll accept the observation," Moran said.

"Don't act like a reporter, Michael. It'll take lotsa diggin' to pin this down good enough for the DA to indict. But I think Carly would like to know about the hair sample. You want to call her?"

"She isn't home. She had an appointment."

"Appointment? You workin' her nights? Shame on you, Michael."

"Just an appointment with one of her doctors, Victor. Gordon Slesar."

Suddenly Hoover clutched. "Gordon—"

"What's wrong? He's a shrink here in—"

"You *sure* she went there?"

"Yes. Why?"

"You listen. I just got a report from surveillance. That's where Laval went."

There was a dead silence.

"She couldn't have known," Moran said, his voice quivering. "She wouldn't do that. Victor, she may be—"

"I know. I'm rocketing up there. Michael, get a cab. You go too."

"Wait a second," Moran broke in. "You've got men watching them both. Warn them!"

"Negative," Hoover replied. "They're in private cars. They call in from phones. No radios. No way to call 'em. We're short on equipment."

"Short on equipment," Moran seethed.

"It's real life, Michael."

Both men hung up. Then dashed for the street.

Carly pressed Slesar's buzzer again.

She heard footsteps. Oddly, they seemed to be going *away* from the door, rather than toward it.

"Come in, Carly," she heard. The voice was muffled. Slesar must be in a back room.

Carly turned the knob and opened the door. She stepped in, but found no one there. "Dr. Slesar?"

"Coming," the muffled voice said. Probably with a patient in the next office. Carly sat down and waited.

She waited almost a full minute.

Then, from an entranceway behind her, footsteps again. A door opened.

She looked back.

"Dr. Laval!"

Laval quickly placed himself between Carly and the outside door. "Ms. Randall, how nice to see you. I was just consulting with Dr. Slesar."

Now a river of fear surged through Carly. "Here?" she asked.

Laval shrugged. "Doctors visit doctors."

Carly stood up, her heart starting to pound. Laval wasn't the type to visit other doctors. They came to *him*. "Were you consulting about me?"

"Not at all."

"Where is he?" She was getting numb with fear.

"Ms. Randall, you seem nervous."

"I am. Where is Dr. Slesar?"

"He'll be with you in a moment."

"Tell me where he is."

Suddenly, Laval stepped back and clicked the master lock on Slesar's front door. Now it couldn't be opened, even from the inside, without a key.

"Why'd you do that?" Carly asked.

Laval dropped all pretense. "Still snooping around, aren't you, Carly?"

He knew. Somehow he knew. Carly edged back. "Where's Dr. Slesar?"

"Indisposed."

Carly stepped into a hallway. She glanced to the left, into an adjoining room. "Oh my God!" she gasped. "What did you do to him? What did you—?"

"Carly, please. Don't be common. We have needs. Don't we? We *all* have needs."

"I've got police with me!" Carly burst out. But then she remembered with a shudder: she'd sent her bodyguard to a coffee shop.

"I'm sure your policeman won't object to anything I do," Laval said.

Maybe he'd return, Carly prayed. Maybe he'd sense something was wrong, or simply ring the doorbell to check.

"I made you beautiful, Carly, but that wasn't enough for you," Laval said, now walking slowly toward her. "You suspected my art. You found out about my experiment."

"Yes, I found out!" Carly admitted, with sudden defiance, with anger.

"Admirable energy," Laval said as he approached. "But you should have been more grateful. You know what I was doing, Carly? I was working to create the perfect face. I wanted to create the face of the nineties. I wanted to make a woman immortal."

"You wanted to make *yourself* immortal!"

"Yes. Yes I did. And I could have been, through you. The others were inferior imitations. But you . . . the highest expression of my personal art. But you weren't grateful. So now you will join the others."

Carly kept moving back, easing around Slesar's body, looking for a way out, not finding one. "Why kill me?" she asked. "Any damage I could've done I've done already."

"I don't know that!" Laval snapped back. "Besides, this is a beautiful plan, isn't it, Carly? You and Slesar were having your little chat. A neighborhood kid broke in to steal drugs. Slesar tried to resist. The punk killed him with a paperweight, then realized he had to kill the only witness. A beautiful plan, just as my plan for your face was beautiful."

Slowly, ceremoniously, Laval took a scalpel from his jacket pocket. "You won't be so pretty any more. They won't be able to open the coffin, Carly. It'll be just like old times, won't it? Just like after your accident."

Carly was trapped. She saw no escape. He lunged at her, going directly for her face.

He slashed out, missing her by inches as she spun away, throwing her hands up. "They'll get you!" she shouted. "They'll know who did this! The police know. My editor knows!"

Laval ignored her. He came at her again as she spun around furniture, knocking over chairs to keep him back. He froze for a moment, as if taking aim, then charged toward her.

"Just another pretty face!" Laval shouted. "No more!"

Carly spotted the paperweight Laval had used on Slesar. She knew, because she knew Laval so well, that he had one fundamental weakness. "What about *your* face?" she screamed.

A quizzical look flashed in Laval's eyes.

Carly grabbed the paperweight. She went at Laval, hurling the hunk of stone directly at his face.

He thrust his hands upward, but he wasn't quick enough. The paperweight hit him in the left cheek, marring that magnificent face, sending him to the floor, the scalpel flying from his hand.

Now Carly grabbed the scalpel. Hold him off. Just hold him off and call for help.

Then she heard car tires screech outside. A man running up the steps. Someone hurriedly trying to turn the knob, then pounding at the door.

Hold Laval off.

But Laval got to his feet. In one last desperate move he charged at Carly, lunging to grab the scalpel.

There was no choice. No holding off. It was one life or the other.

Carly plunged the scalpel into Laval's chest.

For a moment, he seemed to stop in space. Then he fell to his knees. "Great art is immortal," he whispered, then collapsed to the floor.

It was over.

Carly stared at him, unbelieving, numb. André Laval was dead.

And yet she knew, even in that moment, that he would always be a part of her. Her face was his gift, and it was—as he had dreamed—a magnificent face. He had given her hope. He had given her a future.

She heard the crash as they knocked the door down. Moments later, the place was crawling with cops. Carly was vaguely aware of them, of Victor Hoover touching her arm, of the flashbulbs popping. "Don't worry," she heard Hoover say. "It was self-defense. There won't be any problem."

Then, suddenly, amidst the blur, there was Mike Moran's arm around her. Pulling Carly closer, without saying a word, Mike eased her through the crowd and toward a back door. Carly turned. For an instant, she caught herself in a mirror. She saw that face, that wonderful face. But next to it now was another wonderful face—Mike Moran's. Somehow, Carly knew that face would always be there, next to hers. Smiling, laughing, protective. This was the future that André Laval had given her.

They left the brownstone and walked into the New York night. The morning tabloid would soon go to press with its glaring headline: FACEMAKER SLAIN. But only Carly and Mike knew the full story.

They went back to Mike's Brooklyn apartment to start telling it. Together.

#1

HIS THIRD CONSECUTIVE NUMBER ONE BESTSELLER!

James Clavell's
WHIRLWIND

70312-2/$5.95 US/$7.95 CAN

From the author of *Shōgun* and *Noble House*—
the newest epic in the magnificent Asian Saga
is now in paperback!

"WHIRLWIND IS A CLASSIC—FOR OUR TIME!"
Chicago Sun-Times

WHIRLWIND

is the gripping epic of a world-shattering upheaval that
alters the destiny of nations. Men and women barter for
their very lives. Lovers struggle against heartbreaking odds.
And an ancient land battles to survive as a new reign of
terror closes in ...